THE BLACK DOLPHIN

THE HUNT SERIES BOOK 8

TIM HEATH

Copyright © 2020 by Tim Heath

All rights reserved.

No part of this book may be reproduced in any form or by any electronic or mechanical means, including information storage and retrieval systems, without written permission from the author, except for the use of brief quotations in a book review.

❦ Created with Vellum

ALSO AVAILABLE BY TIM HEATH

Novels:

Cherry Picking

The Last Prophet

The Tablet

The Shadow Man

The Prey (The Hunt #1)

The Pride (The Hunt #2)

The Poison (The Hunt #3)

The Machine (The Hunt #4)

The Menace (The Hunt #5)

The Meltdown (The Hunt #6)

The Song Birds

The Acting President (The Hunt #7)

The Black Dolphin (The Hunt #8)

The Lost Tsar (The Hunt #9)

The 26th Protocol

The Penn Friends (Books 1 & 2) by T H Paul

A Boy Lost (Books 1 & 2) by T H Paul

Short Story Collection:

Those Geese, They Lied; He's Dead

PROLOGUE

Far Eastern Russia

An anguished cry rang out as thorns from the undergrowth caught him once more, gouging his leg again. Blood soaked the front of his trousers, tears streamed down his fear ravaged face. He would die, he knew that; he kept telling himself that, though flight took him away from danger. The fight to survive was now so strong in him, despite his old age, despite a life lived in harsh times and in good.

He didn't want it ending like this, his killer upon him, life no more.

So he kept running, pushing through the greenery, wading through the grass. The safety of the city now far from him. Vladivostok was over five hundred kilometres south––this was meteorite territory, the crater from the huge strike over seventy years ago close to the forest through which he now fled.

Yet his killer was following, closing in on him, toying with him it would seem. This was now a battle of wits. The man knew he was at the disadvantage. He hadn't run like this in decades, his body knew it, his knees certainly did. Yet faced with death if he stopped, he found the energy; found the long-forgotten muscles and for the time being kept moving.

His opponent was on home turf, however. Siberian, male, and lethal.

His groin stung again, the injury already inflicted reminding him now there would be no escape. They'd taken his manhood from him already, why couldn't they have taken his life just as quickly? One bullet and the lights go out. Why the chase, why the fear?

He knew why.

He knew who.

He ran all the faster.

Trees stood ahead, the darkness of the denser coverage also a factor––did it advantage him or not? He couldn't think straight, a drone heard overhead, high above. They were closing in; they were hunting him too. Probably able to lead his attacker to his location, alert the killer to his hiding place. At least the trees might blind the military-grade drone to his location somewhat.

He leaned against the trunk of a large tree, gulping oxygen into his starving lungs, trying to slow his racing heartbeat, fear and adrenaline making that impossible. He needed to remain pumped, needed to survive a little longer. Pain shot down his legs again. He cursed, though kept his voice down.

The tree he had stopped at bore markings on the trunk. He did not understand what types of animals or predators lurked in the shadows. He already had a more dangerous beast on his tail.

He pressed on again, his breathing still heavy, sweat still pouring, blood still leaking. He stumbled crossing a log; the drone hovering above. *Damn, they had spotted him*. He stood, not looking up, not confirming his discomfort, not giving them the pleasure of his terror.

Birds scattered into the sky above, from in front of him, the direction he was heading. The way birds fly when startled. *Had his deadly pursuer doubled around on him? Was he now heading right towards his demise?* He pressed on anyway, staying steady, running from what had been. The memories, if he were to survive this––no doubt with him until his final breath——but he would refuse to dwell on them now. The desire to stay alive was great for making focus easier.

Another log, another stumble, this time falling on one knee, the pain in his legs instant. *The bastards.* They'd cut him to make him suffer. They'd cut him to make him shamed.

Birds scattered erratically overhead, this time possibly set off by his appearance. Then a rustle in the undergrowth ahead told him he might not have been the cause.

He stood slowly, hiding behind a tree, the cover of tall grass twenty metres away, across open ground. If his killer were watching, running for it would expose his position. Getting to the grass might help him hide, even if not from above. He ran.

Standing in the grass, birds of all descriptions circled in the air, letting out cries he'd never heard before into the night sky. Were they warning him, or warning of him?

He stood still. He could hear the movement of a body through grass, the careful but unmistakable sound of death closing in. This was it, he knew it; he feared. He should have stayed at the tree, should have tried height instead. He was no climber, however, hadn't been in his youth, hadn't been in his heyday, wasn't in his old age, balls or no balls.

The drone that had been following hung above his spot now, hovering about twenty metres as the two parties came closer. The old man stationary; the tiger moving in for the kill.

He barely heard the sound as it leaped from one side, the claws lashing, the hungry beast's jaws going for his neck. It was clear they had teased the animal's thirst for blood with the offering of thirty minutes before, enough to give it the man's scent. Enough to tell the tiger that a feast awaited.

The old man collapsed to the floor immediately, his fate now sealed, the drone hovering in position above the banquet, though the tiger soon dragged off the now dead body into the undergrowth.

1

Penal colony № 6 Federal Penitentiary Service, Russia
May 1994

One of the oldest prisons in the country and near Orenburg, it had been the first to accept lifers, those criminals sentenced to spend the rest of their years behind bars. It was now four years since that change, and there had been no escape attempts since.

That year, the fourth since the prison opened its seven-hundred capacity doors to murderers, child molesters, cannibals, terrorists, serial killers, political prisoners and maniacs, one particular prisoner would try an escape. It would be the only attempt ever made. Nothing now existed on record, the documents at the time put under lock and key. Soon they would get lost in a system of paperwork and reports. Soon nobody would remember.

Boris Mihaylov was forty-two when captured. A notorious criminal kingpin in and around Moscow, his organisation had been responsible for countless deaths, many at the hands of Boris himself. He thrived on bloodshed, made that clear. Anyone who crossed his path—criminal, political or police connections regardless—he made sure they never did again.

Tried, sentenced and found guilty—the trial nothing but a formality, he'd killed the deputy of the State Duma and the police chief in the last months—Boris was sent to Russia's highest security prison under heavy guard. It was a known threat that his organisation had vowed to free him.

In the years that followed, the prison would start several measures that they would put in place as unique practices in this prison. No other facility in the country would do it the way they would, but they learned this through mistakes with Boris Mihaylov, a man given too much time, too much opportunity to have a go.

Four weeks before the planned escape, someone visited Boris for the first time at the prison. Inmates were allowed one visit a month, plus one longer visit—of up to four days—a year. Boris had been behind bars for six months before his second-in-command showed up, a family member, this being the reason they allowed him to be there. As far as Boris knew, the authorities did not suspect his cousin of being part of the organisation.

They guarded their conversation, each word picked carefully. Both were sure the authorities would listen, though these men had been well used to that threat for decades. The KGB had been their biggest challenge for a long time, the dark days of Communism behind them now, when you could trust nobody, where every stranger posed a potential threat, as did many friends.

It had been the word of a friend that had put Boris behind bars.

The conversation moved to Aunt Olga. There was no Aunt Olga, this the signal for both of them that what they now talked about had double meaning. They could pass dates between them as they discussed Olga's imminent birthday, or who she met at the market the other day. It was a well-rehearsed practice, Boris immediately aware of the planned escape. If there was anything they didn't understand, a clarifying question would follow, usually asked in rhetorical fashion, and always aimed at dear Aunt Olga.

By the end of his allotted time, Boris had a date for his escape. June 27; seven weeks from then. He had the method, too; a tunnel was now being dug underneath the prison, currently at the outer walls, coming into the basement where they located the workshops. This would be the meeting point, the cousin only coming back for the June visit if there needed to be a delay in the plans. They both assumed there would not be. Boris knew they had put great expense into the operation, his cousin confirming—via reference to fifty people attending Olga's birthday party—that there were several dozen men working around the clock on the digging effort. They would get there in time.

"Give Olga my best wishes," Boris said, standing in front of the glass that separated him from his cousin, from freedom too, now that the guard was once more behind him, visiting time over.

"She'll perhaps see you next month," the cousin smiled. "I'll see if she's up for a visit here," and the guard ushered Boris away, a bag over his head as they led him by the arm along concrete corridors, Boris doing his best to map out the layout in his head as he walked, knowing he would need this come the last week of June.

In his cell, now alone to his thoughts once more, he marked up in chalk on the wall the seven weeks that remained of his time behind bars. He would count down the days, make sure he was ready. He didn't expect to see his cousin the following month. He knew they would finish in time.

Alicante Region, Spain
Three months ago

THE SUN BEAT down as it often did in the city, Jose standing in the marina, his men with him, though pacing two steps behind. The Don was in no real danger in his own town. And Alicante was that, despite the actions of an unknown individual or group. While the world watched political events unfolding in Russia that month––elections were imminent, a new dawn heralded––the Don homed in on something much closer to his heart. Was there Russian involvement in the death of his son? While identities remained hazy for the time being, the Don's ability to drill down on something until it became clear had already kicked in days ago.

Now he had a credible lead.

His team had put word out on a man, a suspected rapist. Someone had spotted him in a hotel room in the city centre. Don

Zabala had gone in person to confirm from the CCTV if it was in fact the same guy.

Inside the hotel, the air cool, the entrance and foyer areas elegant, Jose Zabala walked casually over to the reception desk. Just an elderly man with a cane and designer suit. His men had waited outside.

"I'm here to speak to Sergio," Jose said, his team having passed him the name of their contact in that establishment. It always paid to keep listening ears in such hotels, as you never knew what they might turn up.

"I'll call him now," the young receptionist said. She was young enough to be his granddaughter, something he would never now have––the elderly couple's only son, who'd been unmarried and childless, had been gunned down earlier that year. The Don, however, was never not around family, never not around children. His wider relatives were extensive.

Five minutes later Jose entered a small room down a corridor from the reception, a few screens relaying feeds from various entry points.

"You understand that there are no cameras in the rooms," Sergio said, nothing Jose had ever expected. "The occupant of room twelve-eleven had forgotten the *Do not disturb* sign one morning." The plan showed that to be a penthouse suite, over six hundred euros a night. This was no backpacker's room. "When the cleaning staff approached, they knocked on the door and not hearing an answer, they entered the room. They spotted a man tied to a chair."

"They did not inform anyone about this?" Jose asked, the situation seeming to demand that they would have done so.

"No," Sergio said, his tone suggesting he wasn't happy about it either. He had only found out earlier that day when questions got put to the hotel via Jose's men. Then the story had come out, though it fitted the account from the two women who had been there. It all seemed to make sense. "The guest was also still in the room. He came out of the bathroom when the room door opened. They said he seemed calm and spoke with an accent."

"He wasn't Spanish?" the Don asked, raising one eyebrow at that thought.

"No, and he tried speaking in English first, before breaking into basic Spanish."

"I see. So what happened?"

"The guest did not threaten the cleaning women. He merely walked over to the man tied to the chair and told the women that this was a bad man. Without any weapon or obvious threat, the guest asked him to tell them what he had done."

"And he confessed to being a rapist, just like that?" the Don asked, his mind jumping to the natural solution.

"Yes, he did," Sergio replied. "You know this man?"

Jose wasn't sure which of the two he meant, though wasn't about to divulge knowledge of either at that moment.

"What happened after your staff heard the man tied up confessing to be a rapist?"

"The guest told them he would not hurt the man," Sergio said. That seemed strange. Nobody had since seen the man. Someone had got to him, and there were no other suspects aside from the guest. "He said he would see that justice got done. Then he paid the cleaners off in rubles."

"He was Russian?"

Sergio looked around a little cautiously. "I can't give you a name-- believe me, even if I had access to that, it would be more than my life was worth, but someone arranged the booking via a Russian contact. So yes, I believe a very wealthy Russian rented the suite."

"Super wealthy?" Jose probed. A Russian oligarch had reached out to the Spaniard that year presenting him with a plan for revenge. He had given the Don the name of a contact inside the prison that had housed a British man named Clifton. The same Brit who'd murdered Don Zabala's son. Now Clifton was also dead.

"I think you could say that, yes." Jose need ask no more. This guest could have been the same man Jose met, though the idea there was not only one Russian oligarch in Alicante that same week raised new thoughts in his clever mind.

The Don pulled a photo he had taken from the home of the rapist. "Can you confirm if this is the guy they saw?" and he passed the image to Sergio.

"I will check," he said.

"You can let me know on this number," Jose added, passing his own card, a number he thought very few people had, though the Russians had. Someone called him on that number to arrange a meeting, the same meeting at which Clifton turned up and confessed to killing the Don's son earlier that week.

Jose Zabala left the hotel five minutes later. He would get a call that evening that the man in the photo was the same one that his staff had seen in the room. It closed the circle, put the fate of this rapist onto the actions of this Russian or group of Russians. The Don's sixth sense had been on overdrive all day. However the confirmation had not surprised him. He'd been certain it was the same man.

Finding out where he was, and what these Russians were doing in his city that week, might move him one step closer to his biggest question, and his biggest fear; if they were up to no good that week, did one of them have a hand in his son's murder? He had always known that Clifton Niles, the man who fired the gun, had no reason to kill his son. Had no motive at all. Unless he had no choice, that is.

2

Berlin, Germany
Present Day

"Is he not here today?" Anastasia asked, the Belarusian looking around a room slowly filling with people, though the man who'd put the whole thing together was noticeably absent.

"Doctor's appointment," the club treasurer confirmed. "Said he couldn't avoid it."

The Belarusian took in the gathering masses. The twelve tables she had help set beautifully with teacups and small plates seemed to fill quickly. There were plenty of new visitors this month.

"I think we need to set more tables," she said, her German coming on after a few years in the country, though they were speaking Russian on that occasion.

"I'll give you a hand," the treasurer smiled.

Having Anastasia onboard had been a huge help. They knew of her within Russian circles there in Berlin because of her marriage to Dmitry, who had run for President at the 2018 election, ultimately finishing third and going out in the first round of the vote. At that point, their marriage was already as good as over, the combination of her not wanting to move to Russia had he won––something they barely talked about––coupled with her sleeping with a British agent which arguably didn't help either. The campaign had been brutal, Dmitry slaughtered in the press as various weaknesses became exposed, many of them not his doing. He was now in a British prison, there on evidence Anastasia had provided to the police. Without her involvement, there would have been no trial, no long sentence. She might still be trapped in a marriage she knew was over, had been for a long time.

She loved Alex, the British MI6 agent who'd somehow fallen into her world, or she into his? In fact, they created their own world together, looked away from a raging planet that only wanted to harm them. *Safe*. Until it wasn't.

Now Alex had vanished. She had informed on her husband to make a clean break, though before that had all happened, Alex had gone, presumably disappearing in Russia. Deep down she feared he was dead already, though in her last call with Anissa, the British MI6 agent and former colleague of Alex, Anissa had hinted they had intelligence to suggest Alex was still alive. Hidden and off the radar, but alive somewhere, most likely in a Russian prison.

She'd never given up hope on him since that phone call. It had been three years, nine months. Dmitry's men had followed her for a while––she never knew officially, and when it was clear she didn't care, they went, just like that. Various suitors had pursued her, some introduced by well-meaning friends, some by her cousins, but she'd rebuffed them all. This heart wasn't available to anyone else. She still loved Alex, wanted with everything inside her to believe he loved her too, to believe he was still alive. The longer the weeks and then months passed, the fainter the hope grew. She knew it. But she had decided.

Wealthy beyond all normal bounds, she had no need of anyone's support––either financial or romantic. She was free. Free to do as she wished, free to live her own life. And she lived a good one.

Her involvement in the Russian community over the last year had surprised even her at how much she missed it all. She had volunteered to help Slava--the man missing today for that doctor's appointment--run the monthly Russian Tea Parties, an initiative the older Russian had come up with to grow a cultural understanding of his homeland, even though he had lived in Berlin since before the wall came down. While not Russian herself--she was from Belarus, the same in her mind, yet crucially for many in Moscow she would have been regarded as a foreigner had Dmitry won that vote, had she moved into the Kremlin with him--she thoroughly enjoyed helping to put together these monthly socials. To recreate something that transcended nationality, culture, even language. There were plenty of German speakers now coming, curious folk looking in on proceedings.

Today was no exception. The regulars were mostly present, as were the older Germans who had been coming for the last six months. They largely sat on tables by themselves--their age and lack of Russian, not to mention being on opposite sides in the war for those old enough to remember--seemed to create natural barriers. However, Anastasia knew the power of a cup of Russian tea. She would drop into each group, her German useful with her more elderly guests, and aimed to mix things up. The wall in that city might have come down thirty years before, the concrete now only standing in museums around the world, but cultural divides lasted much longer and were far harder to destroy.

Everybody liked Anastasia's presence there. She was young, beautiful and full of life. Those organising the event, Slava especially, knew some men were only there because of her. They might be a lot older, but they all had a pulse. He too knew about beautiful young things, though those days were long behind him.

English was spoken occasionally, usually by Russians visiting as they met with non-Russian guests around a table. Today they could even hear Spanish, three men, middle-aged so falling between most age groups there--which consisted either the older locals, there monthly, or the young traveller, passing through town that week and hearing about the event from someone.

"Thank you all for coming," the treasurer announced, a spoon against the side of his water glass enough to draw the crowd to silence. "Welcome to another Russian Tea Party," he said, speaking his native language. Those present, even without Russian, knew the routine by now. All cheered the introduction. Trays of food came out of the kitchen area at that moment, the trolley delivering one to each table. There wouldn't be as many leftovers this time, perhaps none at all.

An hour later, the conversation flowed, a few guests moving between the tables––Anastasia one of these, a strong encourager to the others to follow suit, though most didn't. The group of Spaniards seemed to be rather sociable, she noticed, which initially brought a smile to her face. One of the three spotted her watching them, smiling back himself, then coming over.

"A fine gathering," he said, offering her his hand. "I'm Pablo," he added, once Anastasia had taken his hand, which felt in need of either a soothing cream or perhaps a roll of sandpaper. He had to be nearly twenty years older than her, and her guard went up immediately, though what they ended up talking about surprised her.

"I'm Anastasia. I help organise these events," she said, taking back her hand, her eyes watching the other two men on the table behind, the mention of the club's chairman coming up at least twice now in the conversation around that table.

"So you'll know which one of these people is Slava Alkaev?" the man asked.

"Our chairman isn't here today," she confirmed, which seemed to disappoint the man. "A doctor's appointment, apparently."

"I see," he said, glancing over to the other two, an almost unperceived shake of the head presumably conveying the news to his friends.

"Why do you want to speak with Slava?" she asked, a nervousness entering her tone, which she tried to hide, but she'd been around too many men like her husband to miss the signs.

"Just business," he smiled, his eyes piercing, cutting, ruthless.

"Slava doesn't work anymore," she said, well aware he had retired many years before, his involvement in the Russian circuit enough for him to focus on now.

"Is that so?" the man asked, as if it were news to him.

"Where did you say you were from again?" she asked.

"I didn't," he said, his head turning back to his two friends, who were watching him for further instruction. He flicked his head a fraction towards the door. *Time to go.* They got up and moved almost immediately.

"What is your business with Slava?" she asked, stepping in close to the man. This seemed to startle him, Anastasia's persona changed in a split second. She knew how to handle this type. Her voice was low, however, kept between the two of them for the time being. The man took a half step back, restoring the more natural space between two strangers, not wanting to draw anybody's attention.

"My boss wants a word, that's all," he said, handing Anastasia a card, the name *Jose Zabala* embossed in gold in the centre of the card, a family emblem or something the only other thing visible, besides the name and a telephone number. It was a Spanish number, though that figured, given the nationality of the three visitors. They apparently intended their presence there to put fear into Slava. She couldn't imagine how he could have got caught up in something that required such tactics.

"I think you've got the wrong Slava," she said, taking the card anyway.

"Really?" he asked, his two friends now outside the venue, only he remained. "Why do you say that?"

"The Slava I know is an old man," she said, "who has no issues with anyone. He lives a quiet life, keeps his head down, helps where he can. He's elderly, so there is only so much he can do."

"Why don't you ask him about Spain? Ask him what this old man did a few months back," he said, taking a few steps away, though Anastasia went after him, grabbing him by the elbow, stopping him in his tracks. A few heads turned nearby, Anastasia waving them away.

"What do you mean about Spain? He hasn't been to Spain," she said.

"You know this for certain?" It was clear she didn't.

"He hates flying," she said, something she knew. "He holidays mostly in Germany; sometimes Poland given the proximity of the border. Anywhere he can reach by car. He loathes the autobahns, hates vehicles racing at high speed past him."

The man didn't seem to know what to say to that, his mouth open a fraction, but words failing to come out right now.

"You take him that card," he finally managed, "and see what he makes of it. Get him to call," the man finished.

"Are you threatening him?" she demanded, following him to the door, so that nobody else could hear them.

"If he calls my boss today, there is no threat," he said, his grin suggesting what might happen if Don Zabala didn't hear. "You'll take this card to him?" he asked, now halfway through the door.

She nodded, no intention of doing any such thing.

TWO HOURS LATER, the last of the guests were leaving, the event a tremendous success. Anastasia had mentioned nothing to the others about what the three Spanish visitors were doing there. As she cleared the tables, she had started conversations with the people she knew the three had joined. This told her they'd been asking about Slava, asking if they knew where he was, if they could point him out. As these tables were mostly new people––Slava kept a low profile at the best of times, did nothing vocal at the tea parties despite being Chairman of the organisation––nobody knew much about him to answer the questions posed.

She knew there had been some mistake. Slava couldn't have been in Spain, and even if by some miracle he had driven that far, he was a gentle old man. Wouldn't hurt a fly. Probably couldn't now, either.

However, as she left the venue that afternoon, it was the obvious tail she now had that pushed her over the edge. She had spotted the other two men following her, presumably under orders from the third man, who must have assumed she would not recognise his two friends. They thought she would lead them right to Slava, the desperate woman running to pass the man their message.

She wouldn't be so foolish, nor would she go home. She didn't want them knowing where she lived, either.

After an hour, ending up once in the same spot she'd been before, she tired of the charade. She headed into a nursing home––she'd once visited an elderly relative there two years before, the lady long since dead––vanishing behind the doors, but sure the men had seen her enter. Watching from a side corridor, she watched them approach the building, but stop. They didn't follow her in, one man pulling out his mobile phone, presumably informing the man she'd spoken with of the location of Slava, if not calling the name on the business card directly. She pulled the card from her pocket, looked it over, front and back, but there were no more clues besides what she had already seen.

No company named. No address. This wasn't any business card her husband Dmitry would have issued, where logo and image was everything. This was personal.

Seeing the men walk down the street along which they had followed her, going away from the nursing home, Anastasia slipped out of the building through a side exit which led in the other direction.

At home later that night, she'd searched the name on the card online, no clear business connection noted. The biggest results came back from Spanish-speaking countries, Anastasia looking naturally at the ones on mainland Spain itself, given what the man had said to her earlier. She didn't speak Spanish, the articles in only that language, though rough translations by her search engine into English suggested one reference to a mafia connection in Alicante. An image of an old man, the caption claiming to be one Jose Zabala, had him dressed in black, an old yet elegant lady by his side, standing over a coffin of what the article said was their only son, murdered earlier that year.

She shut down the pages she had searched. Nothing fitted anything that Slava might have done.

She called Slava, heart pounding for the five rings it took him to answer, fear rising that they might have already got to him.

"You're there," she said, Slava answering before the sixth ring.

"Just a routine appointment, my darling," he said, a term he used for almost any female below the age of seventy. Anastasia was over forty years his junior.

"There were three guests there today asking after you," she said, making it sound like old friends had come calling, though both knew he had few friends left, even fewer he ever talked about.

"Who were they?" he asked, half way between curiosity and concern.

"They were Spanish," she said, waiting for any hint of recognition, getting only the opposite.

"Spanish? I don't know anyone Spanish," he said, confused.

"You've never been?" she probed.

"Too far to drive, darling," he explained, enough of a reason for her. "What did they want?"

That she knew, though why, she had yet to figure out.

"Gave me the number for a Jose Zabala, wanted you to call him. Today."

"Today?"

"I know. Does the name mean anything to you?"

"Jose?"

"Yes, surname Zabala." She spelt it out after he asked her to.

"Not at all," he said, naturally confused. She sensed no falsehood in him, no sense he was playing her along. She had become an excellent reader of people over recent years.

"I thought as much," she said. "When I asked them, they said it had something to do with what happened in Spain. With what you did in Spain this year."

He laughed at that. "If I could get to Spain without requiring days to drive, believe me, I would love to go," he joked.

"So you do not understand what they might have wanted?"

"I guess I could call, get this all straightened out. It's clear they have me confused for someone else."

"That's what I said."

"Did you?" He appreciated the way she looked out for him. "You'd better give me that number then, let me get a pen," he said, the sound of him rummaging around for a while all she heard at the other end. "Go on then," he said, "slowly though, my hand's not as obliging as it once used to be, you know."

Three minutes later, after repeating the number three times––and how to call abroad from Germany––and spelling the name, they ended the call. She hoped she'd done the right thing. Part of her had wondered about not passing on the message at all, though having led the men to the nursing home, if they had heard nothing that day, perhaps they would have become angry, even coming after her. She wanted nothing to do with them more than she had already.

SLAVA ALKAEV CALLED the number at eight that night, seven Spanish time. Zabala answered it immediately.

"I take it I'm speaking to the man who ordered the killing of my son," Jose said, waiting for the call, the German number indicative that his message had found its way through.

"I'm sorry to say you have the wrong man," the croaky voice of Slava said. "There's been some misunderstanding, I can assure you."

"Enlighten me," he said. They always claimed innocence right up to the point the bullet ripped through their skull, dumping their brains out through the back of their heads. Denial never brought them any good. He knew they were guilty.

"I've never been to Spain," the man said.

"You didn't pull the trigger," Jose confirmed, well aware of the man who did, "but you set him onto my son. You targeted Luken for the little games you play. You and the others."

"Others?"

"Yes, others. I know about them all, too. Even met one of them.

Roman came to me, offered to give me a way to get to the killer. But soon I realised Niles had never worked alone in my son's death. Somebody forced him into it. And that man was you!"

"I assure you, I…"

"Shut up!" Jose snapped. "You're dead, you hear me!"

"I didn't kill your son!" Slava shouted, his voice finding a strength he'd not known for years. Perhaps it was a final resolve, a final rally before the inevitable?

"She gave you up," Jose sneered, knowing he had the son-of-a-bitch, claims of innocence or not. "Gave me your name the moment I asked for it."

Panic raced through Slava. *What had Anastasia done to him*?

"You spoke with Anastasia?" he asked, terrified to hear an affirmation to his question.

"Anastasia, who is Anastasia? I'm talking about Volkov. President Volkov!"

Slava swore, in Russian, so that Jose didn't understand the words, but he knew the tone of a defeated man regardless of language.

"Svetlana Volkov gave you my name?" Slava asked, his breath short, the wind taken from his lungs with the mention of her name.

"Yes," Jose smiled, aware they were getting somewhere now.

"Look, I'm sorry about the death of your son," Slava started, his mind racing, his thoughts in free fall. He'd feared this moment more than anything else those past four years. "It's true, I had nothing to do with his murder," he added, and before Zabala could cut him off with another angry comeback, he said. "But I know why Volkov would want you to think I was responsible," his head hanging in shame, the conversation pausing for a long while.

3

Berlin & London
Present Day

Anastasia sat cupping her morning coffee in her hands, going over things in her head. A call from Slava had woken her that morning before eight. She knew he was an early riser, but soon she realised it was more than that. He'd not been able to sleep. The name of Russia's new President soon came up--Slava didn't say why he was a target, but informed Anastasia he was afraid. She tried asking if the Spanish men she'd seen had threatened him, but he didn't answer her. Said he didn't care about them; it was Volkov who had caused him to stay up all night.

None of it made sense. Slava had not been back to Russia in years, for the same reason she knew he couldn't have been to Spain. It was too far away. Slava didn't even have a vote anymore, not that he had shown any sign of interest in his country's election race. Whenever Anastasia had raised the subject, he would soon move the conversation on to something else. She told him he could call her if he needed anything. Told him to stay safe. He didn't reply before hanging up.

Anastasia got out of bed, dressed quickly, and went down the road to her favourite café. Her phone lay open, a number displayed, one she hadn't called for a long time. A link to her past she just couldn't ignore for ever.

She checked the clock. It would be seven in London now, Anissa up early, kids in the house. Anastasia caught herself. Anissa had no children, not anymore. She would wait. Another half an hour, perhaps, take another coffee. Willing herself to leave it, to not make the call. Perhaps she would hear news from Anissa that she wouldn't want to know? Perhaps Anissa had found something out, the information too terrible to have called, though Anastasia knew that was foolish. Anissa didn't know her number, it was how they had worked it. Anastasia knew the British agent's phone number by heart, changing her own regularly, though she hadn't bothered for nearly two years now. She wasn't being followed anymore, didn't care much if she was. She knew she couldn't live like that, always on the run, always looking over her shoulder. She remained careful, but after several months on the move, taking in multiple European countries, she had circled back to Germany, the only close family she had left, and while living in a different part of the city than before, she had settled. She would meet up with her cousins regularly, one having taken her in when she first moved to Germany. They were close. This was home for her now. This was all she had.

At nine, Anastasia placed the long-empty mug onto the table, the second coffee she'd had in as many hours. She grabbed her phone, pressing the call button before any doubt could divert her actions, and put it to her ear. Each time she feared she might have forgotten the number, or that Anissa would have changed it.

The phone rang, the tone confirming she was calling a still-working British number.

"Hello?" came Anissa's voice, the sound of music in the background.

"It's me," Anastasia said, her still distinctive accent enough for Anissa to understand who it was. Anissa gave her private number out to very few people. Outside of Six, she knew few others.

"Look, I'm driving," she said, using the car's inbuilt hands-free system. "Are you okay?"

"Yes," Anastasia said. "I'll call you when you get there. How long will that be?"

"Give me one hour," Anissa confirmed. She had to finish the thirty minute commute and clear up a few things first.

"I'll call you at nine UK time then," Anastasia said, ending the call.

ANISSA HAD BEEN in the office for half an hour when her mobile vibrated again, the appointment she'd made having completely slipped out of her mind once she got into the office. Sasha looked up from his desk as she swore at her lapse, but said nothing. He watched her leave the room, mobile in hand, putting it to her ear as she went down the corridor. There had been a frosty relationship between the two agents ever since Sasha had confronted Anissa about the murder of their former DDG, Bethany May. The Russian, a former FSB agent himself, had worked out that Anissa had been the one to kill May. He'd kept his word not to say anything to anyone at Six, however.

"I've not heard anything," Anissa said, taking the call, heading towards the canteen which would at least still be quiet.

"I'm not calling about Alex," Anastasia replied, though that was never entirely true. She was desperate for information, any snippet of hope which might help her sleep a little easier.

"Then why are you calling?" Anissa asked. They had no other connection apart from Alex. Anissa knew her former colleague had been a fool for getting involved with the Belarusian. Even if she believed Alex didn't know who she was initially––Anissa still not one hundred percent decided on that one––he had soon found out. Her advice, even the advice of Sasha, had been to end it immediately. Alex had agreed, though he never had. It had nearly cost him his job, perhaps his life. Had the newspapers followed up the stories of the mysterious affair with an actual name, it would have finished him.

His days in the Service would be over. Kaminski would also have known his identity. Men of such wealth did not take kindly to finding out another man had moved in on their wife.

"I had a call this morning from a friend here in Germany," she said. "He's scared." There was a pause, Anastasia not knowing what to say but knowing she'd not said anything that gave reason for her to call a member of the British Security Service that morning. "It's Volkov."

"The President?" Anissa said, still not used to that title, having been on Svetlana's trail for many years already, knowing better than most there was a side few people saw in the now popular President of Russia.

"She's coming after my friend."

"Why?"

"He couldn't tell me," Anastasia said, something that had annoyed her that morning too, Slava unable to give the reason, though she knew one existed. There was no doubt of that.

"And this friend is who?" Anissa knew Anastasia showed a strange taste in men, oligarchs and secret agents included.

"An old man, harmless," she said. "That's the point. He's no threat to her."

"He must have done something?"

"Not anything to my knowledge. Took no interest in the election. Hasn't been to Russia in decades."

"So he is Russian?"

"Yes," Anastasia confirmed. "He's in his eighties now, retired twenty years ago, maybe longer. Well before her rise to political fame. It makes no sense."

"And he was certain it's her specifically who is after him?"

"Yes. Somehow it involves a Spanish man––I think he's mafia. Apparently Volkov gave this Spaniard my friend's name as the man who killed his son."

Anissa was scrambling to keep up, but anything involving these Russians––and after Filipov, who was now long dead, Svetlana Volkov had become her chief target––she would hear them out.

"She set the mafia onto an old man?"

"Yes. Look, if it's the same Spaniard I found when searching online, his son got murdered earlier this year. I'm certain my friend had nothing to do with it, however."

"So why would Volkov tell the grieving father he had?"

"Exactly," Anastasia said, pleased her hunch to call Anissa had proved worthwhile.

"And the threat is real?" Anissa wanted confirmation.

"He's petrified, I can see that. He knows what she has against him."

"You must get more from him," Anissa said. There was nothing yet which would warrant British involvement. "Or get him to go to the police there."

"He won't do that," she said. She'd told Slava the same that morning when he called her, the man in a panic, seeing things that weren't there. Very much the rabbit caught in the headlights, frozen, awaiting the inevitable.

"Get something," Anissa said. "Call me back when you have it," she said, ending the call. There was nothing more she could say. If she were to get involved, it had to be credible this time. *Watertight; no messing around.*

Penal colony № 6 Federal Penitentiary Service, Russia
June 1994

THE TEAMS WERE WORKING *around the clock now, the tunnel fifteen feet underneath the prison compound, the entrance they came in through now over one hundred metres away. They had purchased a house eleven months before with that specific purpose in mind. Tunnelling had started almost immediately, the initial effort slow, the first couple of metres thick clay. Deeper down, the clay turned to sand and soil, and progress could speed up.*

It worried them what they would find at the other end, when it was time to dig upwards. More clay, then concrete? They wanted to get to that part of the tunnel two weeks before the deadline, though with ten days to go, they had yet to make it far enough.

It felt like trying to land a fighter jet on an aircraft carrier, the margins for error small, the risks great. Come up too early or too late and it would all be for nothing, their position revealed, their plot uncovered.

It would be tight.

At the house from where they worked, a full renovation was being carried out. The men could work on that during the day. They could explain away the bags of rubble coming out from the house continually—in reality all soil from the tunnel—as the ongoing work, the number of workers enough to move the neighbours on and raising no suspicion.

Most of the men stayed in the house, only five or six going out through the front door during any shift, the bags piling up; the container emptied several times already.

The heat in the tunnel was becoming an issue, though as they drew nearer the end, only working at night helped somewhat in that regard. Still, in the tunnel, the surrounding earth warm, the summer sunshine hot above ground, it felt like an oven, the space compact with little airflow.

They reached the clay layer on the twentieth of the month, one week before the date they'd given Boris. Visiting day had now passed a week ago, the cousin with no option but to make sure they finished in time. It would be close, and now that they were digging upwards, they had to make sure they kept noise to a minimum. Through the clay they still had cover—nobody would hear anything—but once they got to the concrete foundation, the instructions were clearer. Night-time only.

Lanterns hung from the sides of the tunnel now, boardwalks put down along the floor. They increased effort that final week, the men during the day making a larger space underneath the basement, allowing more men to wait there, aiding them in the night-shift rota which started that night. They had something like five feet to get through, and all their measurements showed they were exactly where they wanted to be.

Seven nights of frantic work and they could tunnel through. They would only break the floor on that final night, in the hour Boris was due to be there, so as not to alert anyone to their presence.

A heavy supply of weapons was loaded into the tunnel, ten men now in the house, guarding things from that end, the visible construction work that had been going on suddenly coming to an end. The remaining bags of debris could stay in the house.

They had purchased five large trucks, five drivers hired ahead of time, though they would only get their instructions an hour before the escape. They would be ready to evacuate everyone from the area, Boris included, the men in the back of each truck—ten per vehicle—weapons ready. All being well, they would have got away without the alarm being raised. The first the prison would know about the tunnel would be the following morning, when the inmates arrived at the basement for another day of work.

They would be miles away by then.

The first few nights had been hard, the tools they had not adequate, though to use any power tools would be too noisy, the vibrations sure to sound somewhere above ground. Still, with three nights remaining and only half the concrete chiselled through, they purchased several smaller drills during the day, an elaborate cable system sorted out to get plugs to the far end of the tunnel. They would make lots of small holes, using less power, the risk therefore of anyone hearing them minimal. It was all they could do. When they got to the final foot, they could revert to doing it all by hand, working continuously, each man taking ten minutes at full speed. There was only room for two men to work comfortably by that point, the number of people meaning rotation and freshness played to their advantage.

By that last night, they were close. The end was in sight. They put away the drills; they watched the clock closely. They knew the working day finished at five, when the inmates went to dinner, when the basement would get locked up. Boris should have cut himself on something that day so that he would have to spend the night in the hospital wing. He had no other way from his cell to the basement except from the hospital ward. The security was still heavy there, but the doors were less impenetrable.

Boris too looked at his watch expectantly.

4

London
Present Day

When Zoe rang the bell at Sasha's flat one evening it was Anissa who opened the door, even though she no longer lived there. To be exact it was Alex's apartment but he'd not been there for over three years. The gathering hoped to address that. It seemed the right place to meet. Sasha had the space, anyway, and they couldn't do this in the office.

The sound of laughter came from the lounge at the end of the small corridor.

"Hang your coat anywhere," Anissa instructed Zoe as she slipped off her denim jacket to reveal a rather elegant black number underneath, a little too tight, or perhaps that was the point. Zoe looked up as another roar sounded from Charlie and Sasha, who'd got there already.

"What's going on down there?" Zoe asked, turning to Anissa and seeing the funny expression now on her face.

"Never mind them; what's going on with you and Charlie?" Anissa asked, the dress suggesting her MI6 colleague had assets she wanted others to know about—perhaps someone in particular. Zoe rarely dressed for any occasion. It was interesting that an informal gathering to discuss what they all might do about Alex seemed to warrant such a carefully selected outfit.

"Nothing," Zoe said, somewhat deflated.

"Still?" Anissa knew about the fling, the one night Zoe and Charlie had shared several years before, not long after Charlie's former-girlfriend had been killed. They'd both been drunk, Charlie remembering even less than Zoe did of their time together.

"We work together. It's complicated," Zoe said.

"I work with Sasha," Anissa replied, as if that meant anything. Zoe knew things were not now as they had been between the two colleagues. She'd often walked in on frosty conversations between Anissa and the Russian, both going silent, neither able to look at the other. Zoe knew there was tension there, knew they were no longer seeing each other outside of work. Another roar of delight went up from the lounge, Zoe now moving towards the source of the noise, seeing both Sasha and Charlie playing a video game, Sasha talking his colleague through the role-playing game as the action unfolded. They each had their own screen, presumably playing the same game together.

"Besides," Zoe said, "he won't even notice." She whispered this to Anissa and the validity of what she had just said was proved as they walked into the lounge, Zoe dressed to impress, and neither man even noticed their appearance.

"Zoe, if there's one thing I know about men," Anissa said, whispering back, "dressed like that, they'll notice." The words brought a small smile to Zoe's face, Anissa not sure if that was an appropriate reaction, but let it go.

"What are you playing?" Zoe asked, sitting down on the sofa, Sasha two spaces to her left on the same sofa, controller in hand, operating a soldier on the television in front of him. Charlie sat at right angles to Zoe, a laptop on the table, his eyes glancing at the flash of leg as Zoe sat down, the dress ending at least nine inches above the knee.

"Bloody hell, Zo," Charlie exclaimed, mouth slightly open, though a shout from Sasha to watch out, drew him back to the screen, those long slender legs––making a very rare appearance––constantly in his peripheral vision. His gameplay went downhill fast from there on.

Anissa stood in the kitchen, pouring two glasses of wine, and mouthed over to Zoe, who had looked her way, smiling. *See, I told you.*

"It's Call of Duty," Sasha said, answering Zoe's initial question. "I'm giving Charlie a little tutorial." Charlie's character died again at that point on cue. He flopped his head back as if dead, before standing up from the table––his eyes constantly glancing at those legs.

"I'm done," he said, taking the seat next to Zoe, Anissa passing Zoe a glass of wine, winking mischievously as she did so. Zoe shook her head, embarrassed, but smiled anyway.

They watched Sasha finish the task they were on, before he said something into the headset––there were apparently others in the team besides Charlie––and he logged out of the game and switched off.

"You look beautiful, Zoe," he said, coming over to greet her properly now, giving her a kiss on each cheek which she rose to receive.

"I thought, why not dress for a night out for once," she joked, taking her seat again, Charlie passing back her glass which she'd passed to him when she stood up to greet Sasha. The four friends clinked glasses now that they were all seated, Anissa taking the sofa opposite––a good view of Zoe's thighs had Charlie opted for that seat––but he seemed perfectly happy sitting next to her.

Nobody could work out why they were not already an item.

They were there to discuss Alex. The only other member of the group was Gordon Peacock, head of IT and cyber-security at Six. He couldn't make it that night, the four agents deciding to meet together anyway to discuss a way forward for them all.

"So, how do we get to Alex?"

"We don't even know where he is," Charlie confirmed. Charlie had been in Mexico until less than a month ago and Zoe had flown in from New York the previous weekend. "Do you have any contacts that might know where to look?" he asked Sasha, a man he'd grown to appreciate increasingly over the last few years. Their frosty start in Stockholm following the murder of Anya in Zurich was now long forgotten.

"None that could help me now," Sasha confirmed. He'd been out of Russia and the FSB for too long, presumed dead for just as long, though he knew Filipov had known about him, and therefore so did the current President. Following the sending of Rad to London to kill him––the pair going back longest of all, though they hadn't seen each other since they were boys––there had been nothing further. It appeared the new President was a little more forgiving than the previous incumbent.

"Is there anything the DG can do?" Zoe asked, she the least senior of the other two Brits there, in Six a little longer than Sasha, but the newest to the Security Service of them all, following her transfer from New Scotland Yard in the wake of the Zurich bombing and its connected scandal. The Director General ran MI6, the chain of command streamlined to miss out the role of Deputy Director, a post which the DG had once asked Alex to fill, and one that had produced two consecutive duff characters, both now dead. Both colluding with Russians in the worst sort of way. Anissa's husband and two sons were dead because of the second DDG.

"We can try," Anissa said, knowing full well that nobody at MI6, especially the DG, had sanctioned the mission to send Alex to Russia with Phelan. They all knew he would never have signed off on it.

"He won't go for it," Charlie interjected, certain of that fact as much as anything. "Alex overstepped the mark," he said, glancing at Anissa, then Sasha, who'd both been in that decision process, both therefore party to the same fault, though Charlie didn't seem to blame them. "He knew what he was doing," Charlie added, having time for Alex, even if they'd never hung out much outside of the office. He regretted that now, had enjoyed the immersion into Sasha's online gaming life, and though he would never make a pro-gamer himself, he missed not having close friends around anymore. He missed nights like this one, made easier, he saw, because they all had the same thing in common. They all worked at Six. There needed to be no awkward cover stories, no long silences when a stranger asked how they knew each other, or what they did for a living, asked them where they worked, wanting to catch lunch together at some point.

"But he's still alive," Anissa reminded them all, something they'd learned from *Gremlin* the previous few months, the Russian whistle-blower having shared that much with Anissa, even if he didn't know where they were now holding Alex. Rad too had confirmed he had not shot Alex, telling them of his order to kill Phelan, which he did, though Alex needed taking alive.

Alex had quickly outlived Filipov, though Svetlana Volkov seemed in no hurry to release him. They assumed she had to know of his existence, therefore knew of his location, and for whatever reason, had kept that a secret still, even if it had not directly involved her.

"Look, I had a call from Anastasia Kaminski today," Anissa said, Sasha turning at the mention of the name, it also ringing a bell with Charlie.

"The woman Alex had an affair with?" Charlie asked. The mention of the affair seemed to send Anissa's nostrils flaring.

"Yes," she confirmed. The affair had been Alex's one huge mistake and sole reason he was now missing. "She called about another matter, in fact, something about Volkov," Anissa added.

"Anything worth knowing?" Sasha asked.

"Later," she said, dismissively, coming back to her initial thought. "Anyway, I know Anastasia still loves Alex. Do I tell her what we are thinking?"

"Can you trust her?" Zoe asked, somewhat sketchy with the idea of speaking to anyone outside that group, especially someone like Anastasia, whom she didn't know.

"I do," Anissa said, no small thing. She'd not liked the woman one bit in the beginning. Time allowed her to see the risks Anastasia had taken for Alex.

"Is there even anything she could do?" Charlie pointed out, aware Anastasia's ex-husband was in prison in the UK, the Belarusian herself somewhere in Europe. She wasn't in Russia. How much could she know, and if it was not a lot, how could she help them?

"No, Anissa has a point," Sasha said, his tone suggesting he was seeing it differently from both Charlie and Zoe at that moment. The four of them––not only working for MI6 but their history too––were far more high-profile to the Russians than nearly anyone else might be. "As much as I would like to go, I'm not sure I could."

"You can't!" Anissa said, strongly. She wouldn't allow Sasha to travel back to Russia, it wouldn't be safe.

"And I'm not sure you're ready yet, either," Sasha added, ignoring her words for the time being as he looked at Anissa, whose five-year ban had ended but not the nightmares. She shrugged, as if to say she wasn't sure, which was confirmation enough. "Charlie, you also have history there. They'll have your passport logged."

"I have other documents," Charlie countered, the most qualified of the group––besides Sasha, who he knew couldn't go––to travel to Russia. Charlie spoke Russian. MI6 had posted him there early in his career.

"That might be, but it's too dangerous," Sasha said. "However, we need someone who can sniff around."

"I could," Zoe offered, not on Russia's radar, as far as she knew, though she had helped Charlie take out a rogue FSB unit in Switzerland several years ago. She didn't speak a word of Russian, though.

Sasha shook his head. "I think we could do with a local," he said.

"What about your friend?" Anissa asked, aware of Sasha's connection to Rad––a connection strong enough to save his life. They were hardly friends, however. They'd spent time in the same orphanage for two months. Sasha had saved Rad's young life and helped him to escape. He'd even given the boy a name, the same name he still carried to that day.

"He works directly with Volkov now, heads up her security." Anissa recalled that now, nodding in acknowledgment.

"So you think I should sound out Anastasia?" she asked, coming back to her original thought.

"Do you think she would help?" Charlie asked, Anissa laughing at the need to even ask the question.

"Charlie, she's madly in love with Alex. She'll do anything."

"But should she?" Zoe questioned, aware that feelings often impeded reason.

"We might not have any other choice," Anissa pointed out. "I'll speak to her tomorrow," an unspoken consensus now reached among them.

5

Zabala Family Compound, Alicante Region, Spain
Two Months ago

Don Jose Zabala sat at the family table, plates of food still being put into position, his wife working away in the kitchen. He'd been doing a lot of research that last month.

Two of his men sat on the two nearest chairs along one side of the large wooden dining table. A young woman sat on the other side.

Señorita Zabala had turned her nose up at the girl the moment she set eyes on her. She knew a *puta* when she saw one.

"Tell me what you told my men earlier," Don Zabala said, turning to the young woman to his right.

"I reached out to them, to you, for help," she said. Despite what his wife might think, she wasn't actually a prostitute. "I was walking home, three streets from where I live, and someone grabbed me from behind, dragging me into the bushes." She stopped speaking, the Don leaning forward a little, his voice fatherly, gentle, safe.

"This was a man, I assume?" She nodded. "And?"

Her eyes told him the inevitable, the woman unable to form the words, yet deep hurt and shame clearly evident.

"Why didn't you go to the police?" he asked.

"I did." Jose looked at his two men. They'd not told him this, and a shrug confirmed they'd not known this either until that moment.

"Yet here you are anyway," the Don smiled. He controlled much of the region; it was why so many looked to him for help, usually before going to the police.

"They couldn't find him."

"You knew who raped you?" Don Zabala asked, not flinching to say the word, having also picked up that she knew more than she had said.

"I gave the police the name of the man, yes."

"I see," the Don said, taking it all in, allowing his mind to fill in gaps he might be missing. "And they said they couldn't help?" he asked. That could mean many things. It could even mean the man in question had protection, or was in the police himself. That last part bothered the Don the most.

"They couldn't find him," she confirmed. "Said he'd vanished."

"I see," the Don sighed, happy that it had broken that way. His men had an uncanny way of finding people the police couldn't. They'd hidden enough themselves; they knew where to look. "And the name of the man you want us to find?"

She slipped him a piece of paper. It was enough for her to write the name of her attacker. She would not voice it.

Jose looked at the name which meant nothing to him, as he had assumed. Had this been one of his own men, he would have known. He would have already put a bullet through his skull long ago and would have been able to confirm to the victim the scumbag was dead.

"And you want my help to find this man?" he asked. She smiled up at him, Señorita Zabala coming back into the room at that moment, placing down a plate of meats, and turning away with a flick of her hair without saying a word.

"I want justice," she said, tears welling up in her eyes.

The mafia only dished out one kind of justice, she knew that. It would have been why she had come to them now.

"I'll see that you do," he said, his men standing at that moment, one of them going around to lead the woman out, the meeting over. She got the idea eventually, standing up and thanking him, before following the two men out.

Jose's wife came back in, setting down the last dish––she'd been waiting for the conclusion to the meeting, Jose sensing that fact––and they began to eat in silence, his wife occasionally looking up at him, though Jose seemed deep in thought throughout dinner, and didn't say a word.

IT TOOK him a few days to pick up another clue, but finally Don Zabala knew he was onto something. And none of it made initial sense.

The man suspected of the rape had vanished without a trace, and that meant he either had help or even stronger enemies. No mafia Don ever liked the prospect of an unknown force on their territory, someone able to do something like that––protection or murder, it didn't matter––on his turf without the Don's knowledge. He would say he knew every criminal in the region; kept most of them in line, too. This was his town.

Yet someone else had got there first.

They managed to track down the house of the man in question and found nothing had been touched for weeks. The fridge was full of out-of-date products, the fruit bowl containing nothing fresh. Looking through the rest of the house, Zabala took in everything, his men going through the downstairs, Jose going upstairs. A passport was on the dressing table, travel cases remained in the wardrobe, a toothbrush, toothpaste and shaving equipment in the en-suite. This wasn't the home of a man away on a trip anywhere; this wasn't a man in hiding.

Someone had got to him.

"Don Zabala!" came the call from downstairs, the distinctive tone of his right-hand man drawing Jose to the door which he pulled closed again behind him, his gloved hand sure to leave no trace of his presence. He slowly descended the stairs. His man stood waiting in the kitchen.

"What have you found?" Zabala asked, aware that it had to have been something important. The other man held up a small shard of glass, the pane of a small square window next to the door broken.

"There were at least two of them," the right-hand man confirmed, moving away from the part of the kitchen that had a section where someone could have hidden and not been visible initially. "There are two different footprints in this corner." Jose went over to the spot and saw the marks on the floor. "I believe they broke in and waited for him to arrive home," the man concluded.

Jose reached down and examined the dirt. "Find where this came from," he said.

"That's already clear," his man replied, going over to the back door next to the smashed window. Outside, there was a small garden, most of it dry and unloved, apart from a bed of colourful flowers planted directly underneath the windows. They could see two clear sets of footprints––the smaller pair perhaps size ten, the larger at least a twelve, maybe more. The soil was fresh, though it had dried considerably in recent days, its owner not there to water it anymore.

"I don't understand why they both needed to stand here?" his man said, Jose thinking it over, wearer of size tens himself.

"Shut the back door," Zabala ordered, stepping outside, his mind coming up with the only reasonable explanation why both intruders would have stood there before breaking in.

"The first man is shorter than the other. I bet the taller was the leader of the pair." Not an unreasonable assumption, he thought. "He asked the first guy to break the window, which he did. Glass smashed, access to the inside door lock now possible. Except he couldn't reach," the Don enacted, now with his arm through the hole, aware he was a few inches away from reaching the lock.

"So the taller of the two had to step forward to unlock the door," his man finished.

"Exactly." They didn't need to get anyone to join them from the inside to test the theory. "He opens the door, and they wait inside for their prey to return," Jose continued, reopening the kitchen door and stepping back inside. He closed the door behind them both.

"They stood here and waited," he said, in the spot where both muddy boots had been, his shoes now adding something from the flowerbed, though he kicked this away. "See if there are any other traces anywhere," he ordered, his men going off as instructed, a call coming back to him less than thirty-seconds later.

"In here."

Jose walked down the hallway into what would have been the lounge, a study area beyond. His man was standing in the doorway between the two. A chair behind the computer lay on the floor.

"There were traces of mud across the back of the lounge and one here," his man said, Jose seeing the larger boot print against the wall and two feet behind where the chair would have been.

"They waited for him to settle, perhaps inside for a while, before creeping down the hallway, across the lounge, then back behind him here and pulling him off his chair." There was no other sign of a struggle which seemed strange, though a new thought took hold of him.

"They drugged him," he said, which suggested these were no common criminals. They had targeted the man. Someone wanted him alive, and an unconscious victim was a lot easier to drag away than one kicking and screaming. "They approached from behind," the Don acted out, stepping over the chair––he would move nothing more––and up to roughly where it would have been by the desk, "probably got the needle into his neck before he heard they were there, and with a strong grip around the mouth and shoulders from behind, they dragged him off the chair, probably out cold in seconds. Then they would have taken him to wherever they had orders to take him."

"They were working for someone?"

"Undoubtedly," Jose said, once himself having ordered someone brought to him, once himself having used his men to drug the target. "The question remains, who? And where did they take him?"

The Don looked around. There was no computer on the desk,

which seemed strange. No sign anything was missing, either. Jose moved to the desk, using the end of his cane to open the first of the drawers, nothing but stationary inside. He opened the larger bottom draw, which housed a box. On lifting the lid, it suddenly made perfect sense.

"Keepsakes," Jose said, somewhat disgusted at the find. They both looked down at a box filled with perhaps fifteen pairs of ladies' underwear. "This wasn't the first victim that this man had pounced upon, but I sense it was his last. The question remains: who got to him before we could?"

He would ponder that the entire drive back to his compound, getting nowhere at all in his thinking by the time he reached home.

Vauxhall House, MI6 HQ, London
Present Day

ANISSA HAD BEEN in with the Director General for twenty minutes. Despite what Charlie had said the night before about his willingness to allow them, she knew she had to ask. She had to push every angle.

"Anissa, you know my hands are tied on this one." He had missed Alex being around, the man was a good agent. How they'd both got caught up with Phelan, a wanted terrorist, the DG still couldn't work out. He thought Alex would have known better. He expected much more of Anissa.

"We can't just leave him!" she said. It'd been three years and counting since anyone at MI6 had seen Alex. They'd already left him.

"Why are you coming to me with this now?" he asked.

"Because I didn't know for sure before," she said, doing her best to keep any emotion out of this, knowing it would not make the matter any better. The DG saw any emotional response as grounds for regarding an operation as highly dangerous.

He shook his head slowly.

"I'm sorry, we've been over this. The British cannot acknowledge we had any awareness of his presence there. Hell, Anissa, I didn't know he was!" the DG snapped, raising his voice a little, his own emotion coming out more forcefully than he had expected.

"I know," she said, not entirely clear which bit she was agreeing she knew: the MI6 stance or him being left out in the cold. "So that's it? We leave him there?"

The DG stood up; he had been in that world for too many years already and it was all beginning to catch up with him. He thought he might have been considering retirement by now, though the absence of a safe pair of hands to pass things on to, coupled with the shaky last few years, meant he had needed time to steady the ship. Needed the government to put their faith in the Security Service again. Those beaches would have to wait, the golf courses too.

"The thought of leaving any agent in the field is not one I ever wanted to happen, Anissa," he said, guiding her to the door, but in no hurry to usher her out. "Believe me, I wish Alex Tolbert were still here. God knows we need agents like him. But we both know you all overstepped the mark on this one." It was less of a reprimand, more of a statement of how the landscape looked. "I've had it from the top, too," the DG said, the first mention that someone had passed this verdict down from a cabinet level in the government, meaning the DG had raised the same question with them, perhaps even with the Prime Minister. "We can't sanction an official MI6 mission," he confirmed, a finality in his tone suggesting there was no wiggle room, yet he added one additional comment. "So I wish you luck in finding him," he winked.

"Sorry?" But she got him. This couldn't be official, but he wanted them to find Alex through another channel.

He remained silent, opening the door for her.

"I'm sorry I couldn't give you any better news," he said, smiling now, the pair in earshot of his security and office staff.

"I understand perfectly," she said, not one to wink usually but offering one back at the DG anyway at that moment. He smiled before turning and shutting himself into his office again. Anissa made her way back to the office. She needed time to think, Sasha working at his desk.

She headed to the park.

THEY ALL AGREED to keep things between the four of them, Gordon happy for them to use him for his technical expertise, but not involved in the ongoing planning. When they met again, Anissa let Zoe into the apartment, the two men popping to the shop for more wine––they were planning a games night together once the four agents had got the planning done.

Zoe, dressed this time in jeans and a loose sweater, followed Anissa into the kitchen, glancing around the apartment given the chance.

"I never came here when Alex lived alone," Anissa said, continuing their conversation, Zoe asking about how long she'd worked with Alex. It had been over ten years at the time Alex vanished.

"That's understandable. He's a nice-looking bloke," Zoe said, with a smile.

"No, it was me, really. I owed it to my husband, mostly."

"You and he…" she started, Anissa knowing she meant Alex, the topic hovering on office affairs.

"No, never," Anissa said, honestly.

"Never?" Zoe repeated, a little unbelieving.

"No, I mean it. We were a team. We worked together. He respected that, knew my husband. It worked. I just didn't want to cause my husband any concern. I never once came here." It wasn't as if Alex held lots of parties, anyway, but that wasn't the point. Whenever she met Alex outside of work, it would usually be with others, for the odd drink, but mostly the hours spent together at Vauxhall House were enough. She missed them all now. Missed his smile, his sense of humour, his stubbornness.

"I work with Charlie," Zoe pointed out, as if that meant anything. She'd slept with him once, Anissa had lived with Sasha for a while.

"It was only ever friendship with Alex," Anissa said, her tone indicative that this was the final word on the subject.

"Fine," Zoe protested, taking the glass offered, the bottle now finished, which was why the boys had headed out.

"And what about you? Aside the obvious, anything in the air?" Anissa grinned.

"What's that supposed to mean?" Zoe quizzed back, though she knew precisely what she meant by it. She and Charlie was the obvious, and nothing had happened there in years, despite their chemistry. Perhaps because of their chemistry. She seemed to be nothing but the little sister to Charlie—when she would have taken much more.

Anissa didn't answer. She didn't need to, Zoe instead knowing the truth of what her colleague had just asked, speaking up again next.

"No, that boat sailed a while ago I think."

"You went to New York together the other month, surely you had plenty of time together, no?"

Zoe had travelled to New York, Anissa had helped to organise it. She'd been there to find out information on Gremlin, Zoe staying when they discovered the Russian whistleblower was hiding in Mexico. She stayed there to keep the CIA guessing, while Charlie sneaked away, apparently returning to London before heading off to Mexico himself.

"We talked, yes, but he's off the booze mostly now," she added. The men might be out buying wine at that moment but when it came to drinking it, Charlie would probably limit himself to a glass, if that. Drinking and women didn't go well for him. He knew his vulnerability. Anissa couldn't help but see her colleague talking herself down yet again. *Charlie would only be interested in me if smashed out of his mind. Sober Charlie would never look twice at me.*

"There are others at the office, though," Anissa pointed out, the choice of eligible males in short supply, granted. Two of them were coming back in through the door at that moment; another was in prison in Russia. She assumed that Alex was already spoken for.

Anastasia had that area taken care of, Anissa certain the feelings between Alex and the gorgeous Belarusian were entirely mutual.

"What, you mean gormy-Gordon?" she laughed, Anissa nearly choking on her wine as Sasha and Charlie entered the living room. Once she'd stopped coughing, their conversation went remarkably quiet, neither answering the men about what they were talking about.

Ten minutes later, they sat around the lounge in their usual spots, two bowls of snacks on the table, a bottle opened with two more in reserve. Charlie had said how they planned to have a late one, Sasha continuing to educate him in the world of online gaming. His laptop sat ready on the dining table, but the focus for now was Alex.

"So, the DG won't stand in our way," Anissa confirmed, Zoe looking at her female colleague with surprise. They'd been chatting for the last ten minutes since she arrived and she'd failed to tell her that.

"He's sanctioning a mission?" Charlie asked, astounded.

"No, he's not," Anissa interjected quickly, hands raised for calm, as she explained the double-sided conversation she'd had with the DG earlier in the day. She chatted through her call with Anastasia. "She couldn't wait to get involved," Anissa finished, picking up her glass.

"She knows what she's getting into?" Sasha questioned, aware this might quickly put her on the Kremlin's radar, if she wasn't already on it.

"She loves him," Anissa said, not for the first time in her account of the day's events, and as if that made it all okay. As if that enabled them all to put the Belarusian in harm's way.

"It will help to have someone like her running point," Charlie said. She could lead the search from inside the country better than any of them could manage outside. She spoke Russian, could cross the border freely, had the money to back herself up too.

"My point is, she knows the risks. She's onboard with this," Anissa clarified, a consensus reached around the group now. They should use Anastasia, there was no conflict here.

"And presuming she finds where they are holding him, then what?" Sasha asked.

"Then we break him out," Anissa said, Charlie nodding, having already asked Anissa about this over coffee at the office.

"We break him out," Zoe echoed, with a smile.

By ten, they had finished the second bottle, the four friends chatting freely, though as the night pressed on, the ladies sensed they were encroaching on game time.

"We'll leave you two boys to it," Zoe joked, Anissa standing, Sasha already reaching for his controller. Charlie saw the two women out, closing the door behind them once they walked off down the corridor, before rejoining the Russian in the lounge.

"Let the warfare begin!" Sasha roared, his avatar logging in, Charlie filling his glass again––playing an online game less than sober far safer to do than spending time around two attractive women drunk––and he then opened his own laptop, soon loading up the same screen, ready to join Sasha's team in a nighttime of missions. He'd not had this much fun since his parents bought him a Super Nintendo for his fourteenth birthday.

6

Penal colony № 6 Federal Penitentiary Service, Russia
June 1994

The workrooms were closed for the day, the inmates already on their way to dinner. Inside the metal and ceramic workshop, the final sections of a fountain were being put together, a black dolphin from which the prison would soon get its name. The prisoners had built the statue, and the ceremony to put the structure in place was due the following month.

In the next door room, the sewing machines of the fabrics workroom now sat quietly, the room empty. Only a matter of inches underneath the floor several men waited. A tunnel shaft three feet in diameter dropped into the ground, along which a tunnel ran to freedom, out beyond the prison walls. All fifty men stood guard, ten men remaining in the house, watching the rear. One of these men would call through to the trucks, their drivers waiting for the signal for their night's work, aware and on standby that this was the day.

Ten men grouped in the space carved out directly underneath the basement workroom, weapons ready. They didn't want a gunfight, nobody wanted that. All being well, they wouldn't need one. They'd made it this far *without detection, though the final inch or two were perhaps the most dangerous yet. If there was anything but an empty room above them as they broke ground—or if they were anywhere other than where they planned to be—the game was up. The shaft was hard to fight from, weapons difficult to hold. Anyone above ground had a huge advantage—one grenade dropped into the shaft would take out most of the men in no time.*

A fight was the last thing they wanted.

Boris lay in his bed in the hospital ward looking up at the clock. Dinner had come, inmates in that wing given food in bed when otherwise it was the canteen. There were only two others in the room, men who wouldn't last long in a place like that. Child molesters. Boris couldn't stand their sort. Rich coming from a man who killed so willingly, but even he had a line he never crossed with children. There were some things too sick, and the two in his room had got what was coming to them.

His own injury—self inflicted, not that the doctor or guards knew that—was a severe gash to the arm. He'd been close to his artery, a little too close, he realised now. The doctor had told Boris he was a lucky man—lucky being ironic. Surviving meant a lifetime behind bars.

Except Boris knew he was getting out of there. A piece of sharp metal slashed across his own skin, the pouring of his own blood, was worth that kind of opportunity. The scar from the twelve stitches the doctor had needed to close the wound would remind Boris of how close they came to caging him. He vowed he would not allow them that chance again. He knew this was it, his last night behind bars.

The other two patients were largely out of it come nine that night. One was still in a comatose state following his attack—Boris had heard the doctors discussing amongst themselves if he would ever wake up—and the other man was so heavily sedated that he barely stayed awake long enough to finish his dinner each night.

Boris heard the heavy breathing of these sleeping inmates all the way from the other side of the ward. He kept his own eyes closed. The doctor did his rounds, confirming to the guard that all the patients were now asleep, saying goodnight himself as he left for home. He was going off duty, the day over, everything quiet.

Boris smiled as he heard the footsteps fade. Three hours and he would make his own way from that room.

As midnight fell, the lights had gone out in the hall, the footsteps of the guard still heard overhead, though he walked past once every fifteen minutes, and even then, the ward was in darkness. Boris climbed out of the bed, staying low. He stuffed two blankets under the sheets, doing his best to recreate his shape in the bed in his absence. Happy with his effort, he waited for the guard to pass by once more. If the man was suspicious, he would come down—his eyes off the bed during that process, Boris able to get back in and pretend to be asleep.

The guard didn't slow his pace one bit. Boris checked his watch again in the light from outside the window. He had an hour to get into position, a walk he'd never done from there, the dark not helping in that matter, though the cover it now offered him was invaluable. He would work it out.

Sixty minutes and he would be free. He could almost sense the air filling his lungs once more.

The guards worked in shifts around the building, going the same way, the same route, three hours at a time. The next change wouldn't be for two hours. It was the window Boris had. The new guard might want to check on the ward, make sure the men were actually sleeping.

Boris heard the footsteps come once more, as he waited by the door. His plan—his only choice—to get nearer to where he needed to be would succeed or fail in these next few seconds. There was no other option than to follow the guard, albeit at a distance, but moving behind him constantly until he got far enough round to sneak into a storeroom, from which he could make it to the basement. There should be no guards anywhere near those rooms now.

As the footsteps drew closer again, Boris's heart pounded at double the rate of the rhythmic steps of solid Russian boots coming along the prison corridor. The stride did not break even after the final clicks happening and the door silently fell open, Boris having worked the lock from his side a little. Boris waited for any further sounds, though all around him, darkness prevailing, there was nothing. The footsteps grew quieter and Boris pulled the door closed behind him quickly—no going back now, this was it—and tiptoed after the guard. If he were too far behind, on some turns, it would be possible for the guard to see him through the windows. Boris had to be closer, making no noise.

After the first turn, Boris knew he didn't know where he was. He'd only walked these corridors with a bag over his head, and though the surrounding darkness now offered similar light, he had assumed without such a covering, he would have known his way better.

He kept low, shifting down another corridor, the first prison cells visible behind bars soon after. He wasn't where he thought he was. He sped up, looking at his watch, looking all around him, panic rising in him for the first time that night. Get caught where he was now—exposed and very much in the wrong place—and it would all be over. This would be his one chance, his only chance at getting out of there.

Boris paused at the next corner, the steps of the guard having stopped a second before. He dare not look around the corner yet, for fear the guard had heard something, perhaps turning to check. Boris heard a conversation begin seconds later, the sound of a cigarette lighter flicking on, two guards sharing a smoke and a brief chat.

Boris crouched down, risking the tiniest of looks around the corner, catching sight of the torchlight of the retreating guard, his body in silhouette, up ahead and partly obscured by the corner. He couldn't see the other man, presumably not in the actual corridor, perhaps behind some bars in the section that overlooked the cells? Boris had not expected another guard.

And he still didn't precisely know where he was.

Thirty minutes left.

In the tunnel, the cousin drew back into the space underground, allowing the two most experienced engineers to carry out the final procedure. They had taken measurements. They knew there was a matter of centimetres left, perhaps only two. They used hand drills on the four corners to carve pilot holes up through the concrete, the crust giving way so easily proving the closeness now to the surface. A week of heavy work had weakened the floor there. Soon they drilled all four holes, and the men drilled one final one in the centre, ready for the hammer blow they would strike the area with, enough they hoped to break through suddenly. Boris should be there by then, the noise kept to a minimum, and for the life of them underneath, they hoped nothing heavy rested above the spot.

Half an hour later the cousin looked at his watch under the torchlight one final time, calling up to the one man in the space with the sledgehammer, telling him it was time. Two other men did their best to shield him from debris, holding up a wooden box they'd nailed together, a wooden umbrella of sorts. It would stop the final inch of concrete doing any serious damage, but if something substantial were to follow it from up above, they might be in trouble.

The men in the space underground raised their weapons. The call was made to the truck drivers, readying them to sweep into the area minutes later.

"Okay, go!" the cousin said, one, two then three blows from the hammer enough to break through the final section of flooring, one corner the first to drop, the man in the tunnel then using a downward blow having pushed the hammer through to cause the rest to cave in.

Boris was not in the darkened room, however, nothing but silence awaiting them as the man with the sledgehammer peered through the gap cautiously.

One building away, Boris stood frantically pacing around an identical basement workshop, wondering all the while why he couldn't hear breaking concrete.

Then gunfire sounded, the alarms at the prison ringing out a minute after that, lights coming on all over the place, the roar of delight from the waking prisoners telling Boris something had gone wrong.

Armed guards cut three of the men down as they climbed out of the hole, their calling for Boris having drawn the attention of a guard on duty down the hall. The next men out of the tunnel shot the guard though he'd done enough to raise the alarm.

"Get back inside!" the cousin demanded, no response from above. He climbed up through the hole, seeing the fallen men, hearing the approach of feet. For a moment he thought it might be Boris, though the sounding of the prison siren told him he shouldn't have been so hopeful.

"Freeze!" a guard shouted, spotting the head coming up through the floor from the shaft that led down into the ground. The cousin ducked back, dropping to the tunnel floor.

"Make sure nobody follows up," he ordered his men, the group raising their weapons towards the opening at ground level, the cousin racing back down the tunnel towards the house.

Five guards stormed the workshop, weapons drawn. Gunfire up at them from down below told them to hold back. They dropped three smoke grenades into the tunnel, initial panic caused as the objects bounced off the sides of the tunnel and onto the dark floor. The men backed away, able to hear the screamed instructions of the guards above that there was a tunnel leading out of the prison.

Outside the house, five trucks skidded to a stop. The proximity to the prison would make it obvious soon enough.

"Get on board!" the cousin demanded, the men aware fifteen others were still in the tunnel, the rest having followed their leader to the house. He knew three were already dead. He'd seen their bodies.

He took the first truck, the men loading in, the cousin banging on the back of the cab, the driver's sign to move them out of there. He would not wait around.

Shots rained down on the remaining trucks, the drivers ducking from view, the men not on board now rushing back into the house. Soon the area was in lockdown, the army there in force, those men not already dead surrounded and surrendering when they realised they had no better option.

They cornered Boris's cousin at the edge of town, the truck trapped, twenty soldiers enough to take him out as he opened fire. The rest of the men surrendered immediately.

Twelve died that night, including one prison guard. The warder later found Boris in the basement workshop. Right room, wrong building, the disorienting effect of movement around the prison enough to make him not realise they'd moved him to another building entirely when he had cut himself.

They destroyed the tunnel. Over the next five years, authorities drove concrete pillars randomly into the ground right around the perimeter, making it all but impossible to navigate such a path through ever again. They introduced stress positions on all inmates soon after, aimed at disorientating the inmates, keeping them looking down as they moved them around, heads down, arms raised behind their backs. It meant no inmate had a good look at the place as they moved him around the prison.

Boris Mihaylov would be the first and only life-sentence prisoner to get that close to an actual escape. He would spend the rest of his life in prison, still there to this day, in his seventies, resigned to the fact his men were now all either dead or behind bars themselves following the failed attempt.

Boris still hated anyone he came across who messed with children and had put plenty in the hospital wing down the decades. It had become a sport to most there, a rite of passage. He now stood at the top, almost unchallenged. But one day an altogether different type of inmate would arrive on the wing. Even Boris Mihaylov would play second-fiddle. Then he would know his days as the top dog were firmly over. A new king had arrived, and Boris would let the younger man do his thing. His own days of fighting such a rival for control were long past.

7

Zabala Family Compound, Alicante Region
Two Months Ago

The Don had been using his men to ask questions all week, turning over stones, seeing what came crawling out. Jose had not expected his next clear lead to be from someone under his own umbrella of control.

While he had always made sure his empire stayed within lines of morality––to a degree––if not legality, his men ran probably the best brothels in the city. The workers were all legitimate, Jose had been clear on that. It had only been his son in the last eighteen months who had become ensnared in sex trafficking, something that had brought the two men into sharp dispute. Jose still pained at the state of his relationship with Luken, his son, at the time of his murder.

The women who worked in Jose's establishments––his men ran them, his men staffed them, it was all something Señorita Zabala detested––were local. It was their choice to work there, nobody forced them, no drugs allowed on the premises. They were professionals, some students, some working mums, there by choice, knowing the money was good, the protection keeping them safe, and there were few other options open to them.

One of these women, Gabriela, came forward after catching wind of the discussions taking place. Russians had contacted her in the past.

Jose sat once more at his dinner table, this time just him and Gabriela, no food arriving, his own wife practically hissing steam by that point.

Ever since Clifton's trial in England––the Don had kept a close watch on proceedings, a keen eye for detail––he had wondered if something had happened during Clifton's time in Spain. In transcripts Jose had got hold of, and from what the oligarch had told him in person, it was clear the charges being thrown at Clifton were for a rape some time ago in the USA, and something far more recently––no dates given––in Spain. Jose was sure it had to have happened that year, probably even during the same week he now found himself fascinated about, fixated on in fact.

The thing that had puzzled Jose the most when he read the fully published reports of the trial, was that none of the final charges raised related to either a USA incident or one in Spain. These women were not the ones at trial. It was the others, many more silent voices raised in the media storm who came forward, crimes committed in the UK, crimes punishable in British courts. Clifton had pleaded guilty so none of the details of the crimes committed had come to light. But where were the USA and Spanish women? These had been the ones to expose him, but their cases were never raised in court.

"Tell me, what happened?" Jose asked Gabriela, the Don leaning forward a little, grandfatherly. She respected him enough already to tell it straight.

"Someone came to the club. We talked. They put a proposal my way, paid me upfront."

"Was this in rubles?"

"No," she said, a little confused, the Don initially disappointed at hearing that. "It was euros, a lot of euros. They paid me ten thousand."

"They were local?"

"No," she confirmed. "Russian." It was why she'd come forward. The club had asked about any activities involving people connected to Russia that year. It seemed everyone had been talking about Russia in the week it swore in its first female President.

"And what did you have to do for your ten thousand?" She should have paid part of that to her employer, if this was an under-the-table kind of deal, though he would not press that point for the moment. She'd come forward, offering him the story. For that he was grateful.

"The strangest thing," she said, with a smile. She'd done some odd things in her time, not all enjoyable, the memories something she had to deal with, get over, move on. This one she couldn't even remember.

"I had to go to a party."

"A party?" That wasn't overly unusual. Men had used the girls as escorts many times, though sex usually concluded the night in most cases.

"At a villa, a little down the coast."

"I see," the Don nodded, encouraging her on. He would come back to the location of the villa later.

"I went, as instructed, danced a bit, had some drinks," she started.

"You weren't meeting a particular client?" he asked, the setup a little unorthodox.

"No, the instructions were clear. Go, party some, then find his bedroom, and take a pill."

Multiple questions rose in his mind.

"Whose bedroom?" he clarified first.

"The guy who owned the villa. I guess the guy who hired me," she added, though there seemed no certainty there.

"And the pill?"

"The Russian gave it to take with me. It would knock me out."

"They meant him to find you unconscious in his bed, is that it?"

"Yes," she confirmed, now a little ashamed. She heard how it sounded coming out of her own mouth. She'd done some weird stuff down the years, but never unconsciously.

"And he took advantage of you when you were asleep?" the Don said, his choice of words picked carefully.

"Yes," she confirmed. Nothing about the night had been normal. She knew she was being paid for sex, knew her role in it, though in the cool light of day, she still felt somewhat violated, even though she was on the game that night, this another score, and a good paying one at that.

"There were cameras in the room," Jose said aloud.

"Sorry?" she asked, thinking he was suggesting she had recorded the ordeal.

"I'm thinking out loud, nothing more."

"He recorded it?" she said, something not allowed in the club where she usually carried out her business. Home calls were a rarity for most of the women, the club much safer for all.

"No," the Don said, "I don't think he did. I don't even think he hired you. Did not know who you were."

"But he must have done!" she said, the thought a stranger had done that to her causing her to shudder.

"I think they knew he wouldn't be able to resist. A gift horse, they might call it. They knew what he would do when he found you."

"He's done that before?" she asked.

"Yes," he confirmed. "Do you know his name?"

"No," she said, visibly upset now, wanting to help. Everything had got dealt with remotely, however, the money paid upfront, the plan explained to her. She'd had a good time. She'd not seen any danger in it, waking up in the early hours, the place empty, her body sore, the evidence of something happening manifest immediately.

"Can you take me to the villa?"

"You think he's still there?" she asked, the Don shaking his head.

"I can confirm who booked it, however, the night this happened." That brought a smile to her face.

"I know where it is," she confirmed.

Gabriela had taken the Don straight to the house and Jose stood outside with the owner of the villa. The owner had several luxury villas in the city, and further south in the Murcia region too. He scanned through his records, coming up with the name Don Zabala had been expecting the moment Gabriela showed up at his home that day.

"Clifton Niles, British guy," the owner confirmed. "He had the place for two weeks this time, been here at least three times before, I think."

The Don passed him an envelope which the owner pocketed without opening. It always paid well to be generous. Zabala was a man who looked after his friends.

"Thank you," Jose said. "It was who I expected it to be."

He was now sure the Russians had wanted to frame Clifton, though why that was he had yet to understand––he knew he couldn't stop until he made that link. He also knew it all implicated these same Russians somehow in the murder of his son, and once he had the proof of that, there would be trouble.

Berlin & London
Present Day

It was the following lunchtime before Anastasia called back, Anissa taking the call while walking in the park close to the office. It'd been a tough morning, and she needed space to think. She was now somewhere she used to meander with Alex when the pair had been working together, something she perhaps missed more than anything. She rarely visited the park anymore, never walked its paths thinking as she was doing again, though the call from Anastasia had brought it all back. Anissa knew, regardless of the woman's faults, she missed Alex at least as much as Anissa did herself; she couldn't deny it.

"The old man I told you about has gone," Anastasia said, the connection made, the call answered, Anissa acknowledging it was her on the other end.

"Dead?" Anissa said, startled initially.

"No, he spoke with me before fleeing. He's vanished."

"Of his own accord?" she probed. It paid to be sure.

"I think so, yes," Anastasia replied, the best she could know.

"What happened?"

"He said it had something to do with his job in Moscow," the Belarusian started, Anissa cutting in.

"I thought you said he retired years ago?" She had, it had been two decades already.

"He is. It must be about when he worked. Back in the nineties, I think. He still hasn't told me everything, but after he first called me, he made calls to others. He tried to connect with his old gang, I think. Guys he has apparently had nothing to do with in years, from before he left. All that time ago."

"And?" Anissa had stopped moving now, fixed to the spot, an excitement rising inside even though the situation didn't really warrant such feelings.

"These men had all vanished, he told me. All gone missing suddenly in recent months." There was silence for a moment, Anissa not initially seeing huge cause for alarm. Old people had to die at some point. "All gone since Volkov won the election," Anastasia clarified, the thought bringing Anissa closer to the action.

"You think it links them?"

"He does. Told me that much."

"And now he's vanished himself, of his own accord?"

"He said these other men had not gone freely. He spoke to the son of one of them who knows his father was snatched. There are rumours, you see."

"Rumours?" Anissa worked in an industry of rumours. Rumours were usually all she ever got. It was what put her onto the Games.

"Do you remember the revelations from the whistleblower aimed at Volkov before the election?"

"I do," Anissa said, unaware that anyone outside of MI6 had been in direct contact with the man's handler in New York prior to the press getting wind of the story.

"Do you remember the name Yuri Lagounov?"

Anissa remembered the name, the butcher of Moscow. At least one brutal murder had been connected to him according to *The Gremlin*, the US code name for the whistleblower. The CIA suspected the whistleblower was hiding somewhere in New York but the British knew he had been in Mexico all along. Meanwhile the Kremlin had confirmed that Lagounov had gone on the run following a Presidential warrant for his arrest.

"Yes, he's wanted for murder," Anissa confirmed.

"The rumour is they have sent him after these men," Anastasia said.

"The ones who your friend claims Volkov might have a legitimate gripe against?"

"Precisely." That would place Lagounov in connection with, perhaps under command of, Svetlana Volkov herself.

"She's sent him to do her dirty work?"

"It's more than that. He's a lunatic. The name in certain circles is enough to send absolute panic through his targets. The press have nothing on this. Perhaps the whistleblower didn't know the full extent? These men knew, or they do now, anyway."

"You think they are already dead?"

"That I don't know. Slava thinks they are."

"Slava? This is the terrified old man you know in Berlin, who has now vanished?" Anissa asked, not having got the name until then.

"Yes. Slava Alkaev. You might as well have his full name now. See if there is anything you can find out before it's too late."

"Too late?" but she understood as soon as she voiced it. "You think he's next?"

"I think Volkov assumes he's dead already, setting the mafia on him," Anastasia said, pointing out the one inconsistency in the story. They had set Spaniards onto Slava, not a Russian.

"And you are sure it connects them?"

"Slava is. He knew who to call. All six of them are missing. He said he made six calls. There is something that connects the seven."

"These others are all in Russia?"

"Yes, most of them are still in Moscow, I gather."

That made some sense, Lagounov under an arrest warrant, not able to cross the border. Volkov had been making overtures to the press about her stance on crime. She couldn't knowingly let Lagounov escape and she couldn't do anything in Germany directly herself either. How the Spanish had become involved remained a mystery, though Anissa recalled the claims that the President controlled vast reserves of criminal money, and that gave due leverage in that regard too.

"Do you have the names of the other six?" That would give them far more to go on.

"No," Anastasia confirmed, realising asking Slava for these names, had he even given them to her, would have been helpful now. "But they are all suddenly missing. There must be reports, some stories. I'll have a look online, see what I can find," she said, Anissa recalling then that though Belarusian, that also meant Anastasia was a native Russian speaker. Anissa knew Sasha would also be a great help, a task she would hand him once back in the office. Something to work on together, at last.

The thought of Sasha brought her back to the conversation she'd just had with him, the reason she'd come walking in the park that afternoon. The reason she needed space to think, air to clear her head. She'd come to that symbolic place of all places because she'd told Sasha they should look for Alex. Not wait for news, not dig around for snippets, but get to him. Get him out of whichever hellhole he was being held in. Get him home. Though she shouldn't have been saying anything––she'd come to the park to work out what she thought about it, in the cool light of day––she knew she was now speaking to someone who could help. Someone who, despite huge failings, deserved to know.

"We're planning to rescue Alex," she said, the air as if sucked from

Anastasia's lungs at the comment, the shift in the flow of conversation enough to send her into silence.

"You are?" she gasped, eventually.

"We believe he's in a prison somewhere," Anissa confirmed, sure that Anastasia must have assumed that herself. A prison was better than any grave.

"Let me help," she pleaded.

"That's not my place to say," Anissa cautioned, though she still wasn't personally ready to travel to Russia––her five-year exclusion now up––and Sasha couldn't safely do so either, having defected a few years back from the FSB.

"I can travel freely, visit anywhere. I will go anywhere you send me. Anissa, please, let me help," she wept, emotion coming through even as they spoke on the phone.

"I can't officially ask you to get involved," Anissa said, aware there was nothing official about any of it. Alex's trip to Russia to smuggle Phelan in wasn't official. Their conspired plot for Phelan to blow up President Filipov was far from official. Alex's capture was not even official. As far as MI6, and therefore the world knew, nothing had happened. Six had explained away Alex's disappearance, keeping it internal, case closed.

"You need not ask me to do anything!" Anastasia stormed back, hope pressing through between her tears, passion within the pain. "I volunteer. I'll do anything that helps get Alex back. I can get in under the radar. I have freedom to move around Russia, legitimate reasons for being there. Let me do this."

"I couldn't stop you if I wanted," Anissa said, smiling now at the unlikely ally. For too many years she'd loathed the woman with whom, it seemed, she was now in partnership. Alex had only ever agreed to go to Russia to chaperone Phelan because he believed it really was over between him and Anastasia. That there was nothing waiting for him, no-one there to love him. Anissa had found out the truth too late, hearing from Anastasia after the pair had already broken communications in northern Finland. Hearing that the woman still loved Alex, had never stopped in fact. She'd hurt him to save him from her husband, before doing the thing she'd denied Alex all along; giving the authorities the information that would eventually convict Dmitry Kaminski. Anissa had sat with Anastasia throughout the trial, their relationship then allowed time to establish at least.

"Send me what you know. Anything you hear, get in touch," Anastasia said, her focus seemingly so quickly shifted from Slava, though his welfare still concerned her. "I'll go wherever you think he is."

"Stay safe," Anissa said.

"Don't worry about me, just stay in contact," Anastasia rattled back. It was usually her calling the British agent, not the other way round. If she was to be of any help, however, she would need to hear regularly from Anissa whenever they had anything new.

"I will," Anissa said, ending the call, aware that her reason for coming to the park had now manifested itself. They would get Alex, actively searching for him, and from there, find a way of breaking him free. They would do this.

She walked with a fresh spring in her step the ten minutes it took to get back to her small office. Added to the clarity––and help, via Anastasia––around the Alex situation, it had also given her fresh fodder on Svetlana Volkov, several angles emerging in her ten-minute conversation.

Suddenly the world looked bright again, the day swimming with possibilities.

8

Alicante Region, Spain
Two Months Ago

"See what you can uncover between these two dates," Don Zabala said, his man tasked with fishing through events for the two weeks Clifton had booked the villa, and especially the day when his son died. He already had several pointers to events that week, knew a group of Russians were sniffing around, yet couldn't land anything substantial. The Don had put all other operations on hold for the time being--this had to be his sole focus.

Zabala reached out to the one oligarch he knew, Roman Ivanov. The Russian had been personally in touch in the weeks after Clifton had confessed to the murder and fled to the UK. The oligarch had urged caution back then, laying down a carefully thought out plan, and Jose had agreed to call off his men. A Crown Court trial had followed, a confession of guilt, and the rest was now history.

Ivanov did not answer the call and had made no reply. Jose was certain the Russian knew much more about events that week than he did, though he would work hard to close that knowledge gap. His son's honour might still rest on it--whatever honour he had left. Jose shrugged that last thought from his mind. He wasn't doing this for his son, the boy more disrespectful than anyone he knew in the final months. Luken had felt invincible; he'd told his father that he was his own man. He would have pulled the family reputation into the gutter in no time, Jose knew that. Except, he was his only son. You don't kill a Zabala and live to gloat over the feat.

Less than five minutes later Jose's righthand man passed the Don his tablet device.

"Look," he said, Jose putting on a pair of reading glasses, glancing down at the screen slowly and taking in the report. The article was dated the day his son had died, recounting an incident which had taken place at the Santa Barbara Castle the previous day. It detailed a man being seen running naked from the top of the castle, frightening families who were there. It said how shortly after first being spotted, the unknown stranger––the title suggested the man had already escaped––attacked a tourist, pulling the man's clothes from his body before running around a corner with them, still apparently naked. The article concluded that a police officer had confirmed they had seen the suspect fleeing the area, clothed by this point, and a police chase had got as far as the beachfront, but the man had vanished.

As the Don stood there with the device, working through what the report had told him, another man handed him his phone, the website of the same newspaper open at an article which reported an unusual event from the day after his son's murder. No-one spoke as Jose looked at the phone.

A different reporter this time wrote about the strange accounts of a plane falling from the sky and exploding on impact at a mountainside olive grove. Witnesses had reported three parachutes, suggesting there had been no-one on-board at the time of the crash. The article stated that by the time the journalist had arrived at the scene, the only sign that anything had happened there was the five burnt trees in the grove, none of which was expected to recover. The farmer was angry, though it had not been the police who had come. The flight school itself had cleared up the wreckage, paying a little for the damage to the trees, though this had been reportedly far too small an amount.

"Find me this flight school," Jose asked of the man whose phone he was holding. Jose gave it back to him and the man left straight away. Now it was just the two of them, Zabala with his most trusted ally, a man more like a son to him than Luken had ever been.

"So on the Tuesday that week, a stranger runs naked around the castle, beating up a random person, before getting away from the area with the clothes from this other man's back. On Wednesday they kill my son. Then on Thursday a plane falls from the sky, three people spotted jumping out with parachutes, but everything gets cleaned up, the police not even involved. And Friday Clifton Niles confronts me face to face confessing to the murder of my son," Jose spat the name of the Brit as if swearing in a foreign language. "And the week before all this, Gabriela gets paid to drug herself and lie on a bed in a villa Niles has rented in what I assume was an obvious setup." Jose had told his righthand man what Gabriela had said the previous day.

"Four separate incidents, four consecutive days," Jose mused.

"You think it links them?" his man asked, sure of the response he would receive.

"Don't you?"

The man nodded.

"I need you to do two things for me," Jose requested. "Help with the search into that flight school. When you have something, we'll go together for answers. And second, find out who the victim was at the Castle. We'll pay him a visit too, show him the picture of Niles, see if he can identify our guy." Jose's mind was working fast. "And make enquires at the Castle itself," he added, aware that naked people didn't just appear at the top of buildings randomly. "See if anyone hired out the private rooms on the day of the incident. See if you can make any connections there, anything that links to these Russians."

Don Zabala had looked over his city the same way the Castle overlooked everything. The man felt an affinity with the ancient monument, a pride and connection to the region he'd made home many decades before; yet others had come onto his turf, their purpose in doing so not entirely clear. Besides the killing of his son—which had been enough to make Jose their enemy—they didn't seem to have been working against him, only against this British man, Niles. It would appear, he had been their target.

"And get me everything you can on Niles. I want a report done on him," the Don finished.

"The dead guy?" came the confused response.

"Everything he did when alive. His business connections, the circles he moved in. I have a feeling at some point he pissed off someone, and I bet you what happened here that week was more than random. I bet it was personal."

THE FLIGHT SCHOOL had not been too hard to track down. Only three operated in the area, and only one showed that a plane was out of action.

Don Zabala arrived there the morning after being given the news, only his next-in-command making the trip with him. They weren't expecting any trouble, so didn't need a show of force. The flight school would know who had come calling, eventually. Most knew of Don Zabala by sight already, knew to avoid eye contact, knew to vacate any room he walked into, any table he wanted to sit at. The Don never needed to threaten anyone, never needed to ask anybody to move. They just did. It was how it worked. It was how people remained undead.

"I would like to speak to the two pilots who jumped from the Cessna," and he gave the date in question, no hint in his tone that he didn't know exactly what he was talking about, no sign that he would take anything but compliance.

The man the Don was speaking to, who while owning the business, had also been one of the two pilots that day, knew this wasn't the police calling. He knew of the Don only by reputation, the sight of the car arriving moments before enough to tell him the mafia were needing something.

"I was there that day," the man confirmed. Jose took him in, the face nervous, the eyes dancing with trepidation.

"I'm not here to harm you," the Don said, happy the man had been straight with him. Jose turned to his security, a tough guy able to make anybody hurt, make anybody confess to anything, though not needed now. "Wait outside for me," Jose said, knowing the pilot would talk to him. The move was designed to show Don Zabala was true to his word about not wanting to harm anyone. The threat remained outside, anyway. Near. The threat would never go away, not entirely, everyone knew it. Not until Zabala had everything he wanted.

Now it was just the two of them––Zabala and the pilot––Jose paced around the room a little, taking in the photos, not saying anything for a moment, allowing the silence to fill the space.

"Who booked the flight that day?" Zabala asked finally, turning on the spot from the picture he had been looking at of the pilot in parachute gear preparing for a jump, and from the young features, taken a long time ago.

"My partner deals with that side of things," the man replied, Jose certain this partner were not about to come out and join the conversation.

"I see," he said, his tone suggesting he wasn't overly happy with how things had started between the two of them. "And you had Clifton Niles on board?" Jose would try the name first. He had a photo in his pocket if needed.

"I didn't know their names."

"Their names?" Jose picked up on it immediately. "There were two passengers?"

The pilot couldn't look the Don in the face at that question, and when Jose repeated, this time with far more force in his voice than his otherwise calm exterior implied, the pilot nodded slowly.

"Yes," he said, barely a mumble.

"You took two people up, alone?" he said, though the information on the walls talked about a pilot and co-pilot on each flight, the second man there to help get everyone ready for the parachute jumps, able to film if clients ordered that service. A single pilot could never do all that and fly the plane.

"No," he muttered, ever more cagey.

"There was another man on the plane when it crashed," the Don exclaimed, the pieces falling into place now. "What happened up there?" The article had cited witnesses on the ground as spotting three parachutists in the sky, and the debris cleared away before the police could get involved.

"There were cameras," he said, his resolve breaking for the first time. The pilot looked up showing terror in his eyes, but he broke eye contact as quickly as he had made it. "We were told to take the plane high, towards the mountains. They had paid us in cash, for the plane and our time."

"By Russians?" Jose asked.

"Yes," he confirmed, though he offered no more.

"And what happened?"

"One man was on the plane already. I had put him there first, the other was surprised to see him. We were told this first man was a rapist."

"A rapist?" Jose quizzed.

"Yes. It seemed to surprise the foreigner."

"The other man was British?" Jose asked, pulling a photo from his pocket now, showing the pilot an image of Clifton. "Is this him?"

The pilot took the photo, studied it for a few seconds, before nodding silently.

"What happened next?" Jose asked, taking the photo back from the pilot.

"Look, I won't go to jail for this," he said, his finger pointing, trembling uncontrollably.

"I'm not here to put you in prison, I'm just here for answers."

There was silence for the time being, the pilot breathing three deep breaths, his emotions pulled back under control.

"Okay," he said, as if deciding then to share what he knew. "At ten thousand feet they told us we needed to put the plane on autopilot, set a course for the mountains, and then open the door. We already had our chutes on."

"You jumped?"

"First, we had to throw the one remaining chute between the two men."

"I see," Jose said. One lifeline, two lives. It was all forming a picture in his mind now, he didn't need to probe further. Clifton had made it and the next day would confront Jose in the restaurant. The bruising around the eyes that Jose had looked into now made more sense too. It would have been some fight, a fight for life, a fight for freedom.

"The footage they shot, how did they recover it? Was that why you cleared the crash site up immediately after?"

"No, and they made us remove the black box flight recorder when they came to fit the cameras. They were broadcasting live. Nothing survived the explosion, it couldn't have. I think they cleaned up because perhaps there might have been parts of someone still around."

There had been cameras at the villa, too, Jose was sure. They would have used that to blackmail Clifton. It suddenly put things on a much higher trajectory.

Don Zabala thanked the man for his time, promised not to tell anybody their secret, and reminded the pilot not to mention to anyone that he had been there asking questions. They had an understanding, and Jose returned to his car, his man driving him back home.

"Did you get what you came for?" he enquired from the front.

"Yes, and plenty more besides," Jose smiled.

9

Far Eastern Russia
Present Day

Svetlana stood, white fur coat moving in the gentle breeze, a strong hint of winter in the air, though at ground level it was still several degrees above zero.

In the far distance, snow already topped some of the highest peaks.

Roman Ivanov left her by herself; it was the first time he'd seen Svetlana since a conversation with her three days ago at the Kremlin. The context now couldn't have been more different. He stood with the four other oligarchs--Popov, Budny, Markovic and Utkin--the group of five men, the same five who'd been present at the event Svetlana had hosted in Spain.

They were here once more to witness an altogether different spectacle.

Roman had said nothing to Vladimir Popov about Zabala's demand for the oligarch's name, nor his own suggestion to the President that she should have given it to the Spaniard at the first time of asking. Roman had nothing against Popov--and might have warned his fellow Russian had he heard the President passing on his name—but he saw more danger in Zabala than Svetlana Volkov did.

He'd not heard what they had done against Zabala since his meeting with Volkov at the Kremlin.

Svetlana stood alone. She knew what was about to come, this the third gathering that month, the time away from Moscow welcome, even if for all six of them—the five oligarchs and the President—getting away so frequently and needing to travel so far had not always been easy. They'd found a way. When the President demanded something of you, there was no choice. Following Alicante, they'd agreed to this path. They were a privileged few now, in on her activities. The Games had included many oligarchs over the years, always twenty at any one time across the two groups. Now they were five.

An ominous foreboding settled upon the scene as her security slowly led four hooded men from the back of a van. The oligarchs knew who the four were—they'd been there the first time, when it was six. Now two were no more, four remained. Today would be another's turn. Today one more would die.

The four old men each had their hands tied behind their backs, not that they were a flight risk. Not at their age, not out here. They each knew they would die imminently and this had nothing to do with their age.

The security men forced the four to kneel on the ground, difficult for all, but doing so regardless. They removed the hoods, the faces frail, wrinkled, frightened. None of them looked up at Svetlana Volkov, who now stood in front of them, a mocking reversal of the position they'd all once put her in. The very reason for their involvement in this now.

These men, with others who had since died of old age, and Slava Alkaev who'd evaded death in Germany, had all once worked in the Moscow film industry. They had been top-dogs in their day, arrogant, ruthless and cruel. They had all at least once forced a young and vulnerable Svetlana to kneel before them as they stood there, belts unfastened, trousers lowered, and made her do a degrading thing. All so she could pass her audition. All because they had the power of her future in their hands, or so they claimed. All because they were sick and ready to abuse and use their position.

How the tables had turned!

Kneeling down, the four old men looked at nothing but the ground. They'd been here before, they knew what to expect.

Svetlana paced before them, standing while they knelt, the one in power while they felt powerless. Now the one to punish them while they died inside. Death wouldn't only be internal for another of those monsters that day.

She felt alive in that moment, her body electric, the thrill of retribution tantalising. They deserved everything coming to them, she assured herself.

As always, a team of technicians ran the show from the sidelines. This one relied on the use of drones. Anything else would have interfered too much. They had set up a clock which displayed the countdown time of one hour. Sixty minutes for these old men to make their escape, sixty minutes for them to prepare for the inevitable. There could be no escape, the distance too far, the time too short, the threat too powerful.

The tiger they'd used on each of the previous two occasions sat once more in its cage. A man-eater now, hungry and expecting food again soon. Nobody could miss the low growls coming from the animal on the far side. It only added more focus to those gathered there.

"And here we are again," Svetlana spoke at last. The oligarchs, while knowing the brutal reality of the action, loved the chase. They would bet with each other, millions often at a time, on the exact minute after the first hour was up that the tiger would catch its prey. A sixty-minute head-start and then the cage door opened.

"Here I stand before you, again at last, you filthy, despicable men," she spat her words, only a foot in front of each of them, pacing from one end to the other as she spoke. "You didn't deserve to live the lives you've had since doing what you did to me and countless other young actresses all those years ago." Her tone was aggressive but her pace of speech was steady. "I can't say for certain, but I doubt any of these women are now in the position I am to do something about it." She smiled, something lost to the four old men, whose heads hung only in shame and defeat. The smile was also lost to the oligarchs who stood behind her, twenty metres away, but able to hear her perfectly.

"What you did to me then has been the fuel which has driven me," she said, something she'd voiced on each of the previous two times. "It strengthened me. Showed me I needed to be the solution. Drove me on to change. And here I am," she said, pausing for effect. *The President, the billionaire, the woman with everything.*

Her pacing stopped, standing before the first man who'd auditioned her, the first man to destroy a small part of her on the inside.

"Stand!" she ordered, two of her men coming from the sidelines, the same group who had led the four prisoners forward minutes before, coming up behind the old man and lifting him to his feet. The old Russian started to weep, only now looking up into the face of Svetlana, nothing but terror in his eyes.

"Please!" he pleaded. "I'm sorry! I was a fool. I have grandchildren," he said, but she raised the stick she was holding in her right hand and pressed it onto his lips, to stop him talking.

"Open your mouth," she said, the same ritual as the two previous times. Her eyes showed him she wouldn't ask a second time, and he did as told, the terror already racing through his body, the two guards holding his trembling shoulders a little tighter. She pushed the one inch thick piece of wood between his teeth. "You can bite down now," she smirked. He'd once forced something into her mouth too. He'd not offered her the option of biting down then, however.

Tears filled his eyes, the anticipation as bad as what was to come, though he knew the pain would be worse. The stick in his mouth there to stifle his scream.

One of the two men holding the prisoner in place now crouched down, reaching forward and after undoing the old man's belt, lowered the trousers, underwear and all.

Roman Ivanov paced awkwardly on the spot, as any man would now, aware of what was about to happen again. The exposed groin was hidden behind Svetlana as she stood right in front of him, though they all saw the knife she pulled from the sheath tied around her waist. The metal flashed in the sun. This blade had already taken the manhood from the two previous victims and the third now standing there with his trousers pulled down to his knees was left in no doubt of his fate.

Svetlana raised the blade to eye level, nothing but a whimper coming from the old man now, though his eyes couldn't help but look at the nine inches of blade gleaming before his face.

Then she reached down suddenly with her left hand, grabbing his genitals. With one rapid movement of her blade-wielding right hand, she cut them clean from his body. He screamed in sheer pain, his teeth clamping down into the wood, his eyes wild. The two guards held him in place. They then pulled up the man's trousers and fastened the belt in place. The oligarchs could soon see blood seeping through, the Russians looking away, unable to watch the scene again.

She held her left hand up, raising it to within inches of the face of the emasculated man. She walked over to the caged beast, the growl of the tiger rising the closer she got. *Dinner time.* She threw in the fresh meat, nothing but a pre-dinner snack for an animal that size, but enough to give it a taste––and a scent. The clock started its ominous countdown immediately. They took the handcuffs off the old man and led away the three other prisoners shortly afterwards. A drone took to the sky.

"I suggest you get moving," Svetlana said, the old man standing still for the time being––it was too painful to move––and yet the knowledge that worse awaited him if he remained was enough to force the taking of a step. None of the remaining four men knew anything about what happened next. They had left the scene by that stage, as the other three just had. They had known their fate––emasculation––but perhaps the others had escaped? Had made it out of there alive. In pain, for sure, and devastated by the injury, but even that didn't compare to being eaten alive by a tiger.

He staggered off at a painfully slow pace.

The oligarchs moved up to the building. They would all be safely indoors when the one-hour countdown reached zero, when the cage door opened. Screens in the room already showed the escape this far, the old man moving steadily, but there would be no getting away. They all knew he was a dead man, even if he didn't yet know it.

"Ten minutes," Ivanov said, eyebrows rising right around the room. He was betting the tiger would catch up to its prey within ten minutes of being released, bearing in mind the man, old and much slower and with a terrible wound, had a one-hour head-start. The quickest kill the animal had managed in the first two events had been twenty-one minutes.

"Ten minutes?" Motya gasped.

Roman nodded.

"How much?" Motya asked.

"I'll bet ten million he is killed in ten minutes or less," Roman proposed. The other four oligarchs were prepared to stake that same amount against Roman. If the tiger killed the Russian when the clock showed ten minutes elapsed––rules stated that ten minutes, fifty-nine seconds still counted in Roman's favour––or less, Roman would be forty-million up. Once eleven minutes elapsed, he would be forty-million down. The next closest time was chosen by Vladimir Popov, who'd gone for twenty minutes.

Bets could go the other way too. Arseni Markovic had stated the old man could last forty minutes. Twenty-million rested on that result.

The room watched quietly; the hour ticking down, the old man moving painfully through the grass and forests of the region, perhaps getting as far away as a kilometre within the first half hour. He soon realised how barren the area was, no sign of human habitation anywhere as far as he could see. Blood now covered his trouser legs and thighs. He stumbled a few times, the sound of the hovering drone a constant reminder that these sick people were expecting his death any time now. He'd lost all track of time. For all he knew, the tiger might pounce at any moment. He stopped for breath.

WITHIN THE ROOM from where they watched, the tension grew as the first hour ticked by, the last few seconds observed in absolute silence. The tiger paced around its little cage as if it too sensed that time was nearly up. The door slid open suddenly, the animal initially cautious, smelling around the opening, picking up the scent. It jogged out, its pace not in full hunting mode––the animal could move, its top speed impressive, but only over a short distance. It also didn't need such speed with this prey.

It vanished from sight, three other drones now carefully controlled, all three watching for the animal from different positions. A map on the main wall showed the progress of the tiger, a chip in the big cat represented by the flashing yellow light that moved across the terrain. The red light, on the drone above the Russian flashed, indicating the probable location of the prey. There could barely have been two kilometres between the two at that moment, the distance easily the shortest of the three so far, Roman aware of a severe lack of movement in this man, something apparently overlooked by the other four.

Whether that knowledge was enough to win him forty-million in the next ten minutes, remained a mystery. The hunt was very much on.

Svetlana had joined them now. The events, besides the technical side, required little else. Gone was the role of odds maker, gone the need for catering staff. That had all been easier to arrange in St Petersburg, when the original Games took place in the Volkov mansion. Now she kept it to the bare minimums, the oligarchs themselves an exception, and only five of them, anyway. She knew she could trust them.

The President watched them all carefully, the men aware of her presence there, a few acknowledging her arrival, but this was not a politician and her people, this existed before all that. She was still the Chair, they the Hosts, even if now they provided neither the prize nor the Contestant. She'd delivered it all.

Five minutes after the tiger left its cage, it was clear from the map it had the man's scent. The stats of the animal refreshed constantly on the top right corner of the screen. Heart rate, pace, distance covered, and the distance that remained. There was less than one kilometre between hunter and hunted now, the pace increasing all the time; the drones picking up shots even David Attenborough would be proud of, yet these shots would never appear on any of his shows. In fact, the live transmissions were not even being recorded. They were privileged relays, for those wealthy and well connected enough to be there.

Another three minutes and the animal was into a fast jog, the four drones all within a few hundred metres of each other. It wasn't sprinting full pace yet, which in a normal situation, it could only maintain for about one hundred metres, anyway. The Russian was moving again, having been hiding in some dense trees for a while. Did he sense the approach of the beast? How could he have?

It would be tight, the ten minutes now nearly upon them, seventy minutes since Svetlana had sliced the Russian, seventy minutes since his final humiliation. Death remained the only certainty. She hoped it would be as painful as the removal of his manhood had been. She didn't wish any of them a fast, painless death. They had it coming to them; they deserved it all. There would be no escape.

She looked across to the five oligarchs, the tension clear between them. She'd picked up word on the betting, aware that Roman Ivanov had been rash, perhaps, though she'd learned he was rarely reckless. She'd seen a similar streak in him as with men like Matvey Filipov and Mark Orlov, both former oligarchs more wealthy than Roman, both more dangerous too. She needed to keep Roman onside, however. She had left Filipov unchecked for too long, alone, hidden, secret. That had allowed him to creep up like the tiger on their screens. At that moment the old man heard three other drones high above, their presence there ominous.

Ten minutes clicked around, the maps showing the prey and hunter now within proximity, the map unable to display any more detail. All eyes fell to the screens.

Ten minutes, twenty-seconds.

The tiger broke cover, a burst of speed taking it towards the man.

He saw the flash of orange and black all too late, not that there would have been any escape. He ran anyway. The animal pounced, knocking the old man to the ground. He was unable to put up any real fight against an opponent far too powerful--far too hungry for death--for him to cope with.

It severed an arm from its joint.

Ten minutes, forty-seconds.

The tiger stood above its victim, the drones close, the camera zoomed, picking up the last seconds of action, looking the man in the face, his eyes ablaze with pain, his face set in terror as the tiger went for his neck, in for the kill.

"I'll say that's my win," Roman called, turning from the screen, six-seconds still to pass before eleven minutes were even up, the blood visible as the tiger started to move the mangled corpse into the grass evidence enough that the old timer was already dead. Nobody was about to dispute the result, the money lost of little importance; it was their pride that took the biggest hit. No oligarch enjoyed losing, especially to another oligarch.

"How did you know?" Popov asked, just the two of them for a moment, Svetlana watching the exchange from the other side of the room, but unable to hear what they were saying.

"The way they walked him over," Roman said, happy to divulge something he'd noticed since the first event, waiting his time for Svetlana to choose this man. "I could tell he usually walked with a stick." They had taken away his cane as soon as they'd captured him, the man barely able to move at all initially. "When the guards kept bringing him out, I could tell," Roman elaborated. "I knew of all the six, he would struggle the most." He was happy to divulge that now, giving nothing away about the remaining three men, who would all last longer than ten minutes--one might even make it half an hour-- but none would live.

"Well, I'll give you credit for that," Popov said, pleased he had not used any prior knowledge, merely observation, something any of the others could have noted but had failed to. "Well played," he finished.

Svetlana watched them walk away, the screens now blank, the

final shots being of the bloodied grass, and the arm lying by itself on the ground, a path of red leading to where the tiger had taken the body. Her team would track the animal which, now full and having run the shortest distance of the three events so far, would be easy to find, especially with its tag guiding them in. She would let it have its fill first. The animal would be easier to capture a day after the kill, the meat eaten, the animal resting. She wouldn't leave it too long before doing it all again. Three more feasts awaited, the three men who had been let off yet again but the dread of what was sure to come no doubt keeping them awake at night.

She revelled in that thought for a moment, smiling as she left the room, the oligarchs big enough to settle their own accounts with each other. Svetlana had no intention of acting as mediator in that regard.

10

Orenburg Region, Russia
Present Day

One week after speaking with Anissa, Anastasia was in the city of Orenburg, not too far north of the Russian border with Kazakhstan. She had first flown to Samara, avoiding Moscow entirely. She didn't want to risk being in the capital and most political prisoners were housed elsewhere.

Alex Tolbert appeared on no official report she could find there, which didn't mean a lot. It was clear he had been imprisoned on the quiet; no trial, no charges, no official crime having taken place. Phelan had failed, President Filipov was still alive to carry on for a while more. His end came soon after.

A few helpful voices in Samara pointed her to penal colony number six, in the city of Sol-Iletsk, which lay seventy kilometres south of the regional hub city of Orenburg, and not even half that distance again to the border with Kazakhstan.

She had travelled on to Orenburg the very next morning.

It took her only an hour to make the drive from the city down to

Sol-Iletsk, a small town of under thirty-thousand people, made famous by housing the country's most notorious prison.

Anastasia hoped her search there would prove fruitless––difficult, when she wanted to find Alex, but she would be relieved if she discovered he was not in a place that swallowed up and rarely gave back. It wasn't long before she discovered the dark reputation of the place and the fact that, in the long-term maximum security wings, nobody had ever escaped. The prison also housed local prisoners, whose sentences were not life. These were kept away from the others, and one of them had reportedly made a break for it two years previously.

She booked herself into a local hotel, reading up as much as she could on the prison that evening. Now there, she had to think carefully about her next moves. She had the element of surprise, but if Alex was there, it wouldn't be publicly acknowledged. Turning up and asking for a man whom no-one was supposed to know was there would only attract the attention of the Kremlin and Svetlana herself. She had to be smart.

The following morning, Anastasia casually started asking questions about the prison. In a town that size, every guard lived locally, meaning there were many families connected to the prison. She even discovered several relatives of inmates who had moved across Russia so they could be close, able to see their husbands when visiting days came round.

Anastasia found these women most useful. One prison-wife had introduced her to two others, the three all married to men now serving long sentences. All three had moved once sentences were confirmed. They had visited every month, and once a year they were allowed four day conjugal visits. Most women left their man, they informed Anastasia. They liked the fact she too had come looking for hers, the Belarusian initially a little light on actual details, though she sensed she could have trusted them with a name. She would remain in touch with them. The next visiting day was not for another two weeks, so there was nothing any of the three women could do to help until then.

What she was looking for were the families of those who worked there, and in particular, a guard who was single. Someone she could get close to, tease information from, find out if there was an Englishman inside. She knew she couldn't rush this and she would not betray Alex's trust by going as far as sleeping with anyone. She might allude to it being on the table, suggest they were headed that way, but she couldn't go there. She wouldn't. That wasn't who she was.

Sitting in the nearest bar from the entrance to the prison on that second night, she sensed she'd found such a man. He even still had his guard's uniform on, sat alone at the counter, working through three beers slowly before upping and leaving.

Anastasia stood, following him quickly, calling after him, asking for a cigarette. He seemed eager to oblige. She turned down the offer of a light; she had no intention of smoking the thing.

"Do you drink here regularly?" she asked, turning on the charm, which for a guy with three pints in him at the end of a no doubt long day, must have seemed like magic.

"Yeah, all the time," he said, somewhat coherently.

"I might see you here tomorrow night then, same time?" she winked, going back inside, hoping against hope he didn't take his chances and follow her in right away. He didn't, and she hoped he would remember the encounter. She was certain he would. She waited five minutes, dropped the cigarette into the bin as she left, and walked back to her hotel. She would wait for him the following night, unsure of when he finished his shift, but trying to be there before him. She didn't want him arriving, seeing nobody, and telling himself it had all been too good to be true.

Madrid, Spain
Two Months Ago

IT HAD BEEN several years since Jose Zabala had been in the Spanish capital, though he didn't miss the heat.

It had been three days since his visit to the flight school, and two days since his men had handed him the name of the tourist--thankfully from Madrid and no further--attacked by Niles while visiting the Castle on his summer holiday.

Zabala had travelled with five other men this time--Madrid far riskier for him than the sleepy nature of home turf. There were others who would happily see him dead and who would then try to move in on what remained, like a victorious lion.

The street they were in was common in the city, apartments tightly packed together, parking impossible to find, his men having to drop him and three of the others off, while they drove both cars away and met up with them later.

One of the three rang the bell, Don Zabala stepping forward as a man's voice called out. He let Zabala in after a brief conversation, the occupant hesitant until Jose had finally said he was there to make sure the man responsible for the attack would see justice.

Now in the modest apartment, the host stood cautiously behind his door. Jose ordered his men to stay outside, the Don stepping in once he opened the door fully.

"You can never be too cautious," the Don said, waving to his three men outside, as if he was more vulnerable than the stranger he was meeting. It was a trick he often used to put the other person at ease.

"You said you know who..." but the man could not finish his own sentence, Jose seeing humiliation there, shame too.

"I know it was difficult what you went through," Jose said.

"I don't want to talk about what I *went through*!" he snapped back, stress put on the final two words, making it clear to the Don that he would have to avoid discussing that if he was to get any credible information.

"The police didn't catch anybody," Jose mentioned.

"No," the man said, shaking his head in disbelief. "Someone does that to a complete stranger, and they let him get away. It's a disgrace."

Jose had discovered that the victim had spent three weeks in hospital after the incident, the first week in Alicante, the last two back in Madrid. Counselling brochures lay on the living room table, the trauma of the ordeal far from healed.

Don Zabala reached into his jacket pocket, pulling out the now dog-eared but still clear picture he had of Clifton.

"Is this the man who attacked you?"

Jose watched the other man glance down at the picture, initially as if too scared to look. His eyes went wide, his head beginning to shake, looking away entirely after a few seconds. Utter panic there now, the man needed to sit down, unable to speak.

He'd said enough, Jose putting the photo back inside his pocket.

"Thank you," Don Zabala said, moving back towards the door.

"That's it?"

"Look," Jose said, turning, "This man was a rapist and a murderer." Utter shock filled the face of the man in the chair, his hand trembling as it covered his mouth. "He killed my son as well, so we've both lost something because of him," Jose added. "But, I have learned that another prisoner took out his own revenge on him while he was in prison in London. Your attacker is dead."

"Dead?" he said, hope, relief, even pleasure filling his eyes now where only sorrow and fear had been before.

"Killed, yes. Dead."

The Don turned, enough time spent there. He had what he came for, had the confirmation that Clifton had been at the Santa Barbara Castle that day, at the start of what seemed four carefully programmed days. His men could find nothing that had taken place on the Monday, if there was anything. The only other thing had been the week before, the incident at Clifton's villa during the party.

Zabala had the main pieces of the puzzle, his job now to make sense of what they all revealed, aware that there were many pieces missing. He had enough though to know something significant had happened that week, and his mind moved closer to working out who it all involved. It wouldn't be long now before he had that figured out too.

Orenburg Region, Russia
Present Day

Anastasia had been sitting at the table for half an hour when he walked in the following night, this time with two friends—both guards, probably there to prove he was lying to them—and they walked to the bar, not initially seeing her. The man looked around the place as he ordered, spotting Anastasia at last, panic and delight filling his cheeks. She waved at him. The man turned to collect his beer, a word spoken to his two companions. She spotted them both looking her way moments later, one with his mouth falling open as the guard punched them both on the arm, and left them. He walked over to Anastasia.

"Can I sit with you?" he asked, his friends staring from the counter, dumbstruck.

"Sure," Anastasia said, moving her jacket from the one spare chair, her way of keeping the table somewhat reserved, not that there was much of a crowd yet. It seemed to get most of its business from prison related matters. She'd seen several uniforms of various roles. There were plenty of pickings available, if this man didn't come through for her.

An hour later the table was littered with glasses, the guard offering to buy more, though Anastasia had said she couldn't.

"Do you want to go for a walk then?" he asked. "I can show you the sites." He smiled, both aware there wasn't a lot to see, even less that interested her, besides the contents of the prison across the road. It was as if being potentially a matter of one hundred metres from Alex at that moment had birthed in her a new energy, a new willingness to do whatever it took to see him again.

"Lead the way," she said, happy to get some fresh air, happy to get him alone, away from listening ears. She needed to move their conversation onto more sensitive things, to questions she could not have asked in there, for fear of people eavesdropping from other tables. It would be clear to most the couple made an odd match.

They both stood, the man smirking at the looks of his two friends, who turned from their drinks and traced with their heads the movement of the other two as they headed towards the exit. The guard put one finger up to his two mocking friends. *Who's having the last laugh now, suckers?*

"Have you worked there long?" she asked, now outside, the prison visible a short distance away, the first she'd directly asked him about the Black Dolphin. He still wore the uniform, so it was obvious she knew where he worked.

"Five years this winter," he said, Anastasia delighted on the inside with that answer. That was before Alex went missing when they were still together.

"Is it dangerous?" she asked, feigning fear that he risked his life daily for the job.

He considered his response for a while, Anastasia noticing him puffing his chest out before he spoke.

"It can be," he said, "but I'm not scared."

"Is it only local prisoners there?" she asked, again playing the tourist, something she'd done throughout their chat. He knew she lived in Germany and was born in Belarus.

"Here?" he said, thumbing across the road to the prison, the two black dolphin fountains visible in the grassed area out front. She nodded. "No, this place holds the country's most brutal criminals," he said, an element of pride in that knowledge. "Local prisoners get sent here too, but I don't work in that wing." He wanted to set the record straight. She smiled.

"How bad are these men?"

"You're kidding, right?" and he raised his hand, counting off his fingers. "We've got all sorts. Murderers, and not the lone type. We've got serial killers in here, even cannibals who ate their victims."

"Really?" she sounded both disgusted and shocked, though this only swelled his pride all the more. He was the man, keeping women like her safe.

"Only the most dangerous, most vile men get sent here."

There was silence for a moment, the walk taking them past the prison now, and Anastasia struggled to think of how best to continue probing.

"And these are all Russian men, these terrorists and cannibals?" she asked.

"No," he said, jumping in as she had hoped, wanting to prove not all Russian men were monsters. He was no monster. *I'm a good guy, remember, keeping you safe. Please sleep with me. Please.* "There are two bombers from the middle-east. Muslims, you know."

"Any Belarusians?" she teased.

"No, I don't think so. Look," he said, starting to turn the subject if he could, though she jumped in.

"Any Germans?" she smiled.

"Nope," he said, happy to play this game, happy to be talking with her at all in fact. They'd doubled back, now approaching the prison once again, the local no more leading her than she led him.

"Any Brits?" she added, oh so subtly, naturally too.

He paused, standing still, Anastasia stopping also now. He turned away from the prison, as if they might hear, and lent forward.

"Actually, there is one," he whispered, Anastasia's stomach doing somersaults inside.

"Really? What did he do?" she whispered, matching his tone, mirroring his actions as if this were their little secret, their little thing they shared with each other.

"Come back to my place and I'll tell you everything I know," he said, winking at her now. He started walking, Anastasia rooted to the spot. "You coming?" he said, seeing she hadn't moved. "It's not far." He wondered if that was the problem, willing it to be the problem in fact. Better that than she didn't like him the way he thought she did. She smiled, catching up with him quickly, working through in her mind what she was doing, deciding she had no option but to go with him, though knowing she wouldn't cross the line. She wouldn't go there. Sex had to be on the cards, had to be there, until she knew for sure. Until she had the confirmation. She would use the time to the house to work out her exit strategy.

The walk to his apartment took less than ten minutes, the pub they had started in was less than five minutes from his home. He seemed to grow more nervous the closer they got, which made her happy. He wasn't used to a woman. She would use that.

Inside, the place was messy, as she had suspected it might be. She asked to use the bathroom. He pointed her down the hallway, Anastasia hearing him frantically putting things away in her absence, dirty plates no doubt finding their way from the lounge floor into the sink at last.

She pulled her phone out, rapidly typing a text message to Anissa.

Call me in twenty minutes. You're my exit strategy. Might have news of A. Will confirm later.

She didn't sign it. She knew Anissa had her number.

She looked at herself in the mirror for a moment, running her fingers through her hair twice. Appearances were everything. And it would be all he would get. She flushed the toilet, running the taps moments later, sure he wouldn't have noticed either way, but she would not take any chances.

The lounge seemed remarkably clean, given she'd only been gone for two minutes.

"Would you like something more to drink?" he called from the kitchen which opened onto the lounge.

"It depends how this story of the Brit will go. Mildly interesting, then a beer will do. Scintillating, then I'll need something stronger."

He laughed, reaching for a bottle of vodka from the top of his cupboard.

"This stuff is the best they make," he said, proudly. "Purest vodka you'll find." She smiled up at him as he poured two generous measures.

"So?" she asked, willing him to talk.

"First, we try the vodka," he said, raising the glass to his own lips, Anastasia doing the same seconds later. "One, two, three," he said, downing the liquid in one go, Anastasia taking half of her amount, the burn instant, the potency of the alcohol clear. He smiled at her, going to refill both glasses. "Good, right?"

"Yes," she smiled, straining to keep her head clear, her thoughts straight. "This story had better live up to such high billing," she said, raising the prized vodka.

He placed his glass back onto the table.

"They came in together, actually," he said. "About three years ago. Kept apart from the main population."

"That dangerous?" she said, playing along with the game, unsure if this were heading in the direction she wanted or not, given the mention of there being two men.

"That secret," he said, the worse for wear now. He'd been going rather heavy on the drink since she'd been speaking with him, something she engineered. "The Brit is in for treason," he said, proudly. Hope soared inside Anastasia.

"What did he do?"

That seemed to wipe the smile from his face.

"I don't know," he confirmed, picking up the glass and downing his second shot. She didn't follow suit this time. She glanced at her watch. She'd been there about fifteen minutes. "But he certainly wound up someone important to end up here without a trial."

"No trial? Is that usual?"

He smiled, pleased he had her eating up his words again. "No, it isn't," he confirmed.

"Who ordered him here?"

This he smiled at. He knew the answer to this one.

"The orders came directly from the Kremlin," he said.

"The President?"

"Yep," he confirmed smugly. She didn't need to ask which one. It didn't matter. It was Alex, she knew it already, a sensation now racing through her body she'd not known since he had vanished.

He moved a little closer to her on the sofa, Anastasia counting down the seconds in her head. She hoped for the life of her Anissa had seen the message. Her phone buzzed suddenly.

"Sorry," she said, standing up from the sofa, his beer-smelling breath still in her nostrils. "I have to take this."

She answered Anissa's call, speaking in Russian––she didn't need Anissa to understand, this was not for her benefit––before getting upset, speaking more rapidly, promising to be right there, she would come immediately. She hung up.

"Problem?" he called, somewhat worried. Anastasia was already putting on her jacket in the hallway.

"Yes," she said, that much had been clear. "I have to go."

"Anything I can help with?" he called, her shoes going on, the door half open.

"No," she said, not wanting to add he'd already offered her all the help she needed. She pulled the door closed behind her, the fresh air eventually blowing away the effects of the vodka.

At the hotel twenty minutes later, she called Anissa back, filling her in on what she'd learnt.

11

Santa Barbara Castle, Alicante
One Month Ago

The tourist traffic had quietened, most heading down into town, the various tapas establishments full, as the city's best restaurants and bars would soon be. The sun hung low over the mountains in the distance, the crowds on the beaches down below noticeably thinning out, despite the warmth.

Don Zabala had chosen dusk to make his appearance, the meeting scheduled then because the castle would be quieter. It'd been one of the first places Jose had visited when exploring the city as a boy––the place had huge symbolism for him. Now he was returning, very much the king of his city.

Two months of digging had got him this far; he felt sure the final pieces were about to fall into place.

They had arranged the meeting under the impression he was looking to make a booking. A woman had shown him around the various private rooms on offer, Jose making far more small talk than even he thought he was capable of as they moved through the space. Each room lay off the beaten track, away from any unwanted attention. If there ever was a space for high profile Russians to be close to the action but tucked away, this was undoubtedly a prime example.

"Do you have many bookings?" Jose enquired.

"A few," the woman confirmed. "Which dates are you thinking about precisely?"

"Could you tell me if there are already other bookings?" he asked, aware she would have known that.

"Yes," she said, holding up an iPad. "I have all the bookings here. To be honest, there isn't a lot happening for the next few months, so I'm sure we'll be able to fit you in easily. When is it you are planning?"

He gave her the dates for the week surrounding his son's death. These were two months ago as they stood there together in the semi-darkness of the largest room available at the castle.

"You mean next year?" she attempted to correct him, the man having stated the current year, a month and day that had already long passed.

"No, I would like you to confirm to me who booked the venue for the week in question."

This seemed to stop her in her tracks.

"I don't see what relevance any previous booking has with your plans."

"You'll see," he said, a smile in his eyes, a hint that by helping him with this information she might assist him when it came to his own event. Perhaps something linked the two events, or these were two rival firms in the same industry?

"What are the dates again?" she asked, after considering him for a while. He repeated what he had said moments before, the woman swiping back through the calendar, getting to the month in question. "Yes, there was a booking that week," she said, looking up at him. "Are you something to do with them?"

"By them, I take it you mean the Russians, correct?" he asked, the woman not speaking but her eyes flashed *yes* at the mention of Russians. "No, nothing but a casual observer. Have they ever booked with you before?"

"No," she said, Jose pleased to have passed the stage where she might have refused to give him information of who else had done business there. The venue was a local treasure. There were probably official records somewhere that he might have demanded access to if needed.

"And they were here all week?"

"Not every day, no. The men were here mostly. Probably three of the days they had booked."

"The men?" he questioned, a strange choice of wording, making it sound like husbands in one room, wives in the next or something.

"The actress was here too," she said, nervously, happy to talk about it with someone. She had been sworn to silence for so long and was eager to share what she knew. "I guess I should call her the President now," she corrected herself; Spanish media were full of coverage of Volkov's first months in power.

"The President?" he asked, though the penny finally dropped. The new Russian President--and former actress--had been in Madrid the week before the events in Alicante, then officially back to Moscow. "She was here?"

The woman nodded, beaming at the recollection.

"Svetlana Volkov, the new Russian President, was in this castle that week with a group of Russian men?" he pressed, hardly believing his own words, but needing absolute clarity now, making sure they were speaking about the same person, and not two different women.

"Yes, I spoke to her myself," she confirmed.

Jose took a step to the window, the view down onto the city below spectacular, shadows starting to work their way up the sandy beach towards the sea as the last of the sunlight peaked over the mountains to the west.

"What did they do here exactly?" Jose asked, turning around now, his mind still reeling from the confirmation that his son's murder might go as high up as the Kremlin itself.

"Video conferencing, I think. Had a whole team of people bringing in screens the day before. I didn't see the venue when it was ready. They were clear it was off limits to anyone but them."

"But you saw them bringing in displays, electrical equipment, cameras?"

"Cameras? No, there were no cameras. Just screens and boxes. Perhaps in the boxes there were?" she said, though it didn't matter. If the cameras were feeding live footage back from the city itself, all they needed were screens and receivers in the castle.

"How many days do you recall seeing Svetlana Volkov here?" he pressed, working through the timeline in his head of what he knew as having taken place that week.

"I wasn't here all the time," she started, thinking a little, before offering an answer to his question. "Perhaps two of the days. I know they didn't show for the last few that week. I had a question and came knocking. They had already cleaned out the place, screens, equipment, all gone."

"Which day was that?"

She thought for a moment longer. "Maybe the Friday?" she said. That was the day Clifton confronted Jose and confessed to the killing. It meant they weren't in this room watching. They were already mobile, planning their exit. He made a mental note to look into that later.

"And the viewing platform itself," he added, the final thing in his list. "Do these rooms offer direct access to that part of the castle?" he asked, the woman smiling, perhaps sensing things were getting back on track, this potential client about to make a firm booking for the future.

"Yes, I'll show you," she said, leading the way, Zabala carefully taking each step when it came between the rooms, his cane knocking rhythmically on the stone floor. The passage cut through multiple interconnecting rooms before, finally, she stood behind a small window, next to a door that opened out onto the highest public viewing point.

"I don't have the key with me for this door," she apologised, "but you can see you have direct access from this room." Jose was able to see that himself.

"And this room is private?"

"All part of the suite of rooms you book when you have a function here," she confirmed.

Clifton had undoubtedly been standing on that very spot where they both now stood, relieved of his clothes––Jose knew the Brit had not done it voluntarily––and soon running through the open door into the crowds that mulled around that day. Eventually he would beat a man unconscious for the fabric on his legs and back.

"Thank you," he confirmed, "you've been very helpful."

He refused the offer to provisionally book a date with her there and then, and after several protests, told her he would be in touch. Sensing this was the best she would get, they walked back the way they had come, into the room they had started from and Don Zabala left. Outside it was getting dark.

It took another two days to find out about the yacht booking for the week. He'd been focusing on the airports, but the only official flight to Moscow from Spain on record had been the returning one from Madrid at the end of the week of diplomatic meetings, the one the new President was meant to have taken.

Jose now knew Svetlana Volkov had never been on that flight. How she got to Alicante, he couldn't tell. If anyone knew, they were not saying. It hardly mattered. He knew she was not in Moscow as she wanted others to believe.

He had to think like the super-rich.

Once he ruled out private jets leaving the area––he had widened the search to not only the airport in Alicante, but the ones in Murcia and Valencia too––he shifted to private yachts, and here he struck gold. Someone had booked the biggest one the main firm in the area had available that week. No names given, nothing more known about them; all too secret. All too clear. The yacht had gone from Alicante to Ibiza on the Friday, the day Clifton confronted him and then fled himself. A quick call through to his contacts there had a ten-seater private jet flying from the island's airport late morning the following day. It flew to Moscow. The firm collected the yacht from Ibiza and returned it to its mooring the following week. He hadn't found out how Svetlana had travelled from Madrid to Alicante, but that didn't matter anymore. He knew she had been in Alicante, and that she wasn't alone.

Jose had them. He knew that Roman Ivanov would have been one of these people, President Volkov perhaps the only woman. That left a maximum of eight others, though he sensed the group would have been smaller than that. Perhaps four or five. Enough to make the crossing in the boat, enough to fit in the rooms at the castle watching events unfold, enough to fly back to Russia together in the jet.

One of these Russians, maybe even the President herself, had forced Clifton Niles onto his son, making the man kill Luken and then confess to his face. The thought that this could be the case caused him great concern, however. The papers that week were awash with rumours from an unknown Russian whistleblower sensationally claiming that Volkov had the Zurich loot.

Don Zabala had personally not had anything in *the Bank*, though he knew plenty of criminal groups who had. If there was any truth in the rumours, it made her far more of a threat than he had previously expected, not to mention the fact she'd now won the Russian vote, very much the public face of change, of freedom, of openness.

How open would she remain when confronted with what he knew?

Orenburg Region, Russia
Present Day

ANASTASIA DID NOT RETURN to the pub, did not go looking for the man whose apartment she had left in a hurry. She stayed in the hotel, counting down the days, meeting with the three wives of prisoners with whom she had previously connected.

She would join them on their next monthly visit, which was now only days away.

Anastasia had quizzed them thoroughly, understanding as much as she could about the place, about the whole procedure. She'd told them eventually who she was visiting, though none of the three women said their husbands had ever mentioned a British man being there. They asked her if she was sure. She told them what the guard had said to her.

"Some men they keep away from the main wings," one woman said, the older of the three, somewhat of a leader in their midst. "You know who else I heard they have here?" Her face wore the expression of someone in the know, certain that her piece of gossip would impress them all.

"Who?" Anastasia asked, the other two apparently already in the know.

"Putin," she said, the name slipping across her tongue like silk.

"*The* Putin?" Anastasia asked, as if there could be another. That added even more validity to the story she'd heard from the guard, his mention of two inmates arriving at the same time now popping into her mind.

The older woman merely smiled, all knowing.

"If your man is anywhere, I would bet you it's in those same cells," she added, implying wherever Putin was, Alex would be.

"And they'll let me visit him, regardless of where he is?" she asked.

"State rules demand we have monthly visitation rights," the older woman repeated, becoming the spokeswoman for the trio for the time being. "However, if your guy is off the radar, they might not abide by those rules."

"You think they'll deny my request to see him?"

"That or deny he's there," she pointed out.

"But the guard; he's told me he's there."

"He named him, did he?" Anastasia shook her head. The guard hadn't needed to name Alex for her to know it was him.

"I know he's there," she said, determinedly.

"Then you'll need your little guard friend to get you in," the older woman said, no smile on her face, spoken matter-of-factly though a smirk appeared after a few seconds as the Russian took in Anastasia's understanding of what she was saying. She wasn't asking Anastasia to do anything unethical, but it was clear she needed to do whatever it took to get him to help if Anastasia ever was to see Alex. The Belarusian didn't like that prospect. She'd hoped she'd already got all she needed from the guard.

"Can't any of you help?" she asked the trio sitting with her, "with the guard, I mean."

The youngest of the three raised her eyebrows at this, her tone suggesting she realised their new friend had gravely underestimated the problem.

"You think our husbands will stand for any of us fraternising with the enemy?" she asked. Anastasia smiled. They wouldn't, she got that. This was a guard keeping the inmates subdued, humiliated, trapped. "Anyway, you've already got the inside track." Anastasia had already told them she had him eating out of her hand. "Offer him more of the good stuff and he'll do anything for you," she smirked, the look naughty, mischievous.

"I'm not having sex with him for a favour!" Anastasia snapped, adamantly.

"I didn't say you had to," the younger woman replied, not elaborating on what she had meant. It was no doubt much further past the point at which Anastasia felt comfortable, that much seemed plain. "There are things other than a hard screw that these men seem to enjoy."

That comment caught Anastasia off guard. She thought there was only the physical, and she wouldn't go there. Not to save Alex, not to rescue the man she loved. She wouldn't sleep with a stranger to get to Alex.

"Like what?"

The older woman chirped up again now, the trio well aware of who their guest was, even if Anastasia had not told them.

"You have money," she said, rubbing her fingers together as if to illustrate the point.

"Bribe him?"

"Or better," the younger said. "Involve him in your scandal."

"My scandal?" though the look on all three faces in front of her told Anastasia that these women knew her ultimate connection to Alex. Knew he had to be the British agent conducting a secret affair with the wife of Dmitry Kaminski, news that had been big in Russia too, the story pressed home as it severely weakened Dmitry's status as a credible presidential candidate.

"Join the dots for this man. He'll love a story to tell his mates. Tell him why you're here, who you're here to see. *The lovers' reunion,*" she smiled, though the four-day visits were not for another seven months. Any visit she could get that week would be on separate sides of a pane of reinforced glass. There would be no physical contact this time.

"You think he'll go for that?" Anastasia said, thinking alongside sex or a hefty bribe––only one of which was even an option––such a story could only come a distant third.

"What? The former wife of an oligarch, sleeping with a spy while her husband ran for office? It could be a movie, my dear."

"I still don't think it's enough."

The older woman stood, going to the window, the day warm, sunny. She turned after a moment, silence still among the others.

"What's your goal in seeing Alex?" she asked Anastasia.

"To confirm it's him. To show him I know he's alive and that I still love him." She wanted to say that they would free him, that MI6 were working on a plan, but she knew she couldn't. It wouldn't be fair on the other three, and she couldn't tell anyone. Neither had she heard any plan from Anissa should she locate Alex. If she were about to confirm she'd found Alex, then what?

"So you need to get in there at least once," the older woman said. "One visit does all that."

"I'd like to see him more than once," Anastasia said, weakly, the older woman shrugging her shoulders as if that were not on the table as an option.

"You give this guard your story, promise something good for afterwards to keep him sweet, and he'll get you in."

"I told you," Anastasia started, though the Russian cut her off.

"I'm not saying you follow through!" she pointed out. "He merely needs to think you will."

"Lie to him?" she said, as if the thought seemed criminal to her.

"He's a bloody guard, for god's sake!" the older woman snapped. It was clear as far as they were all concerned, these men were less than human.

12

The Kremlin, Moscow
One Week Ago

They had first reached out some time before but confirmation was only just coming through that the message had been passed on to Pavel. That a mafia family in Spain wanted to speak to the President was nothing new--everyone who had lost money in Zurich when Filipov stormed the Bank and then stole its loot had been trying to contact her ever since the story broke. It was the personal, if not cryptic message Don Zabala wanted to pass to Svetlana Volkov that made Pavel take this one directly to her.

Pavel was a hard man, responsible for his own criminal network in Moscow yet pulled into her ranks when the President had reached out to him prior to the election, and used him to get the underworld onside. She had promised them the return of their wealth if they kept her safe--she was still alive--and if they helped her win the election; she'd been in office for two months.

Publicly, President Volkov continued her charm offensive. She would be hard on crime, hard on corruption, especially in her own government.

Pavel knew these were sound bites, had seen a side to the woman he guessed few knew of, saw a danger too.

He was now starting to get pressure from those on the outside wanting in. Groups pulled into the protection and election race, all desperately trying to survive. All wanting their treasure returned to them by the only person who could. Some had even threatened Pavel's life if he didn't sort it out, a threat that didn't go down well with a gangster like Pavel.

The Russian criminal kingpin waited outside the door to the President's office, his first visit to the Kremlin. All previous meetings had been elsewhere, away from people, away from watching eyes. Having such a high profile villain there––they had never caught Pavel, though he had been around plenty of men now serving long sentences––would cause a stir among any watching journalists. However, police had moved all the reporters from where they were standing minutes before Pavel arrived. They had cited a gas leak, the area in lockdown. Nobody would see the arrival or departure of Pavel.

Svetlana Volkov was no stranger to the criminal underworld, however. She had first met her future husband during his only prison sentence. Sergei had remained the wolf of Moscow, a man with a fierce reputation and a ruthless streak when needed. *Her dog on a leash.* She'd put him to good use many times during their outwardly happy marriage, though it was nothing but one of convenience. He offered her a way into the big leagues, a move away from only being a famous and glamorous actress, to someone to whom men would listen. For Sergei, she offered him credibility. No starlet like Svetlana would stay around a criminal. It crowned the remaking of the man, his image post-prison very much that of a changed man.

Their connection had been mutually beneficial. Svetlana Volkov––keeping her surname even now, despite the death of her husband, very much the wolf herself, as her name meant––knew she would not be in the Kremlin as President had it not been, in small part, to her connection to Sergei.

"You may go in now," an aide told Pavel, having just taken a call from the President. Pavel opened the door, Svetlana standing on the far side of her desk, the door closed behind him as he walked over and took a seat.

"You said this couldn't wait," she said, not looking up for the moment, a pen in hand, her signature added to a couple more documents before he offered her an answer. She didn't like him being there. This had to be the only time.

"A credible threat might have emerged," he said, Svetlana glancing up at him immediately, pen placed on the desk as she straightened up and sat back in her chair. Her face radiated beauty––it always did––but her eyes were cold, like those of a shark.

"Tell me what you have," she said, aware Pavel had got her attention. She'd not expected there to be any credible threats; it was why she had brought Pavel and his minions onside. They had free rein to step in and act. If they could prove any action had stopped a threat to her personally, she had assured them the authorities would turn a blind eye to anything criminal.

"It's not a threat in the usual way," Pavel smiled. "A Spaniard named Don Jose Zabala has reached out to me." The mention of the name caused a twitch in the President's eye, telling Pavel she might well know that name, as he had assumed she did.

"What did this man say?" she demanded coldly.

"Says he knows about your week in Alicante. Knows all about it." Pavel stopped, studying the face of the woman before him. The message meant nothing to Pavel. He assumed it was blackmail, something from years before, perhaps decades. Something to shame her with now if she didn't return him his money or something. Pavel wasn't aware Svetlana had been to Alicante in any official capacity since taking office.

"And?" Svetlana demanded, carrying as good a poker-face as Pavel had ever seen. He couldn't read her at all.

"He wants to talk with you, one-to-one."

"He does, does he?" She seemed intrigued at that prospect for a moment. "I'll call him," she said, after thinking it through a little. "You can tell him to expect to hear from me soon."

"I see," Pavel said. "If he's trying to blackmail you," he started, Svetlana cutting across him.

"I don't know what he wants, yet," she said, picking up her pen, ready to return to her document signing, which she did seconds later, "If I need you again, I'll be in touch," she added. "You aren't to come here in person again, okay?" She looked up at him, her eyes meeting his, Pavel standing.

"I'll await your contact," he said, backing his way to the door, the President returning to the paperwork as Pavel left the room.

IT WAS LATE NOW, Svetlana alone in her office, her staff gone. Security would be around the building, they always were, but most had left for the day.

She didn't want anyone around for this call.

Holding the handset to her ear, she dialled Zabala's number, sure that the Don would expect her call, certain the message would have got back to him already.

"I take it this is Moscow calling," Jose Zabala said on answering the unknown number on his private phone. He spoke English, Svetlana fluent herself.

"Your message left me little choice," she said, the first time they had ever directly spoken.

He pondered that for a moment. The very fact he was now speaking directly with the President confirmed, if he needed it, the validity of his findings.

"I know about Alicante," he said.

"Know what, exactly?"

Over the next five minutes, he pieced together the facts, Svetlana impressed with how much he had worked out, even if there was much he still didn't know, much she wouldn't tell him.

"I could have gone to the police with this straight away and not even bothered to inform you," he finished, the fact they were speaking now actually a good sign. She'd had enough of secret whistleblowers already; one man still lurked in the shadows, silent for the time being, but a potential threat if there were any further revelations.

"So why didn't you?" she asked, sure he would tell her that shortly.

"Because I want something more valuable from you instead," he said. If this was about the money taken from Zurich, it would disappoint Svetlana greatly in a man she had suddenly come to respect during their phone call. He'd worked out plenty. That showed resolve, resource, intelligence.

"Which is what, exactly?" She looked at her watch. It was nearly eleven. She should be home, winding down for the evening––probably through half a bottle of quality wine.

"I want the name of the man who killed my son," he said.

"You had that name," she pointed out, aware of Roman Ivanov's intervention with the Don, something she'd orchestrated.

"I'm not talking about Niles, the man who pulled the trigger. I'm talking about the Russian who must have travelled back with you, the one who put a target on my son."

"A target? What do you think this is?" she laughed, her hand reaching for a bottle. She suddenly couldn't wait any longer for that drink.

"What do you think people will make of it if I share what I know?"

"Are you threatening me?" she demanded. Since the election, she would allow nobody to threaten her again, not in Russia, anyway. It seemed the message had yet to cross national borders.

"The name of the man responsible," Jose repeated, equally forceful himself now. Politicians came and went, he'd outlived many in his own country. He wasn't overly afraid of the woman he now spoke with, aware of the potential for trouble she possessed.

"The name for your silence, is that it?" That was blackmail in her book, but she didn't mind playing that game for the time being, seeing how she could quickly work it to her advantage. "If I give up this man, you had better keep your word."

"You know I'm good for my word," he said, assuming his reputation had somehow reached her office, which it hadn't, but she'd formed a fairly good impression of the character of the man during their conversation. He could have gone to the police or the press, yet he hadn't. They both knew how their worlds worked.

"And he'd better not know it was me," she added.

"He killed my son," Jose said, reason enough for him to have gone after the man responsible.

"Okay," she said, pulling out a piece of paper from her top drawer. She knew the oligarchs by heart, knew which challenge each had set. It had been Vladimir Popov who had proposed Luken Zabala as the target for Clifton in his challenge.

She looked at the list before her.

"He's in Germany," she said, giving Jose the city, though she didn't know the address. "His name is Slava Alkaev."

13

Orenburg Region, Russia
Present Day

When visiting day finally came around--the anticipation by that final morning of waiting nearly overpowering--Anastasia had her plan memorised. She walked with the three women, getting cleared through security with the larger group of other visitors there that day. They were people who presumably had travelled to the town for the day for the same reason as the trio.

They pulled Anastasia to one side; the guard she had got to know smiled at her. The Belarusian waved to her three friends as they went their usual way.

"This way," the guard said, leading her in the opposite direction, away from the departing group of mostly women. "We'll collect him shortly," he confirmed, a dirty look on his face. He couldn't believe his luck with this woman and he knew the inmate, the forbidden lover, was not leaving imminently. "I can't wait for later," he said, almost trembling with energy. They'd paused in the corridor outside a door she presumed was where she would finally meet Alex. The guard turned to face her, barely a foot between the pair. He ran his hand through her hair, leaning forward as if to kiss her, his groin pressing forward, his hand on her thigh. She pulled back.

"My mother always told me," she said, a firm hand on his chest, which pushed him back a step, though done all so playfully, "that when you have a feast coming later for dinner, snacking in the day only ruins your appetite." She spoke delicately and extremely seductively.

"You are so hot," he laughed, a red flush racing across his face. His initial shock at being denied soon turned into a sexual tension he couldn't wait to release. "Later, I hear you," he winked, opening the door that stood in front of him, and he ushered in Anastasia instructing her to take the only chair there was in front of a glass window. Beyond the glass there was an empty cage, a matching chair waiting for an occupant, an inmate soon to appear whom Anastasia dearly hoped would be Alex.

She'd been waiting nearly fifteen minutes before she heard chains and locks, not initially knowing where they were coming from but as they grew louder, her anticipation equally grew. It had been so long since she'd last seen him. Would he still look the same? He'd always been strong, but would his time there, lost to the world for all he knew, have changed that? Would he be different now? If not in appearance, but in character. Would he even still love her? Could he, when as far as she knew, he'd been living in the belief that she had chosen Dmitry over him?

As the final door opened, the head and then the shoulders of a prisoner came into view, his body bent over, arms raised high behind his back. She couldn't see who it was for the moment, the hair dark, the face bearded.

Then he sat down, the guards locking the cage door behind them, giving them a little space, though she knew they wouldn't go far. They probably didn't speak English, however, the language she switched to immediately.

It was him, *her* Alex right before her in the flesh! His face lost behind weeks of beard growth, but his eyes were the same. They'd not changed, and they raced now with affection, with recognition, with utter shock.

Anastasia burst into tears, everything suddenly too much for her, the years of longing, years of not knowing, nights spent awake fearing the worst, had suddenly dissolved into this. He was alive; he was here. Their hands met on the glass--the cold divide an inch thick between their fingers--but their hands mirrored each other.

They stayed like that for a while, eyes locked, hands raised. No words needed.

"It's so good to see you again," Anastasia eventually said, still crying, though these were happy tears. Hope had returned. She would deal with the impossible next. Right now she'd found her lost soul mate.

"How?" he asked, one word all he could manage. He spoke so little now, surrounded by a life of silence and solitude that even one word voiced from his lips, in a language he understood, seemed to surprise him.

"Anissa," she said. "A long story."

His eyes lit up at the mention of his colleague's name.

"She's not here," Anastasia clarified. "She'll know," she promised. "I'll make sure."

He seemed happy at that. She wanted him to know so much, cautious of what to say, fearful that they were listening. They were listening.

"Do you remember what Dmitry did to me in that hotel room?" she asked. Alex did not understand her initially. Alex had done plenty of things with Anastasia, however. "I will do the same to you," she said, her eyes alive with passion.

Alex nodded. Dmitry had smuggled his wife out of the room. That was the second to last time Alex had seen her; the final time they'd been intimate. However, the recollection of his final meeting with Anastasia, when she told him she didn't love him, soon filled his mind.

"I've been in Germany, waiting for you," she said, as if sensing where he'd just gone.

"Not Italy," he smiled, though there was heartbreak there too. She sighed. He finally understood. Sorrow filled his face. "I'm so sorry," he said, kicking himself, the confirmation he already knew deep down now plain and clear.

"Stay strong," she said, doing her best to do that herself and hold it all together.

She removed her hand from the window, the warmth of her print leaving a mark for a while once Alex removed his, their two prints fading into eternity slowly.

She took in his features, his full appearance, chest upwards anyway. His legs, still chained, were hidden beneath the table. He'd lost weight, which was saying a lot. He'd always been trim when she knew him. His face looked sunken, his skin pale. She'd never liked beards, but seeing the forest on Alex at that moment, she didn't care. It looked good. Despite everything, he looked good.

"I love you so much," he said, the words taking everything from Anastasia for a moment, their truth a power she couldn't handle. And she loved him too, only now believing properly he was real, still alive, that there was any hope of a happy ending. And yet her biggest challenge remained. There had never been an escape from that building.

All too soon the guard returned, a different one from before, and this man seemed angrier. He called the meeting off, helped Alex stand––Anastasia only now taking in his legs, a limp he seemed to carry––and after cuffing his hands together again, he forced Alex into a bent position and manoeuvred him back out of the room. Anastasia was on her feet, pressed close to the glass, remaining there until Alex had gone from sight. Seeing him again had meant the world to her. It changed everything. She couldn't leave him there, not now. Not after seeing him like that.

The door behind her reopened, the guard who'd shown her in standing there, smiling. *Hopeful.* Anastasia put a tissue to her nose–– playing the *too emotional to deal with anything now* role––and scurried out through the open door without even glancing at him, much to his frustration.

She left the building, returning to her hotel. She would not see the guard again.

Inside the prison, after locking Alex back in place, the warder was on the warpath, finding the man who'd let Anastasia in, giving him a firm reprimand for not clearing it with him first.

The prison warden would never have allowed such a visit, by order of the Kremlin. Now he knew he would have to make a difficult phone call to Moscow, informing the President's team that Anastasia Kaminski––he knew who she was the moment he spotted her––had discovered where they had stowed Alex. He didn't relish the prospect one bit.

The Kremlin, Moscow

THE PRESIDENT HAD NOT BEEN in a good mood, the call she was now on not helping in that regard. It was the prison governor from the Black Dolphin. Anastasia Kaminski had found Alex.

"Tell me about the guard," the President asked, "the one Kaminski befriended." The caller ran through what he knew; he had interviewed the man himself around five years ago. The guard in question had never made such an error.

After hearing the full story, she thought for a moment, before telling him what to do.

"As you demand," the governor said. To question a direct order would have been more than his life was worth. He knew how things worked in his country.

"And move the prisoner to the main wing. Come to think of it, move them both," she said, aware that Putin and Alex were isolated from the rest of the inmates in another section. To know of one was to know of the other. It was possible Alex had given Anastasia that information. The prison hadn't been listening to their chat, the guard standing in earshot unable to understand English.

"You want Putin moved?" the governor clarified, though Putin was the only prisoner she could mean.

"Yes, move them tonight. Have the British man's door read *педофил—pedofil*. Paedophile." That would give Alex plenty to worry about, such prisoners were given a rude welcome and did not usually make it through the first year.

"And Putin?"

"No change," she said, his charge the one the Kremlin had publicly stated already: treason.

The Black Dolphin Prison, Sol-Iletsk

THE MOVE CAME the day after Anastasia had visited Alex, the change of routine for a second day on the trot enough to give him hope something special was happening. Two guards came and ordered him to collect his things together––Alex understood nothing––the same words ordered in the next door cell. Alex spotted Putin collecting his belongings, the Brit now beginning to do the same which seemed to appease the two angry guards who'd arrived in his cell.

Hope birthed in him afresh. Alex had not had one visit in his entire time at that prison until Anastasia's shock appearance. He'd also never needed to pack up his cell, either. This was different. Were they finally releasing him?

Yet, Putin didn't seem happy. Packed up, he'd spoken to the guards––Alex not understanding the words but aware enough from body language the former President was demanding to know what was going on.

Alex filled the bag with his few belongings and passed it to the guard. They then handcuffed both prisoners, a black bag placed over their heads, which implied they were being moved within the prison.

This wasn't a release.

A nudge in the back got Alex moving, the sound of Putin ahead of him, the awareness of two guards either side. Doors opened and then closed, and on they walked. On and on they went, left turns, right turns, even once doing a one eighty. They were making sure the men did not understand where they were going, nor from where they had come. Alex got that.

Eventually they came to a stop, the sound of three locks slowly opening, the clear creaking of a heavy metal door swinging, and in they went, Alex now aware that they were in another wing. The many voices around them suggested they were no longer isolated. Sudden panic raced through him.

Stopping outside a cell, both prisoners had the bags removed from their head. The instant silence that followed was absolute. It swept around like a wave, starting with the cells nearest and then moving wider, leaving only the sounds of the cell doors opening. It was the realisation that Putin himself stood in their midst. The rumours were true.

A guard slipped sheets of paper into the slots on the front of both cell doors—the charges. Alex was aware of that much even if he didn't know what the words meant. He glanced at his own then at Putin's. The former President's charge hadn't changed. Putin did the same, glancing at his own then at Alex's door. He smiled when he saw what they had written on Alex's.

"Good luck with that," he grinned, going into his cell moments later, nothing more said, Alex looking at his own notice again. These were different letters to before, different to the sign he'd returned to each day for over three years. Alex knew immediately it wasn't good. He went into his cell saying nothing, the door closed behind him. The surrounding silence broke, chatter and noise all around him now, prison guards high above, making circuits around the wing.

It terrified him.

As they shuffled to dinner that evening, Alex pushed in behind Putin.

"What does my door say?" Alex demanded, the prisoners not meant to speak while moving, but the Brit didn't care.

"It means you have sex with children," Putin replied, not turning, but Alex caught every word. Alex swore under his breath. "And men like that have it very hard in places like this," Putin added.

Putin too was wary. As a KGB officer until the early nineties, there were men he'd sent to prison who still might be around.

They sat opposite one another at the same table, Alex against the wall, Putin with his back to others. He had men loyal to him there, too, he was certain. He'd seen the fear in many faces, prisoners unable to look at him. They knew a strong man when they saw one, and inside a prison like that one, physical strength made little difference. Putin remained strong in every sense, even behind bars.

An old man dropped in unexpected and uninvited, sitting next to Putin but looking at Alex. He spoke to Alex in Russian, Putin finishing his bread before acting as a translator.

"He's offering to make a proposition," Putin said, speaking a few words to the other man, presumably explaining Alex had no Russian.

The newcomer spoke again, Alex watching both him and Putin, trying to read the smile appearing on Putin's face as silence returned.

"He's saying he'll make it a quick and painless death if you don't put up a fight," Putin confirmed, Alex looking at the man.

"Yeah?" Alex replied defiantly. "Who are you?" The newcomer looked almost eighty. Alex fancied his chances in a one-on-one, though he knew it wouldn't be that.

Putin relayed the question.

"His name is Boris Mihaylov," Putin confirmed. "Been here thirty years, and he says he's seen that they teach every pervert a lesson. The real sickos he takes personal delight in dealing with."

"Tell him the charge is a lie," Alex said, his eyes pleading with Putin.

"I can't," Putin said. "They wouldn't believe me, anyway. You might as well accept your fate."

"My fate?" But Alex got it. Putin didn't think Alex could survive much longer.

"Nobody leaves this place," Putin said. "Hell, I wonder if even I will," he joked, as if he somehow didn't count as a normal citizen, a normal inmate. "If it's not today, it'll be tomorrow. Someone will get to you. You can't survive on your own."

"I've been on my own here for three years!" Alex snapped, which was true, though he had spent that time away from the rest of them, isolated, hidden. This was the opposite of that. They had sent him to that wing to die.

Boris, who'd not understood the exchange between Putin and Alex and had then not had anything translated by Putin, merely held out his hand, as if agreeing on a business deal. Alex refused to shake the man's hand; a few inmates watched from other tables, a few shouting out comments.

Boris lowered his hand, a shake of his head as if saying *your choice, dead man.* He stood up and said nothing more, slowly moved away back to the table from which he had come. Alex took in the five younger men huddled around the old-timer, no doubt being informed of Alex's reply, if they hadn't already guessed. One man soon looked over at Alex, his tongue licking his lips, his eyes suggesting he was on another planet. The man pointed at Alex with his right index finger, before running the same finger as if to slit his throat. *You're dead.*

14

The Black Dolphin Prison, Sol-Iletsk
Present Day

The attack came quickly and suddenly. Alex was still learning the schedules in that part of the prison, having been shown into a workroom where he could spend a few hours making something. A guard left him alone with one other inmate.

It was the same inmate from dinner, the one who'd pointed at him.

As soon as the door closed, the Russian leapt at Alex; the Brit was expecting the attack, sure the guards must have known something about it.

The Russian had a blade, something he'd taken from the machinery, and Alex used all his training––thankfully, despite the lack of practice, he'd not lost those instincts––to protect himself as best he could, fighting back when the opportunity arose. It was clear the Russian presumed this child-molesting scumbag would be an easy touch when faced with a real man. He would fully understand his error too late.

Alex was clear: this man was there to kill him, the blade slashing his arm twice, gashing his side once. After finally pinning the Russian against the wall, Alex struck the man's right hand repeatedly, the blade falling loose after the fifth hit, Alex landing his sixth square in the stomach, the seventh in the face as his attacker screamed in pain.

It only seemed to enrage the man further, his eyes suggested he too knew this fight would only end one way, and unless he upped his game, it would be his body the guards carried out later, not the scumbag they had ordered him to kill.

Both men stood, Alex keeping a little distance, bouncing from foot to foot. Nimble, ready, poised. The Russian touched his jaw, rubbing it with his other hand, his strong arm still numb. He eyed the blade lying on the floor. It lay under a workbench, beyond his foe, out of reach.

The Russian thrust forward again, nothing else for it but to fight it out, fist to fist. He landed a blow to the side of Alex's head, the Brit ducking, expecting contact, but catching the knee of the Russian as he swung past, causing him to crash to the floor. Alex was on top of him in a second, his legs trying to wrap around the man's throat, his arms doing their best to deflect the flailing punches. He hunkered down, Alex positioning his body out of reach of the man's reach, on the floor, above his head, legs still carefully coiled around the Russian's throat. It was a position from which Alex knew there would be no escape. He held him down for a last few frantic seconds, the other man going still seconds later, Alex not relaxing his grip for another half minute, controlling his breathing, regaining his calm.

He finally broke away, uncoiling himself from the Russian, well aware the other man was dead. Alex confirmed the absence of a pulse. He dragged the body to the other side of the room. There was nowhere to hide it, and it was clear the guards must have been in on things. A minute later, Alex tapped on the door, the same two guards reappearing, somewhat surprised to see Alex standing there, nothing said as they led him back to his cell.

Alex knew unless something happened fast, he might not be so lucky next time.

THE GUARD whom Anastasia had befriended had not arrived for work the following day. At lunch, they ordered another guard to go to the man's apartment.

They found the body on his bed soon after. His throat had been slit. A pair of black knickers the only unusual thing in the entire apartment. They lay at the foot of the bed, underneath the sheets, presumably forgotten or lost by his attacker. The police gathered everything together.

At the prison, the prison governor had reached out to the three women known to have been in contact with Anastasia. Caught on CCTV arriving with the Belarusian the previous day, Anastasia had waved to them as they walked away from her, the trio waving back. The camera showed Anastasia walking with the now deceased guard. It was a murder investigation.

Shown the video, none of the trio denied knowing Anastasia. Neither did they think anything wrong had happened.

"Somebody murdered this man last night," the prison governor said, someone the trio despised––their husbands had shared plenty of stories from life at the prison, most involving him. He pointed at the screen. The video feed paused on the retreating Anastasia with the guard.

"Murdered?"

"We found a pair of knickers underneath his bed," the governor said. He knew that too well. He'd put them there. "Did you know Anastasia Kaminski was having sex with him?"

The oldest of the three turned her nose up at that.

"Hardly," she said. "She used the guy to get her in, nothing more."

"And yet now he's dead," the governor said. "She's our only suspect."

None of the women had seen Anastasia since waving goodbye to her the previous morning. They didn't think she was a killer, but perhaps when forced to repay the man, she had opted for murder instead?

"Why would she kill him?"

"You tell me," the governor said. "She'd got what she came for; now she was covering her tracks."

"No!" the youngest said, sensing the man was painting a picture that couldn't have been true.

"Yes," he spoke firmly, his voice menacing, the story already fixed in his mind. This was his show now, and one of them would comply. He tapped on the door, two guards coming in shortly afterwards. "If you two could please follow them, I want to interview you each separately," he smiled. Polite, but his tone told them they had no choice.

"Screw you!" the oldest of the three said, though she stood, the youngest one also, leaving their friend in the chair.

"Remember, I will give you the same offer in just a second, once you are all seated. This is a onetime deal, and the first of you to agree to it will get it. The other two get nothing." He smiled, delighted to put them in such a position. He was sure one of them would soon do what he needed, what Svetlana Volkov predicted.

Now there was just one woman remaining, the governor sat down opposite her, looking at his watch. Ten in the morning, the signal to share the proposition with each of them. He had two thousand rubles on one of them accepting within five minutes.

"It's rather simple," he began. "Whoever will go on record and link Anastasia Kaminski to the murder of this guard will receive monthly two-day/one-night visits with their husband for the rest of his sentence." He grinned; he could see the temptation immediately, the fear too. Perhaps the others had already snapped up the offer? Perhaps they had already turned on their friend? Could they all remain loyal? Should they?

Perhaps Anastasia really had killed him, like they said she had? Though sitting across from a man who her husband regularly told her was more crooked than most of the inmates locked away there, she didn't believe a word. They were fitting Anastasia up. She wouldn't stand to let them win. She trusted her two friends would do likewise. She was wrong.

It was the oldest of the trio who snapped first; in eight minutes.

It lost the warder his little wager. She had most to gain. She wasn't getting any younger.

"I'll do it," she said. "I'll stand up and testify for her motive in killing the guard."

"Very good," the man posing the offer to her said. "We'll take you to the police station to make that statement right away."

They issued the arrest warrant the following morning and the story was then leaked to the press. Anastasia was still in the hotel, still in the town when the news channels carried the story. Her name flashed across the screen, no location given for the murder, but the report stated she was the key suspect in a murder of a state official––no job title given.

The Black Dolphin Prison, Sol-Iletsk

If news of the killing in the workshop had circulated, nobody seemed to say or do anything. Two days after the fight, and with no further threats manifesting themselves yet, Alex reasoned it had at least bought him some time.

He caught Boris Mihaylov constantly looking his way throughout the day. That one was trouble; the snatched rumours he'd picked up via Putin––the only English speaker as far as Alex knew, and the only inmate speaking to him––confirmed Boris ran his own little empire inside.

Boris was a man of legend. The closest lifer to have got anywhere near escaping. Alex knew if he didn't achieve what this prisoner had failed to do, his own life wouldn't last much longer. Boris had been there for thirty years, Alex a little over three.

However, the legendary inmate didn't appear to be the only one gathering other inmates around him. Alex had noticed Putin had a growing group of his own. Gangs were how powerful inmates controlled such prisons, and Putin offered many on the outside of Mihaylov's protection a new champion of their own. It was clear these inmates wanted a power shift, and that became possible with the former President arriving on their wing. Quickly, sides were forming. The trouble was, Boris had recently lost one of his wingmen, sent to kill Alex and yet the Brit had been the one to arrive back that day.

The next attack came without warning, Alex on the second floor––Boris's men in the canteen on the first, finishing their food. Alex had checked. He deemed a walkabout was somewhat safer.

Timed to give him no chance to react, as Alex passed a cell, a bottle smashed over his head. The force from the subsequent push sent him over the rail. Suddenly Alex was falling, his reaction enough to put out his hands, the floor flying up to him. The pain was instant though it saved his head and face.

Everyone heard the thud of a body hitting the ground, a not uncommon sound, yet enough to get the alarms sounding, guards running forward.

"In your cells!" the barked orders came, each man compliant, the doors locked. Alex struggled on the floor, movement showing he wasn't dead, an inability to stand up immediately plain it wasn't good. Three guards went over to him, blood on the back of his head from where the bottle had hit him.

"Search that cell!" the officer commanded, pointing to the floor above, outside the cell from which Alex had fallen. It was an empty cell; its occupant was the man who had been found dead in the workshop two days before.

The guards helped Alex to his feet, rough and firm––had he seriously broken something, they would have probably finished him with such a lack of care.

They examined Alex, who seemed dazed, the room spinning, his head throbbing. It also felt like he might have broken both wrists on landing. One guard whistled, two fingers in his mouth, the sound high-pitched, cutting inside Alex's pounding head. Apparently a signal to someone.

A call came from up above, the words lost on Alex as they would have been if he were fully conscious.

"It's empty."

The guard next to Alex looked around, though all inmates watched, their eyes fixated on him at that moment, like animals in a zoo, desperate to have a piece of the zookeepers.

"Who did this?" he ordered, a loud chorus of cheers and shouts going up, monkey chants, gorillas, wolves––any form of pack animal. The message was clear. This was the jungle. And a predator had just got his way.

A wheelchair arrived, a doctor in tow and Alex was lowered into the chair, his entire world now spinning, the sounds coming and going. He was bleeding, he knew that. And he'd just fallen twelve feet. They placed a mask over his mouth, Alex initially pushing it away, though he stopped. His wrists were screaming at him, and one gasp of the oxygen coming through the now attached mask told him he needed this. He closed his eyes as they wheeled him away, the sounds fading behind him, as he drifted into unconsciousness, his eyelids heavy, his body light, floating away.

He would wake four hours later in the hospital wing, his head bandaged, his wrists both in casts, though he had movement in his fingers.

His whole body now ached, the drip attached to his right arm presumably delivering some pain relief, though at that moment, it barely felt adequate.

15

London
Present Day

Sasha had to keep pace with Anissa, his MI6 partner striding towards the park, desperate to talk.

"Wait up," he called eventually, Anissa slowing a fraction though she did not say a word as they entered the park a few seconds later. Anissa took the first path on the right, away from the crowds congregating in the centre. It seemed that a running group was meeting for a lunch break jog.

"I heard from Anastasia," Anissa said, finally able to let it out of her system.

"When?"

"Just now," she confirmed. "She's found him, Sasha." She let the weight of that statement flood the air around them for a moment.

"Where?"

"Where you suggested." Sasha had known Anastasia was heading towards The Black Dolphin prison. Still, the realisation they had confirmation that the British agent was being held there sent a shudder down his spine.

He swore.

"Has she seen him?"

"Yes," Anissa said. Anastasia had been troubled by the agent's appearance, though Anissa kept that from Sasha for the time being. She'd seen how much Sasha was enjoying spending time with Charlie––he missed Alex immensely too, she knew that for certain.

"When?"

"Yesterday. She called me late last night."

"You know, everything I said about that place…" he paused, not sure how to convey what he wanted to say, what hope he might offer. When they were just talking, not knowing that Alex was really there, he'd gone to town on the legend. The place was impenetrable, he'd stated. Maximum security, and it needed to be. They sent only the most vile criminals there. He made it sound like hell––about as easy to escape from too.

"I know," she said, aware he wanted to make it all right, but sure there was much truth in what he said. They would just have to come up with a way in and out that nobody had thought of yet. Where every escape had failed––they had documented only one major attempt––they would have to succeed.

Anissa's phone rang at that moment, and she reached for it expecting perhaps Anastasia had something more for her. It was the office number, however. Gordon Peacock.

"You need to see this," was all Gordon said, Anissa relaying the message to Sasha, as they both headed for the office.

Sasha sat next to Anissa at the screens, dumbfounded.

"It's Volkov, it has to be," Anissa grimaced. Gordon had spotted the reports linking Anastasia to the murder of a prison guard, an arrest warrant issued in the Belarusian's name.

"The President has someone at the prison," Zoe said, "she must do."

"It doesn't matter that much now, but I fear we are losing time,"

Charlie said. If the President now ordered the relocation of Alex, there might be no finding him. Moving him might only make him vulnerable, anyway. He knew too much. They had him beyond reach. Why risk anything?

"You think she'll make a move on him?" Anissa asked, sensing where Charlie was going with his thinking.

"I think she'll do whatever she wants. But yes, I think this has scared her. She probably assumed nobody knew where he was."

Zoe recalled something the whistleblower said. "He'll know about Putin," she said. "If Alex is there, you can bet anything that Putin's there too."

"And Volkov won't want news of either getting out," Anissa said, both impressed they'd reached that understanding and worried about its connotation.

"Volkov knows," Anissa said, certain of at least that much. She pulled out her phone, desperate to reach Anastasia now before it might be too late. The Belarusian's call to Anissa had only been the night before, confirming she'd seen Alex. She'd said how his appearance and condition had troubled her, but noted that he had come alive once he set eyes on her. Anastasia had pleaded with MI6 to do something, Anissa confirming they were working on a plan. They'd ended things there.

Anastasia finally answered on the fourth ring.

"Thank god," Anissa exclaimed, terrified that she might already be in custody.

"I take it you've seen the news?" Anastasia asked.

"Yes. Where are you?"

"Heading to safety," Anastasia confirmed, not prepared to give her location in case anyone was listening. She was close to the Kazakhstan border now, the river and wilderness beyond allowing her to cross the border unnoticed. She would then try to get to the capital.

"Okay, once we finish, lose this phone," Anissa said, Anastasia knowing the British agent's number by heart. "Call me when you are safe."

"Will do," she said, adding, "I didn't kill anybody; you know that, right?"

"I do," Anissa said, not for one moment thinking the Belarusian had been responsible. She'd been around Russian tricks and mind games long enough to know that by now.

They ended their call, Anissa turning to the others, relaying what had just happened. Her thoughts remained with Anastasia for a while, wondering where she would head, wondering if the first they would know of her capture would be television images. Would they even show that?

It all still felt so fragile. It had to be Svetlana Volkov's doing. After hearing the confirmation that Alex was at the Black Dolphin, Anissa had been on a high all night. She'd called Sasha late telling him the news, then called Charlie and Zoe. The four agents were in regular contact. The confirmation that Alex was still alive had rallied them all, though perhaps none more so than Anissa, who had worked the longest with Alex, and knew him as closely as if he were her brother.

"You said Anastasia is heading to the border?" Charlie quizzed, looking up from the screen, a map open. Anissa pointed to the spot Anastasia had mentioned. Charlie looked over to Sasha. "Can you get us in?" he asked the Russian.

Sasha looked at the screen, the aerial view of that part of northern Kazakhstan mostly uninhabited, the border area containing few roads on the Kazakh side, primarily fields and mountains, and the river which largely traced the border.

"Us?" Zoe asked, picking up on what Charlie had asked Sasha about, though Charlie remained silent for now, Sasha speaking next.

"I can," he said, determined that the others shouldn't go without him. He would need to follow them into the country once at the border too.

"Who's *us*, Charlie?" Zoe demanded.

"Do you fancy a trip to Kazakhstan with me, *babe*?" he winked. She laughed.

"I never thought you'd ask, *honey*," she joked back, no doubt that she should be on such a trip with the other two. She could make her dark hair darker. She could make herself look more Russian with little effort. Charlie could speak the language, Sasha was Russian. This might work.

Sasha looked at Anissa.

"I can't," she said, fearing she was being asked to join them, and though it were a long way from St Petersburg, it was still Russia. She didn't feel ready.

"I'm not asking you to, either," he said. "We need you here. Work with Gordon. Keep us informed." She smiled at him. She wanted Alex freed as much as anyone––perhaps more so––but she'd never dealt with her feelings completely regarding Russia.

Charlie had been tapping away on the computer for a few seconds, now speaking up, taking the focus from Anissa.

"We can travel into Kazakhstan without a visa," he confirmed, the website he now had open stating British nationals staying for less than thirty days didn't need to apply for a visa beforehand. He assumed Sasha, being Russian, didn't need one at all. He kept tapping away on another screen, opening up Google Maps to check for the nearest airports. He turned with a smile a minute later. "We can fly to Aktobe," he said, pointing to a city towards the north-west of that vast country, the map showing a car journey from that city to the border area south of Sol-Iletsk where the prison stood to be less than three hours. "Flights are a little pricey, but look at this one," he said, tapping on the link for a flight that took only an hour longer in total but cost a fifth of the price. It cost £469 and took over thirteen hours, a change needed in the capital, but the flight there from London was direct. Charlie proceeded through the process with the web-booking. "They have seats available tomorrow evening," he said, entering the number three, nobody protesting as he booked them. It would take off at twenty past five the next afternoon and get them to their final airport not long after nine in the morning the following day. A drive from the city and they'd be at the border by midday, something like thirty-six hours from then, time zone changes not particularly factored in. He pressed purchase for the three tickets, the fifteen hundred pounds going on the credit card.

He would see if there was a way to stretch MI6 expenses to cover the cost.

"Make sure Anastasia knows we are coming," Charlie said. "We can meet her on the ground in Kazakhstan. She'll be able to tell us a little more about the border area. I suggest the two of you put in for some time off," he said, turning to Sasha and Zoe. They needed to explain their time away from the office. Charlie had a few days carried over from before, anyway. He would do the same.

"So we're going?" Zoe buzzed, the last few frantic minutes catching up with her, the excitement mixing with a little trepidation at what might lie before them. Anissa couldn't help feeling a tinge of regret for not going with them, but they would need help from Six. She would liaise with Gordon. She would see if he could utilise one of the British satellites to watch from above.

"Yeah, baby," Charlie said pleased with himself, pushing his chair away from the desk, the wheels rolling him back with a half turn. He jumped up once it came to a stop. "You're going home, my friend," he patted Sasha on the back. Only Anissa, looking at the Russian at that moment, spotted his face showed only concern at the prospect.

"It'll be okay," she said, now just the two of them. The other two had returned to their office, ready to prepare the necessities for their imminent absence. "I've got your back."

He smiled at her. If things got serious, there was little Anissa could do from behind a desk in London, but he understood the sentiment. He determined it wouldn't be him going missing next, destined to spend a life behind bars.

16

The Kremlin, Moscow
Present Day

Roman Ivanov waited in her office while she finished a phone call, this not an uncommon visit for the oligarch worth over $14 billion. Mostly, when he met with Svetlana, it happened away from the Presidential offices in the Kremlin, often not even in the capital itself. He deemed it safer that way. There were fewer people watching, less chance of a journalist glimpsing him walking in.

Thankfully, the press were getting put back into place as things had been before Filipov hit the scene. A man named Dmitry Sokoloff had been the media mogul then, the oligarch owning the country's largest news networks, including the main television channel. That gave the then President, Putin, unparalleled access to the Russian people, addressing them weekly and when election time came, the sitting-President afforded the prime slots, the opposition making do with whatever scraps were offered.

It just seemed how it all had to be. Until Filipov killed Sokoloff, destroying the man's reputation and life before ending it with a bullet through the skull. They recorded his death as suicide, case closed.

The mogul was no more. Nobody had seen Filipov coming. Like an elusive Siberian tiger himself, he'd hidden in the tall grass, out of sight, but making his move by stealth. Only when it was already too late for his victims did he show himself.

Svetlana Volkov now controlled the television networks, the newspapers, the online blog forums, even the coffee shop gossip, if she could manage it. Nothing showed her name––these firms were apparently open and independent, but they gave a level of access to her not seen since the years Putin occupied that same office. The instructions were clear. The whole country needed showing how radical and effective Volkov was being now that she was their President. Her face had to be before the people all the time, the weekly broadcasts her chance to captivate an audience again. The viewing figures for these shows had been rising, too. The demographics showed that more men were watching. Everything headed in the right direction.

Her team easily managed opposition voices and viewpoints. Everything was subtle. To look at Svetlana Volkov, her make-up light––she never needed much to radiate beauty in any arena she found herself in––she was the picture of openness and transparency. Her in-front-of-camera persona had been honed over decades––playing a Bond Girl or President was not too different. They were both roles, lines to speak. She had a hand in all her speeches, though a team drafted the heavy work first. Svetlana was there to add in the touch of Volkov magic that made them her own.

No President of modern Russia––still in their first year of office––had ever been more popular. She was already thinking through her legacy, a second term affording her twelve years in power. Twelve years of weekly broadcasts, of daily newspaper column inches, of hourly blog posts and discussions. Her films might have stopped being made––they still played regularly on the national channels–– but she was in front of her nation more than ever now.

She could do what she liked.

The President replaced the receiver, getting up from her desk and walking over to Roman, who'd been standing at the window, looking out onto the city sights beyond, no doubt listening to her side of the conversation. She'd called him in for that reason, reminding him she wasn't all talk.

"You had something you wanted to share with me," she said, speaking first, setting the tone of what she hoped would be the flow of things to come.

"I do," he said, though that could wait for the moment. "Were you talking to Pavel?" She'd not said who she was speaking to while he waited there by the window, not once saying Pavel's name, but from what he could hear, it had to be the Moscow-based gangster.

She smiled, though he hadn't turned from the window to see it.

"He was updating me on a few things," Svetlana said, well aware she didn't need to run anything by him, and whatever she might share was totally up to her.

"You still trust him?"

"I wouldn't be speaking to him if I didn't, Roman," she scolded, as if his last comment was a little too near the invisible line he seemed to have more access to than most, but dared not cross.

"Have you given them back access to their funds?" he asked, present when the original deal was discussed, here now because he knew precisely the answer to his question. Pavel had turned to Roman enraged, the multiple groups pressuring the crime-lord about why they'd not had their money returned to them since Volkov had become President. They'd helped her win, kept back any threat, as was the deal. Yet where was the money?

"They will have it shortly," she said, not prepared to speak about the details of her plans yet. She knew Pavel had spoken with Roman, didn't know what it was about, though assumed it couldn't have been merely that weekend's hockey scores. She could well imagine Pavel using Roman to pressure her for the money. She would deliver what she promised them, mostly. Not everyone would be happy.

He turned to her from the window, the grey of the Moscow skyline nothing compared to her charming features now smiling at him, though he knew her face hid a true menace that existed a fraction under that flawless skin.

"You gave Zabala a name," Roman said, the reason for his visit, as Svetlana was now aware.

"I did." She knew Roman knew that much. Aware he realised she'd not given Zabala the real name.

"Why did you lie to him?"

"Lie?" She didn't see that as his likely objection. "I used Zabala for what he is good at."

Roman shook his head slightly as if not understanding her decision.

"Need I remind you, I answer to nobody now!" she snapped, taking a step forward, in the oligarch's face suddenly, though seeing she had produced the reaction she wanted, she smiled. "I can do whatever I need to do to make sure justice gets done."

"Justice?" Roman knew she had given the Spaniard the name of an old Russian living in Germany. He knew that because Zabala had called him that morning, informing him of the whole story.

"You think I should have given him your friend's name instead?" she mused. Vladimir Popov, fellow oligarch and the man directly responsible for targeting Jose Zabala's son during the event she hosted in Alicante, was no close friend of Roman. Oligarchs had few close friends besides their money.

Roman merely shook his head at the obvious attempt to get him rattled.

"I don't think you should have lied to Zabala."

"Please," she said, laughing the idea off. "You think he concerns me in any way?"

Roman didn't know what to say to that. She didn't rate the guy, but Roman wasn't as certain as she was. "I think you underestimate him at your peril."

"Look," she said, suddenly serious again. "He demanded the name of the man who killed his son. He threatened me, threatened to expose what we did in Alicante."

"What *we* did?" Roman spoke, the meaning plain between the pair. This was her doing, as always.

"We were all there," she said, which he couldn't deny. It had been a most spectacular week too. It had changed his opinion of her, enough for him to stand in, take some heat yet crucially to then publicly back her in the election race. His support, and the support he'd mustered for her from his peers, had gone a long way to winning her the vote. As had the underground support of Pavel and the criminal groups, a loyalty she showed very little interest in honouring now the dust had settled. Was he too on sticky ground?

"And the name you gave him. You think Zabala will buy it?"

She looked him in the eyes for a moment, trying to read if he knew something she didn't, but she couldn't tell either way.

"I think he'll pull the trigger regardless," she said. "We both get something we want."

"You want this man dead? It is personal for you, then?" Roman knew she had sent Pavel a list of seven names. Roman didn't know the list himself, didn't know the relevance of the names, though he wondered, if he asked the man directly, if Pavel might let him know. Especially the more Svetlana held out on them all.

"Yes," she said, emotion present but no more words.

"Why?" he pressed.

"You threaten to ask me why?" she spoke through gritted teeth. "How dare you!" He'd never once seen her like that, though he stood there, facing her, forcing her to break eye contact first, which she did. Nobody usually spoke to him like that, either. He would let it slide. She was untouchable, he'd helped see to that.

For the first time, her being in power concerned him.

"Look, Zabala didn't kill Alkaev," Roman stated, looking back out of the window now, the words chosen carefully, the pause long enough before he spoke, but the substance of what he said plain. Jose Zabala was speaking to Roman, the man had given the oligarch the name of his target and the outcome of his action.

"He didn't kill him?" she asked, her tone now suggesting such behaviour to be almost treacherous.

"You didn't stop to think he would speak to the man first? That he wouldn't want to know for sure?"

Maybe she had under-estimated Zabala?

"Then he's used up his worth to me," she said.

"You now intend to go after Zabala?" Roman asked, angry that she had understood nothing, it seemed.

"Yes, I bloody well will," she snapped back, "because this is what I do to people who question my instructions; is that clear to you, Ivanov!" the first name informality she usually used with him now gone.

"Zabala is more than you think," he said, firmly but calmly enough. Roman could see she didn't see the Spaniard the way he did. If the man had threatened her with exposure for Alicante––how did he even know about it if he were a nobody?––then there was way more to the man than she realised.

"He's no threat to me," she said, carelessly.

"Then you are being foolish." There was a frosty silence following that comment.

She walked over to the drinks cabinet, pouring herself a drink–– the other empty glasses remaining so; this was no social drink between two friends. He watched her down the whole glass, her eyes closed, her face confirming both pleasure at the sensation and the quenching of a need that only an addict displayed.

"Standing in this office is a privilege," she said, not immediately elaborating any further on that opening statement. She poured herself another drink, though left this one untouched for the moment, while she continued. "It's an honour for me, but also a rare privilege for anyone who comes to visit the President. Roman, few men now have the access to this office that I've afforded to you." She left Roman in no doubt by the choice of her words he was walking on thin ice, his presence there perhaps a threat.

"I don't take it for granted," he said, which surprised her a little.

"Good," she grunted, not overly convinced at his response.

"And I'm looking out for your interests, too."

"Are you now?" she asked, openly sceptical. She'd been around too many powerful men who did whatever they pleased. For Svetlana personally, that had stopped with the vote. Nobody would have control over her any more.

"If Zabala exposes you, he exposes me," Roman said, ignoring the clear contempt emanating from his President towards him at that moment, a feeling that was growing entirely mutual the longer he stood there.

"I won't allow that to happen," she assured him.

"It might not be your choice."

"You think I should give him Popov?" she quizzed. She assumed now that Roman would somehow gain significantly if she removed Vladimir Popov, though she had seen no direct link between the two, although they were both oligarchs. Both had involvement in the Games for years, had gone up against each other more than once, but there was no direct animosity there, she was certain. Popov had two billion less than Ivanov, but was still wealthy. Perhaps that was the issue? Roman feared Popov was getting close to him? She doubted Roman feared anything. He plainly didn't have the right respect for the office she held or for the access she allowed him to the room in which they stood.

"I don't think giving him Popov's name now will have any impact," Roman said. She should have given it to Zabala straight away the first time of asking.

"Then Zabala has become a threat," she said, pacing back over to Roman, downing the drink as she crossed her office, placing the empty glass on her desk. "I'll call Pavel and have him sort things out."

"You would go after Zabala?" Roman asked, exasperated. She'd not listened to a thing he'd said.

"I have anyone who is a threat removed," she said. "And you'd better not say anything, otherwise it'll be your neck on the line next, do you understand me?" He said nothing, though she knew he understood. He left the office moments later.

SVETLANA PICKED up the phone later that evening, the office quiet once more, the darkness outside the window pressing in, the street lights of the city beyond visible but distant.

"It's me," she said, Pavel answering the call immediately. He'd been expecting something from her all day. "I have two tasks for you, and with these you'll have your money. Complete them both this month, and your share will be double what you lost."

He'd not had everything in the Bank when Filipov stole from the vaults. Pavel's operation had kept going, and they'd pulled in more cash from their local establishments, meaning three years on, they were back up to speed. Still, the twelve million lost, and if Svetlana was about to double that, would represent four times the cash now available to them. Life could get interesting.

"What do you need me to do?" he asked, pen in hand, mind racing with possibilities.

"First, you are to wipe out Don Jose Zabala's entire organisation in Spain. He operates in Alicante, and has now become a threat to us all," she said, drawing Pavel into something to which he had no connection.

"He's mafia?" Pavel asked, aware that it could conflict with some groups he now spoke for; he was the link between the Russian-based criminal organisations and the President. He'd got them all onboard before the election.

"An old-timer, and nothing to worry about," she assured him. "Move carefully, but move quickly. He knows too much." She didn't elaborate what the man knew.

"You said there was a second thing?" Pavel asked. She'd not mentioned how she planned to repay them all the cash they had lost yet, either.

"Yes, and it links directly to the return of all the assets taken by Filipov," she said, Pavel pressing closer to the phone, his pen hovering expectantly over the pad. "I need detailed reports and proof on what each group held in Zurich," she started. "I won't stand for anyone claiming they had masses when all they had was a few million."

"I see," he said, nothing unusual in that. Despite being black-market money, Pavel knew every gangster worth his salt had these accounts carefully recorded somewhere, even if not on the record.

"And I can't allow all the groups the return of their money. There would be chaos everywhere," she said, not explaining what she meant by that besides the assumption that the fresh capital would cause them all to fight each other, perhaps.

"But you promised," he said, aware his role as spokesman allowed him to question her on this matter. The groups would each demand the same of him, too, he knew that much. Most would want to kill him if he told them the news without giving them a reason.

"Look, my country can't see me as hard on crime and yet allow them all back," she said. The lack of finances had seen a drop in crime rates across the country, the stats looking good for her presidency. Coupled with having them all onside, she knew she couldn't lose. Now she could manipulate the situation further to strengthen her position.

"What does that mean?" He felt nervous she was reneging on her promise.

"I want you to select a third of the groups. Target those who stretch the rule of law the furthest," she said, Pavel aware most of them did that. His own group probably bent the rules more than half the organisations for which he now spoke.

"And what will you do with them?" he asked.

"I'll do nothing with them," she said. "Not directly. You will have them destroyed, however."

He swore.

"You're kidding, right?"

"No, Pavel, I'm serious. If you, and the other two-thirds want your funds returned to you, you will make sure it's carried out. I don't care who you target. You will give me their names, and when you've completed the task, between the remaining groups, you will have back the funds, including the funds for the third you destroyed."

Putting that bounty on the line now focused him a little more.

"We get to keep what they owned?" he clarified.

"Yes," she confirmed, not her initial plan, but the money didn't really matter. She knew these groups would not dare challenge her. Not after seeing what she did.

Pavel thought through the prospect. It made the selection process more interesting. He could choose who he wanted––anyone he deemed least onside, anyone he deemed a threat, they would target. With their assets also coming into play, he would factor that in. He knew he needed to determine what each group claimed they had in Zurich. He would get them to list everything, and from these lists he would then confirm which third he would target. He would use the other two-thirds of the organisations to carry out the hits. He could see it working well for Svetlana politically. They would praise her for bringing these groups to justice.

"What makes you think they won't fight back?" Pavel asked.

"Because I have faith in you," she said, which wasn't entirely true. She knew it wasn't her problem, however. Pavel now stood to gain many millions more than he had, perhaps as much as thirty-million, depending on how big the pot became when the other third were wiped out. She knew he would find a way.

"And you want it done this month?"

"Yes," she said, which made it difficult, she knew. But there seemed no point in delaying anything.

"Zabala we can sort out easily," he confirmed. One mafia family in one location was an entirely different prospect from a third of the known Russian criminal organisations spread out across an entire nation. "Here, it will be much harder."

"I'm sure you'll find a way," she said.

"And Lagounov?" Pavel asked, the name bringing her up short.

"You know you aren't to mention that name to me!" she said. "He stays out of things. He is not in your third." Now Pavel was certain she was the real force behind a man he feared more than most. More than her own head of security, in fact: Rad, the sharpest sniper in the country. Yuri Lagounov was a monster, untameable, uncontrollable, ruthless and violent. A man who thrived on violence, relished a slow, painful death, and drew no line to what he would do.

Pavel feared Svetlana Volkov more than ever.

"I see," Pavel said. "I will do as you ask." The call went dead.

She stood by the dark window, the office lights off, her presence behind the glass looking out into her city all but invisible. She allowed the warmth of the feeling to travel through her entire body. The sense of control, of power. Absolute control was getting closer. In three days, she would once again be gathering for another event, this the fourth of six. The fact Zabala had failed to take out the seventh name on her list already saddened her somewhat. She might have to send Rad to Germany instead.

17

Aktobe, Kazakhstan
Present Day

The airport seemed modern, bright, the Russian language dominant, though English-language signs were visible too. The three agents walked out into the sunshine shortly after ten that morning, their heads somewhat fuzzy––they'd spent the night travelling––but each had managed a little sleep on the flights.

They had travelled fairly light, each with a large camping backpack, though most of the things they needed they couldn't bring with them. Sasha assured them both they would pick everything up once there. He'd now gone in search of a hire car, the two Brits standing on the spot for a while, lapping up the sunshine. Twenty minutes later, Sasha swung into the kerb. He opened the boot; the pair dropped their bags in before getting into the car.

"I asked about a camping supply shop," Sasha confirmed, presumably with the people at the car rental firm. "There's a big one about twenty minutes from here," he said. "I've got the directions."

If he'd followed them, neither of the other two could quite tell. Sasha did at least one U-turn, but soon enough, they arrived at the store. Large banners showed people sleeping in tents, Sasha leading the way in, feeling at home in a country where most people spoke Russian.

Forty minutes later they were pushing a trolley full of goods towards their rental. They didn't have a weapon, but had purchased several large hunting knives. Both men claimed to be useful with a blade, Zoe not knowing if it was male bravado or they really could use one. She liked them vying for her attention. Everything would stay in the boot for the time being; they were in no imminent danger.

Anissa had confirmed that Anastasia was now in Aktobe, staying at the Dastan, a four-star hotel in the centre of the city, not all that far from the airport. Charlie confirmed that they would meet with the Belarusian late-morning.

Sasha pulled up in front of the multi-storey hotel just after eleven. The three agents got out, very much friends on holiday, their cover for being in the country. Sasha assured them the FSB had no significant presence on the ground in these neighbouring states, a far cry from when these countries were all in the Soviet Union and the KGB had fingers everywhere.

Anastasia sat in the restaurant, a drink to hand, as she spotted the three-person group walk in. Besides Alex, she'd only ever met Anissa, though she had a fair idea who the strangers were that were now entering the hotel. Charlie smiled at her, the three cutting across the room and making a beeline for her table. She remained seated, remained calm. They could just as easily have been FSB––her number up.

"I'm Charlie," the British agent said, holding out his hand for Anastasia, who took it without hesitation, smiling up at him. "This is Zoe, and this is Sasha." He pointed out the two colleagues standing either side of him.

"Please, sit down," she said, once greetings were over, the three taking the empty chairs around the table, Zoe tucking in next to the Belarusian, the two men facing her.

"You made it across unnoticed?" Sasha asked immediately. He

was directly opposite Anastasia, his dark eyes, dark hair and now obvious accent once he spoke, giving him away as distinctly Russian.

"You aren't British?" she asked, ignoring the obvious. She wouldn't have been there waiting for them if the Russian border guard had spotted her leaving the country.

"Sasha here is what we call in the Service a *special case*," Charlie said, answering for the Russian, in what would remain the only direct response Anastasia would get for her question.

"And the crossing?" Sasha pressed. He wanted to be in the area by early afternoon, giving them plenty of hours of daylight before making the attempt that night.

"Was easy," she said. She'd either been rather fortunate, or there really wasn't much of a physical border in the region.

"Do you remember what this side of the border looked like? Were there houses, farms? Anyone around who might spot us if we went across the other way?"

"No, and it was dark," she confirmed. Sasha nodded. She knew what she was doing at least. "I don't believe you'll have a problem."

"What will you do now?" Zoe asked, aware Anastasia had limited travel options, though Europe would have little concern with a Russian-issued arrest warrant. Moscow had been ignoring European-issued warrants for Russians for many years.

"When you get him out, will you come back this way?" she asked, evidently planning to remain local if they were about to smuggle Alex into the country.

"We don't know what we'll do yet," Charlie said.

"I don't think we can come here," Sasha said, the proximity to the border making the country the obvious place for the Russian authorities to come looking first. She seemed a little downcast at that.

"I'll go somewhere. Perhaps home," Anastasia confirmed, speaking to Zoe, answering the question the British agent had asked her.

"England?" Zoe said, somewhat astonished. She knew of Anastasia's marriage to Dmitry Kaminski before his arrest.

"No, Germany," she corrected, though that was only also an

adopted home to her now. Belarus might not be safe anymore, nor did she have any close relatives left there. She missed her cousins in Berlin.

"So you'll just wait?" Zoe asked, aware of how that felt, knowing it too well. Waiting for a man to come find her. Not just any man, either––the odds of that happening would have been rather slim.

"I have no choice," the Belarusian said, Sasha getting up from his seat now in a hurry to get moving. The others soon followed suit.

"Thank you for your help," Sasha said, wishing Anastasia goodbye. "Stay safe," he added.

"Don't worry about me," she said, her lips rich with colour, her eyes still seductive and tempting, though sorrow lurked there, too. "You all stay safe, and bring him back to me." She didn't even know what life awaited Alex if they got him out. Would he leave that world behind and truly settle with her? Was that even an option for him? Could he walk away from MI6 and that secret world they had wrapped him up in for so long? Could they even get him out?

She stopped herself at that last thought. Getting him out had to be the only priority, and despite the facts, seeing the three agents in front of her, this close––albeit in a neighbouring country––she couldn't help but hope. Maybe they would find a way?

She watched them leave, a few final farewells offered, but she didn't want to delay them any longer than she already had. Alone again, the trio in the car now driving off, Anastasia watched through the windows. She realised she needed to plan what she would do. She couldn't stay there. She was no longer welcome in Russia. Was she now too a prisoner? Panic raced through her for the first time. Might it be that by some miracle they helped Alex escape, only for the police to come and arrest her, the pair switching places? What then?

She pulled herself away from the table as much as from those thoughts, heading to the reception desk, in the knowledge it was futile to think like that. She was free until she made a mistake. She refused to live a life of watching her back, though she would not take any unwarranted risks.

She settled her bill, having stayed just the one night, and asked the man to call her a taxi. She would head to the airport, buy a ticket once there, and take her chances.

The Black Dolphin Prison, Sol-Iletsk

THE HOSPITAL WING delivered Alex back to his cell the following morning, one night spent alone in that ward, a doctor watching him closely, but soon enough signed off, ready to return. Someone had drawn a hangman on the charge sheet outside his cell, the message in his absence abundantly clear.

He pushed the thought away. He would not go to their level.

Alex would eat food that day and the next in his own cell, which suited him immensely. He couldn't yet hold a tray, and it meant staying away from the general population. He needed his wrists back, the damage serious but not a break. He'd dislocated them both, the doctor able to reset them easily, the cast there to aid the healing process. Still, that might take weeks. He didn't have that long.

Putin seemed to have the run of the place now. His group of constant companions had doubled in the time Alex had been away, more than twice the size of the small rabble who remained loyal to Mihaylov. Alex was certain it had been one of Mihaylov's men who'd struck him.

A day after Alex returned, Putin broke free of his men, coming to Alex, staying a foot away from the bars—the guards did not allow prisoners into another's cell. In any case, Alex, despite his need for bed rest, could not sit or lie down on the bed during the day.

"I can offer you protection," Putin said, a smile suggesting he knew Alex already understood that.

"You want to protect me?" Alex asked, waiting for the catch.

"I want to make a deal with you," he confirmed, ever the politician, ever the power broker.

"Go on," Alex beckoned, knowing he had very little to deal with, very little on offer.

"Someone knows you're here, right?" Putin had read the newspaper, seen the story linking Anastasia Kaminski––someone he'd never met, though Putin knew Dmitry––with the murder of a guard, someone used by the woman to get access to a prison. The article was noticeably light on specific facts aside from the guilt of the culprit. Putin knew political spin when he saw it.

"Yes," Alex confirmed, clear Putin already knew this, otherwise he wouldn't have been speaking to him right now. Hanging around with the outcast would not be good for his image.

"She'll get word to MI6?"

Alex had never told Putin he was MI6; perhaps he assumed Alex was, or just that Military Intelligence Six dealt with issues abroad.

"I sure hope so," Alex said, nothing for it but to play along with Putin for now.

"So they'll get you out?"

Alex didn't respond for the moment. Anastasia had implied that in their conversation.

"Is that even possible?" Alex quizzed, Putin a shrewd reader of faces.

"I think you know they'll find a way." Both knew that had never happened, Boris the closest there had been, that over thirty years ago now, the inmate still very much behind bars.

"And what if they do?" Alex asked.

"I offer you protection now, and when that time comes, I'm out with you," Putin said, stepping forward a little, breaking the rule about proximity, but the guards did nothing. He stepped back a second later, his point proved. *I run this place now, no-one can touch me, not even the guards.*

Alex thought the idea through for a moment. He had no way of knowing if an escape plan was on the table, and if it were, getting them both out would make it doubly risky. However, left alone he was dead meat. They had come close to killing him the other day; they wouldn't wait long before trying again. He was still weak, still recovering.

"I can't promise anything will ever happen," Alex said, Putin remaining stony faced, "but if they find a way of blowing a hole in this wall, and if you keep me safe in this place in the meantime, I promise you'll come with me." He resisted holding out his hand to shake on the deal––contact would violate the rules, and his wrist wouldn't cope with it, anyway.

"That's good enough for me," Putin said, nothing to lose by keeping Alex safe. One word and his gang would see the Brit had nothing to fear. The former President was merely playing the odds, giving himself a double chance of escape. He would work on his own route, too, getting word out via the wife of a new gang member. He'd pulled that man in for that specific purpose. If that became his way out, Putin owed Alex nothing. The Brit would then be on his own.

The atmosphere changed the same day, word soon spreading that Putin had covered Alex––the mark of someone like that meaning you didn't touch them if you wanted to be breathing for much longer.

Alex could freely move around the common areas, the time still limited by prison rules––it was still the harshest, most demanding prison in the country after all––but at least he felt safe. Boris Mihaylov would walk the other way, his own group down to two men now, one having joined Putin's gang, another found dead in the shower room.

How long he would have to wait he didn't know. He'd heard nothing more from Anastasia, visiting day that month coming and going, Alex assuming she would have come. He'd been looking forward to it, but no guard arrived at his cell. He lay on his bed that night confused. Had his appearance the previous month frightened her? Had she come to her senses? Or were they onto her? Alex knew she wouldn't let anything stop her trying to get Alex out of there. Thankfully, he knew she wouldn't try anything on her own. Anissa, Sasha and probably others would know. His old colleagues, his own gang. They were out there somewhere, he was sure, plotting and planning, finding a way in. Working out how to break into Russia's most high security prison and release a man who should never have been there.

18

Kazakhstan/Russian Border, Orenburg Region
Present Day

The grass was higher than Sasha had expected, the terrain undulating, which he liked. The grass helped hide them even if the hills were a little harder going on the legs. He'd heard Zoe swear more often that afternoon than ever before, though he chuckled at the thought. He said nothing, Charlie apparently also finding her little outbursts amusing.

The three agents had circled the area. They had a plan of entry for later, but would wait for darkness to fall, the sky cloudy, the moon––if visible––only a crescent. They couldn't have picked better conditions if they'd had months to plan.

Still, Sasha kept warning them, getting into Russia was merely the easy step. He did not understand what challenges might face them on the other side.

The thought they would be on Russian soil soon had caused Charlie to be rather quiet for the last half hour. He had such a history with the nation; it had broken him in more ways than he could recall. Russia was the country of birth of Anya, the only woman he'd ever loved—might ever love. At the point he could see hope returning for them both, following a bitter breakup some years before, the FSB had killed her.

Charlie had spent the next few years following her murder in his own wilderness. He'd gone rogue, tracking down those responsible, a journey that had taken him the length and breadth of both North and South America. It wasn't a formal MI6 mission—he had gone with that cover; his weapons cleared through diplomatic channels. But once Stateside, he'd vanished. Soon the lives of those ultimately responsible for the murder were ended.

His reentry into the world of MI6 had been steady. Anissa, together with Alex, had been getting some results in Russia, the pair working that aspect now that Charlie wasn't. Anissa had been the one to encourage Charlie's involvement when things progressed further, when Charlie was fully back with them; thinking and acting like a British MI6 agent once again.

And tonight he was about to set foot in a place that had caused his own breakdown.

"Are you okay?" Zoe asked, aware perhaps more than most of Charlie's chaotic history which wasn't even that long past.

"I'll be fine," Charlie said, shaking the question away, ignoring the sincerity with which she had asked it. Sasha looked over at them both, aware of a part of the story. Charlie had been Sasha's own entry into the world of MI6, the first time the Russian broke protocol at the FSB by handing something to the British without authorisation.

"We'll hit the river at that turn we found," Sasha said, decisively. He'd been pondering two options, though the river—which they needed to cross wherever they attempted—slowed enough at that point to make getting over to the other side somewhat more straightforward. The approach from their side of the border to that spot was also difficult. Most wouldn't even consider it. That made it the right choice.

"When?" she asked, aware it had to be dark, but not sure when that happened.

"I would say no later than eleven," Sasha confirmed, looking at his watch. That gave them three hours. The sun would set in about ninety minutes, the lack of lighting in the area—coupled with the cloudy, moonless sky—would mean besides torchlight, it would be nearly pitch-black by eleven. "Anastasia said there's a small town close to the border. We can stay there overnight, move on up to the prison in the morning. If we cross too late, we'll arrive in the small hours. I would rather we got there around midnight."

That would be pushing it. They would probably be on foot, though if Sasha could find a ride with someone once they hit any small road, he would try. The cross-country trek was about seven kilometres.

"And if we encounter trouble?" Charlie asked. They were entering the Russian Federation illegally. The last agent to have done that was still in the most dangerous prison in the country.

"We have no option," Sasha said, his eyes sad, though fighting was something he would rather avoid. They only had knives on them, useful in close combat, useless if chased by a machine-gun wielding army truck full of soldiers.

Charlie nodded. *Kill or be killed.* He too hoped it wouldn't come to that. Making it in overnight, staying undiscovered, had to be their main priority. The longer they flew under the radar, the better their chances were with Alex. Charlie couldn't help but sense they would need everything to go in their favour to have even a fraction of a chance of getting Alex out.

DARKNESS FELL QUICKLY, the trio leaving their torches off, trying to adjust their eyes as much as they could. They waited another thirty minutes from when the sun went down before moving, their bags already packed, weapons by their sides. Charlie had spent part of the last hour of daylight teaching Zoe knife skills. She could at least now mostly throw a blade into a tree from twenty feet.

They moved quietly, though there seemed to be nobody around. Earlier, when they'd covered the area, they were looking for any electronic surveillance devices, Charlie having brought with him a scanner from Six. Nothing had shown, which didn't mean there couldn't be something watching them, but they felt a certain confidence in that information.

Retracing their steps in the dark soon became a lot more difficult, however. Sasha flashed his torch occasionally, the advantage of getting a view of the terrain ahead cancelled out by the readjustment of their eyes to the darkness. At least the sound of the river called them forward, though it curved and twisted in that area––it might have been drawing them back on themselves.

Finally reaching the water's edge––it had gone eleven thirty––they were a little further down from the point they had wanted to cross at, Sasha not sure if they were east or west of the bend. He swore.

"It's okay, we can cross here," Charlie said, the water cold, the other side not visible from where they were. Sasha would not risk flashing the torch towards the other bank. There might be patrols in the area at night.

"It's too fast," Sasha said. "It can't be far away. Look, Zoe, you stand here. Don't move from this spot. I'll go this way, Charlie, you go that." He pointed Charlie the opposite way along the edge of the river from which he would go. "Walk no further than three minutes. Then turn around and come back. Keep next to the river. We can't get lost."

Charlie looked at Zoe, who didn't seem overly impressed with being left alone in total darkness in a strange land. He nodded to her she would be all right. Both men set off.

Sasha arrived back first, Zoe hearing the approach, hoping for the life of her it was the Russian and not some animal.

"I found it," he said, stopping next to Zoe, a rustle coming from the other direction suggesting Charlie too was now making his return.

"Anything?" he asked, somewhat desperately.

"Yes, this way," the Russian confirmed, the three setting off the way Sasha had gone, getting to the turn in the river less than two minutes later. They'd missed it by about three hundred metres.

The sound had transformed; the water was moving far slower, though it still felt as cold. They couldn't see the other side now, but earlier, when they'd come across the spot, it hadn't been far. Perhaps twenty metres. In total darkness, it could have been a mile.

"We need to put our clothes in the rucksacks," Sasha said, taking off his t-shirt. Despite being dark, Zoe had enough light to see his muscly chest, thick black hair covering much of his upper half. "You don't want to be walking the other side in soaking clothes," he added, as she watched him pull down his trousers too, rolling his jeans into a tight ball and putting them into the plastic bag he'd just placed his t-shirt in. "Come on!" he urged the other two who didn't seem to move.

Charlie followed suit, a smile towards Zoe at how awkward he knew this would be for her, though in the darkness, he couldn't make out her face. She still hadn't moved.

"Come on!" Sasha repeated, standing in his underwear, though turning from her now, he whipped these off too, dropping them into the top of the bag before fastening it shut.

"I'm not going naked!" she protested, Sasha now taking a few steps into the water, the backpack held high. They would float the packs across. The material was waterproof and would keep most of the water out.

"You don't want soaking clothes," Sasha repeated from the river, his voice suggesting the water was very fresh, though he soon went shoulder deep as he vanished into the darkness.

Thirty-seconds later, Charlie too stepped bare-bottomed into the water, as Zoe stripped to her underwear. That was as much as she would do. She stuffed the clothes in her backpack and followed Charlie, whose head was hardly visible as he too started to swim across.

"Jeez, that's cold," she exclaimed, her feet feeling numb after only the first step.

"Just go for it," Charlie's voice came from the darkness. She could hear a bag being unzipped, presumably Sasha now on the other side already.

Zoe pressed forward, the river dropping quickly, the sensation almost overpowering as the cold grabbed her, starting in her legs and moving up into her chest. She kicked hard, willing movement, the pack floating nicely for her, like a bouncy aid at her swimming lessons when she was a girl. She could hear Charlie too now scrambling out of the water as she got to the middle, the other side still in darkness, though the voices were getting closer.

"Mind the fish," Sasha called, "they bite." Zoe kicked all the harder, a shirtless Charlie coming into view now. He reached forward and took hold of her backpack, guiding Zoe in to the shore.

Sasha had dressed, Charlie getting there. He flashed his torch towards Zoe, her underwear showing.

"Need some light," he laughed, Zoe telling him to piss off. He watched her pull her dry clothes from the bag, turning from him as she pulled on her jeans, removing her wet bra before pulling down the top. She snuck the bra into her bag, trying to do so secretly, Charlie smiling.

"It gets nippy out here, you know," he said, winking at her, a nod towards her chest. She pulled her jacket around her all the tighter.

"Let's go," Sasha encouraged, the crossing complete, Russian soil underneath their feet. He checked his compass, aware of the general direction they needed, movement required to warm them up again, and he set off at a pace, the other two following.

It was half-past twelve by the time they reached the first signs of civilisation since crossing the border. They'd found the small village Anastasia had pointed out, the one which she had passed through not long after ditching the car she'd used.

"I'll find us somewhere to sleep," Sasha said, the other two waited by the roadside at the entrance to the village, Sasha taking his backpack with him and walking up the unlit road, his torch on. The two Brits moved under a cover of trees.

"How does it feel to be back?" she asked, keeping her mind off the wet underwear now digging into the top of her legs.

He looked around. They were in nature. This could be anywhere.

"It's fine," he decided upon.

"You can talk with me, you know," she said.

"Honestly, leave it." There was silence for a while, a single beam of light from a torch eventually making its way towards them, the figure of Sasha--without his pack now--soon coming into focus.

"I've got us rooms for tonight," he said, ushering them forward, the pair picking up their packs and going after the Russian.

Once inside the hotel--the only one that still had a light burning--Sasha collected two keys and Charlie greeted the old woman on duty there in Russian. He felt rusty in that language but the words still flowed across his tongue like old friends. She eyed him cautiously--aware he wasn't Russian--but smiled at his use of her language. She pointed them up the single flight of stairs.

"They had two rooms free," he said. "I guess me and Charlie take this one?" he seemed to ask, adding, "Unless?" and looked at Zoe.

"Unless what?" Charlie said, somewhat bewildered.

Zoe grabbed the key for room four. "I'll take this one, thank you," she said, the Russian smiling, Zoe pushing past him, before opening her door and going inside.

"Sleep well!" Charlie called after her, the door shut before he could hear a reply.

"What was all that about?" Charlie asked Sasha, now that they had entered their room which had twin beds with a table between them. Sasha smiled. Charlie appeared to be the only one at Six who didn't know Zoe's feelings for him.

"Nothing but Russian humour," Sasha smiled, nothing further said. He took the bed nearest the door, Charlie walking over to the other. "I'll shower," he said, the water having gone on in the next door room, Zoe thinking the same. None of them knew what was in that river.

By one, they were all asleep. Neither of the men heard anything more from Zoe until the morning, the day catching up with them all. They had missed a proper night's sleep and had completed several hours' worth of hiking.

19

Alicante Region
Present Day

The call from Pavel had come three days previously and a criminal group based in Ukraine but with strong links into southern Russia had taken on the challenge of eliminating Zabala and his group. Pavel had promised them a fast return on their lost treasure from Svetlana if they carried out the hit that month.

She'd made them no such promise, Pavel going out on a limb to get them to act for the President. He told them it couldn't come back to anyone that this was Kremlin sanctioned.

Pavel had chosen the group––who had sixty-million dollars in precious stones and gold taken by Filipov from Zurich––because they were already working new drugs routes into the Mediterranean and therefore had feet on the ground in Spain. They confirmed they knew of Jose Zabala, a potential block for them a little further down the coast in Alicante. His removal, therefore, would offer them a greater market in the region, not to mention control of the valuable routes for high-end drugs in and out of North Africa.

Ten men flew across to join the three already in the city of Valencia, the orders clear. They were to put everything on hold for the time being and move in on Zabala's operation, the focus being the Don himself. None of them had any concern with taking out the old-timer.

Three cars drove them south, where a little under two hours later they arrived in the city of Alicante, bathed in sunshine, though for the three based in the region for a month already, that aspect was nothing new.

Pavel had sent them the information on Jose, a document Svetlana had put together and then passed to him.

Pavel had informed Svetlana of who was carrying out her orders. Being from the Ukraine, she smiled. It made it even more deniable if it went wrong. Pavel assured her they knew what they were doing. Zabala would be dead before the end of the week, he promised. With no son left to step into the gap––Clifton Niles had killed Luken Zabala earlier that year––the organisation would crumble.

She smiled at the news and asked for confirmation once it was all over.

In Alicante, one car, with three men in it, sat outside the Zabala compound, at a safe distance and with a pair of binoculars between them. They kept a watch on the comings and goings, assessing the strength of security around the grounds. They couldn't see a lot. Word on the street had Zabala as a well-respected guy with few enemies. That gave them an advantage. The man didn't expect trouble. He wouldn't see them coming.

The other two cars dropped in on the various establishments controlled by Zabala's men. The Don himself was not at any of them, not uncommon in such setups. Jose's name appeared on no official document that existed for these premises, the man clean, separate from institutions that many would consider questionable. He had his reputation to think about, and if something criminal happened there, the police couldn't touch him. His name wasn't on the deeds.

Most knew he owned many of the shadiest businesses, though his criminal activities were not enough to cause the police to pay too close attention. He had several officers on his payroll, men who'd ventured into his brothels, men he now controlled with that information. Soon they enjoyed the money, the free sex that went with such employment. These officers caused the police force to look the other way. They had his back.

The Ukrainians would spend the first day staking out the known locations. They knew the clock was ticking; they had only the week, but they had time. It never paid to rush in unprepared.

During their second day in Alicante, one group focused on the electrical supply for the Zabala compound. Of all the locations they watched, the compound seemed the best to hit. Isolated, there were no other properties anywhere near. It seemed also that security was light there, the man safe. He rarely travelled to any of the other businesses. They planned to cut the power to the building and storm it late one night, three days from then. They would hit it that Friday, the businesses in town revving up for their weekend activities, with most security personnel required in these venues. If Zabala left the compound, they would wait for his return. The road to his home might prove another ambush point, his convoy usually only one vehicle, three or four men at most. They had enough firepower to overwhelm them all.

The teams got to work on their plan. By the end of Wednesday, they had located the phone line for the compound, the power box for the area also known. They would take both out late on Friday, switching off the power to the compound together with the phone and internet lines.

Zabala and anyone else in the compound would then be on their own. The Ukrainian team was seeing if they could arrange a jammer for mobile signals, though as yet they didn't know if that was possible.

As darkness fell on the mountainous region that Friday night, the thirteen strong team of men moved into position. One man waited by the power box, another by the phone line. They would leave it until midnight. Zabala had been spotted in his compound and there was no sign of movement outside. His driver and car had been seen leaving without him at nine.

An eight-foot wall ran around the entire compound. The walls formed a large rectangle, several buildings dotting the three-thousand square-metre plot, though none as large or prominent as the main house which stood dead centre, its styles so very Spanish. The man had money *and* taste.

Bougainvillea grew profusely along much of the wall; while the colour of the flowers was lost in the darkness, their scent was still carried along in the breeze. It offered both an advantage and a challenge for getting in. Potential coverage as the men climbed over, though get a weak section of the plant and they risked bringing it down from the wall as they clambered over, which was sure to alert someone to their presence.

As half eleven ticked by, the various teams stationed around the four sides of the compound checked their watches, getting ever closer into position, but staying low. Staying out of sight. The lights going out at midnight would be their cue, by which time the phone lines should also be out. Then it would be a straight shootout. They knew all hell would soon break loose, though with the element of surprise, with the place surrounded on every side, they could come at Zabala's men from behind. That would disorientate the Don's security for a while, though the longer the battle went on, the less advantage the Ukrainians had. Their team leader knew the first blow had to be near fatal.

His men edged ever closer, like athletes on the start line, waiting for the firing pistol. Creeping forward, craning for any advantage that even a few centimetres might offer them.

They were all on radio silence. If anyone was listening for chatter at the compound, they were not about to advertise their presence. As it grew darker, the constant sound of the cicadas had faded too. An acute-eared patrol might have heard the crackle of a walkie-talkie. They would take no risks. They watched the clock, knowing the timing. Knowing the signal.

Midnight rolled around, the lights for the compound going out in unison and the eleven men waited. The other two who'd just taken out the power and phone lines would cover the main road, their distance from the compound keeping them from the first wave, though they could follow up as backup if needed. Should that happen, they would know there had been a serious misjudgement of the situation.

The four groups advanced towards the wall, fanning out a little along each section to offer more coverage. The one team of two––the other three groups comprising three men each––contained the team leader and his righthand man. They were first over the wall, the brickwork exposed, the bougainvillea not yet reaching that spot.

Landing on the inside of the compound, it was clear the sudden blackout had sent Zabala's security into confusion. Someone fired shots, the team leader not aware if these were from his men or not. Either way, the sound of sudden gunfire would be confirmation enough to the Don that his home was now under siege.

Emergency floodlights came on, the sound of a petrol generator kicking into life seconds before connecting the two events. Five of the Ukrainians were lit up as they walked across the centre of the compound. Machine gun fire erupted from the roof of the main building, taking out four of the five men in one sweep, the last scrambling behind the safety of a building where he was pinned, unless help could reach him.

Inside the compound, as the lights went out––not an altogether uncommon experience in that part of the mountains––Jose Zabala got up from the sofa, the television he'd been watching now off. He reached for his landline, which was also dead.

"Go check!" he called to his men. They knew the routine. His wife came out of the kitchen––she'd been preparing drinks before bed.

"Is everything okay?" she asked, aware of her husband's urgent words.

"Go into the bedroom, just in case." She knew what that meant. She would lock herself in. It would take much force to penetrate the specially constructed door.

Then gunfire started, floodlights flashing on outside, Zabala peering out of the window––still in darkness himself––and seeing four intruders cut down, another man fleeing.

He pulled out his mobile, the signal still strong. "Code one!" he called out once the call connected, the signal to his men that the compound was under attack. He then went to his study, pulling out his trusty pistol from a desk drawer, loading it with a full chamber of bullets as more shots filled the night air outside, the sound of return fire too. Zabala checked the doorway before moving back into his lounge. He thought about going into his bedroom––there to protect his terrified wife––but they couldn't get to her in there. Zabala couldn't leave his men to their fate. He went up to the roof.

"How many?" Zabala called to his machine-gunner, who was crouching down behind the wall that surrounded the sun terrace and turned at the sound of the Don.

"Don't know. At least ten." Four bodies lay on the ground in the centre of the parking area; he had taken them out from his roof position when the lights came on. "One's behind the garage," he said, having seen him dive in that direction. "There's been other gunfire from the pool house and the guest accommodation."

That suggested they were on all sides, Zabala crouching low and going to the back wall of the terrace. He could see the silhouettes of three more men working their way towards the house.

"Over here!" Jose whispered, the urgency enough to get his machine-gunner moving, Jose ducking back to the first wall, as the gunner opened fire. Another intruder fell.

The attacker hiding behind the garage––presumably seeing the machine-gun-wielding guard moving position––took the chance to break cover, Zabala raising his own weapon between two turrets and after steadying his aim, took out the running man. His body fell close to the other four men.

Out on the road, the Ukrainian who had broken into the power unit and pulled a lever to take out the power to the compound, saw three Jeeps approaching at speed.

"We've got incoming!" he said into the radio, the only thing he could do. He couldn't engage them even if he wanted. A minute later as he hid in the hedge, the three cars raced past, four men in each vehicle. He swore to himself. "At least twelve of Zabala's men! Get out of there!"

He'd not seen the fourth car, having stepped out of the hedge as the three whizzed past. The fourth was there to reconnect power. They shot the Ukrainian as he emerged from the hedgerow, a radio to his ear, watching the convoy that had not long passed. The Spaniards knew this was one of them.

"Leave me here," the technician said, once it was clear there was no-one else hiding. "Go for the telephone cable." The men from the jeep were aware there might still be another of the attackers there so they would approach with caution.

By one in the morning, Don Zabala still on the roof, his men not recording any casualties, there was a standoff. They didn't know how many attackers there were––seven lay dead, though the occasional gunfire proved at least one was still hiding. When the three Jeeps arrived at the front gates, which wouldn't open with the power off, the remaining Ukrainians were unsure if they should risk climbing the walls. They were trapped inside and that swung the fight in Zabala's favour.

When the power was switched back on, the Ukrainians had few places to hide. The gates opened, the Jeeps charged in––with armour-plated sides and bulletproof glass, they acted more like army transport vehicles than civilian cars.

The team leader of the Ukrainians––still alive though they had killed his companion––was on the radio. Silence did not need keeping, and their fast speech in a language they presumed the Spaniards couldn't understand, didn't seem to matter now.

"How many do you have?" he asked. Between them they realised that of the eleven men who stormed the compound, only four remained. One was pinned down behind trees at the rear, two were together in the pool-house, and that left the team leader alone on the south side. There had been no response from either of the men who'd switched off the power. The lights coming back on was evidence enough that the mafia had got to them. The leader assumed they had restored telephone communication, not that this changed much. Failing to block the mobile signal––they ran out of time and didn't have access to the technology––might have been their fatal mistake.

"We're trapped!" one of the other men said, on his own, his two team members gunned down a while ago.

"And outnumbered, yes," the team leader said, matter-of-factly. They now risked losing their entire Mediterranean operation. "We must take out that gunner!"

The man on the roof––in a prime vantage point with a weapon nobody had expected them to have––had been the difference.

"Pool-house, you have men advancing in your direction!" the man from the trees called, able to see the six men from the Jeep-party now fanning out, clear that they knew the enemy to be hiding in there. He could do little else to help them, not without getting taken out before he got halfway across the garden. He also saw there were four men moving in his direction, each covering the other, the men sweeping the entire area for anyone left hiding. They checked the bodies, confirming that they were all dead.

Gunfire started soon after, presumably the pool-house. Rapid fire filled the sky for two minutes. Six figures soon emerged from the building, sweeping back towards the main house.

The Ukrainians were down to two.

The men in the garden stopped at the edge of the house. A shout came up from the roof, the meaning lost to the Ukrainian still hiding in the spot he'd been in for forty minutes.

"Behind the large alder!" the gunner said, before raining down a volley of bullets into the ground either side of the tree. The men fanned out wide, flanking the Ukrainian on one side, who, seeing they were about to spot his position, made a run for it, firing wildly as he headed for the wall whence he'd first gained access to the compound. It was one of the four men approaching who took him out with two bullets to the spine.

Don Zabala stood up now, high on his terrace. He knew there was one man on the south side, his position somewhat protected––his men risked coming under fire if they tried approaching from where they were––but he was out of sight of the Don at that moment, though not out of earshot.

"You're the last man left!" he called, in English, assuming wherever they were from, these aggressors might understand what he was now saying. "We've killed everyone else. Come out now with your hands raised and we can end this bloodshed!" he demanded, no promise that surrender would stop his blood being shed. As far as his men had informed Jose, they'd suffered no fatalities. A few men had caught the odd bullet in non-life threatening places.

"Okay!" the team leader called, his English much more broken than Jose's, but he had understood the offer. He knew he was dead either way. "I'm coming out!"

"Throw your weapon away first before walking with your hands raised!" Jose called.

Giving up his weapon would leave him exposed, but he was in no position to negotiate. After a brief pause for thought, he threw it twenty metres from him, turning the corner with both arms raised. Four of Jose's security men raced forward, weapons raised, one of them collecting the gun from the ground, the other three taking hold of the prisoner.

"We have him!" one man called up to Zabala, who was still not in view, the man reverting to Spanish again. The Don called down in English, anyway, more for the sake of the prisoner.

"Bring him inside. Don't harm him. I will be down. Search him."

The Don turned, the machine-gunner flanking him as he descended the stairs that took him inside, Jose's wife emerging from the bedroom as he entered their lounge.

"It's all over, but stay in there. You can sleep now, *mi amor.*" She doubted sleep would be possible for a while, terrified for the life of her husband and his men as she had been for the last hour. She'd already had to bury her only child that year. Was everything she loved about to be taken away from her as well?

Ten minutes later, a stiff drink downed in his study as he stood alone, composing himself, Jose was on the ground floor, with four of his men and the prisoner. The others were already around the compound, collecting together the dead, searching them for anything they had on them. Like most in their field, the men had little.

"Who sent you?" Jose asked, coming in low, his face only inches from the prisoner.

He would die; he knew that. His men were dead, he'd come for the mafia and got it wrong. Loyalty now meant very little, his word even less. There was no bargain to make, no way of earning his way out of this. Nobody worth protecting, especially not those who'd put them up to this. Still, he hoped. His heart still sent blood racing through his body. He wasn't dead yet.

"He's Russian," the man said.

"He?" Jose said, the reference to Russia clear.

"A man named Pavel. Some big deal in Moscow."

"And the President?" Jose enquired.

The prisoner's eyes shot to his at the mention of the President, the Don well aware this prisoner knew all about Svetlana Volkov's hand in this mission. He didn't answer, however.

"I see," Jose said, clear enough. "She sends you to do her dirty work and look where that has led you," he said, pulling his pistol from his jacket pocket, screwing a silencer into place. His wife might be asleep, and he didn't want her hearing any more gunshots.

"She instructed this Pavel to send you here to kill me, is that correct?" Jose raised the weapon to the man's forehead, his men stepping back a few paces.

The Ukrainian looked up at the face of the Don, ignoring the weapon in his near-sight. He knew he was dead. It didn't matter now. She was nothing to him.

"Yes, this was Kremlin organised. She sent me to kill you."

"Thank you," Jose acknowledged, squeezing the trigger, sending the Ukrainian to whatever fate awaited him. "Take him to the others," he ordered his men, waving a hand over the body, the instruction clear. They would burn all the corpses that night. The Don had an understanding with a crematorium in town which didn't need paperwork and which never asked questions. Jose emptied the chamber of his weapon, removing the few bullets still there, placing these in his pocket and the weapon back in the inside of his jacket.

He had a lot of thinking to do.

20

Near Sol-Iletsk, Russia
Present Day

Charlie woke first, the light coming in through the only partially sufficient curtains before seven. He checked his phone. There had been no messages, though the signal was not strong where they now were. He couldn't believe he was in Russia.

Jumping up out of bed, Sasha still dead to the world, Charlie stood at the window. He'd visited villages like this one before, the memories now coming back. The buildings were mostly wooden, the paint peeling. A few had chicken coops in their gardens, most growing their own vegetables. The cars he could see were not those found in the large cities. The Soviet-era mass-production Lada seemed to win the popularity vote.

Yet it was everything he had loved about the country. The simple life, the uncomplicated village. This was not Moscow or St Petersburg, where large buildings dominated, where Cyrillic script clung to every storefront, jumping out at him, reminding him he was in some foreign land, some alien landscape.

The village he was in could not have been in England, not modern England, anyway. It was a place that only seemed to exist now in this part of the world. He'd never been to Africa, but he imagined they existed there, too. A hand-to-mouth existence. He took simple pleasure in that thought.

The room was basic. It had a bed, which was really all they needed anyway. They would be out as soon as they dressed. Charlie did that now and he went over to the door. He'd heard Zoe stirring in the next door room two minutes earlier. He tapped on her door three times, the door opening a fraction seconds later, the edges of her underwear that she had slept in showing from behind.

"What?" she asked, not overly rudely.

"I wanted to see if you were up," he said, though that was sure to be the case since he had knocked on her door. "Can I come in? Sasha's still sleeping."

"Yeah, fine," she said, opening the door, not sure what more she could say. He shut it behind him, the room much the same as the one next door. He sat on the spare bed, Zoe pulling on some clothes. She caught him looking at the radiator, Zoe instinctively sweeping over and removing the drying underwear she'd placed there last night.

"Did you sleep well?" he asked.

"Yeah, out like a light. You?"

"Same," he said. He needed a drink to wake him up. "Want to see if they have breakfast ready yet?" he asked. She looked for her watch.

"What time is it?" It seemed early.

"I think they serve at seven," he said, having seen a sign that advertised the fact when they first arrived.

"Bloody hell, Charlie," she said, finding the watch, regardless of the fact that breakfast was already being served. "It's not even ten past."

"I need my morning coffee," he said. A coffee and a run, she knew the routine.

"You go, be my guest," she said, sitting back on her bed now, last night's t-shirt riding high up her thighs as she crossed her legs. Charlie's eyes lingered. Smiling, he stood.

"Suit yourself," he said, leaving her to it as he went in search of something strong and very black.

An hour later, they were back outside the building. Sasha had returned the keys, settling the bill with rubles he'd brought with him from London. They wouldn't leave a trail by using a card. If the cash ran out, they had a problem. They'd eaten breakfast together at eight, Sasha finally up, woken by Charlie coming back from his run, who had then showered and changed. A bus service connected the village to Sol-Iletsk, one bus leaving at ten-thirty, one coming back at half-five.

The bus was less than a third full as they took their seats, the three agents saying little to each other, Sasha speaking the occasional sentence to Charlie in fast and barely understandable Russian. Charlie didn't care that his mind was having trouble getting back to speed, he knew what Sasha was doing. They were three Russians, like everyone else. *Nothing to see here, folks.*

They pulled into the larger town of Sol-Iletsk on the dot of eleven. The stop was across the road from the prison; no need to ask anybody for directions.

"He's inside there," Charlie said aloud, the sheer fact they'd got that far, got that close, now pressing in on him.

"Let's move," Sasha urged. Standing watching the place would not be wise, especially if the authorities were expecting trouble. They headed up the street, away from the prison, the one building they were there to penetrate. They would get one shot at it. They couldn't be rash.

"We should stay in different places," Sasha said after a little while.

"Why?" Zoe asked, not keen on being left alone in a strange land.

"We make an odd group," he confirmed. "You both travel as a couple. Charlie, you studied here once; you're now wanting to bring back your wife or girlfriend to show her the country. I'll book into another hotel. We meet up at a different bar each day."

"If they are watching, they would still know," Charlie said, though he saw the logic in the Russian's reasoning.

"We double back, before each meet. If we think we are being

followed, we flee. If either party is ten minutes late for a meeting, they flee."

"Agreed," Charlie said, Zoe happy to let the boys thrash it out. They knew the country. She was fast catching up with the fear that being there created.

"You think you can handle finding your own hotel?" Sasha asked Charlie, aware it would be far more natural if the Brit did that himself.

"I've got it," he confirmed.

"Okay, we'll meet for lunch over there at one," Sasha said, pointing across to a café on the other side of the road. He headed off in that direction, the two agents watching him go, Zoe very much in Charlie's hands now.

"So, what are we?" she asked. He seemed genuinely confused. "Wife or girlfriend?"

He got it now.

"Girlfriend," he said, their lack of rings meaning marriage or even engagement might lead to their story not adding up. She smiled. She didn't mind being his girlfriend for the sake of getting Alex out.

Once they had booked into the hotel, Charlie spent nearly the entire hour in the room in contact with Anissa. He confirmed where they were, reporting in their passage from the night before, saving some details, Zoe grateful for that.

Anissa confirmed she'd heard from Anastasia; she was safely back in Berlin now and aimed to keep her head down.

When it drew close to one, Charlie stood and put his jacket on, Zoe looking up from her book and, seeing the time, followed him to the door. It was a five-minute walk to the café; the pair watched their tail carefully. There was nobody following them. They went in at one, without the need to double back. Sasha was waiting for them.

"Join me," he said, calling Charlie across, the three sitting down, nobody seemingly at all bothered by the gathering.

"Did everything go smoothly?" Sasha asked now, quietly, and switching to English.

"Fine," Zoe said.

"I've been speaking with home," Charlie added. "The package arrived in Berlin," he confirmed.

"And mum?" he asked, their code for Anissa, home being MI6.

"She's well," Charlie confirmed. *Nothing to report.*

Sasha ordered for the three of them, the food home cooked and delicious, a taste like nothing Zoe had ever had, but she thoroughly enjoyed it. When their hot drinks came, the conversation had moved onto matters closer to where they now were.

"I've started asking around," Sasha said, his eyes watchful but no threat existed in the café, he was certain. "We will need to look at every angle." The situation on the ground was no less impossible than what they'd discovered back in London. "We might need help on this one."

They knew MI6 involvement was off the table.

"Help?" Zoe asked.

"Local," Sasha confirmed. They knew he didn't mean Russian State help. He meant criminals.

"Can we trust them?"

"Probably not," Sasha confirmed, "but we might not have a choice. It's a last resort."

"What do we look at first?" Charlie asked. He didn't want criminal involvement. That would make it too messy, escape too difficult. Besides, criminals would want to get their own men out of prison, people who deserved to be there. Alex wasn't in that category, even if he had willingly aided Phelan in his attempt to kill the Russian President.

"We need to know about the power supply, sewage, laundry, deliveries, guard rotation, maintenance, the workshops," he listed, nearly running out of fingers, the task seemingly colossal.

"The one major attempt before was a tunnel right?"

"It was, and that's now not an option. We don't have the workforce, for starters," Sasha said, looking at Zoe, before addressing Charlie. "They also beefed up security at the prison after that attempt. Drove twenty-foot concrete pillars into the ground, before landscaping the entire area. Nobody knows where the pillars are. That's the point."

"What about the roof? Can we drop in?"

"We need a layout for the prison, and I'm not sure any exist in the public domain. There have been many alterations over time, too. There might not be one accurate set remaining. And there are the guards. They watch from the higher floors. Any roof access takes us right into them. Not to mention the cells are treble-locked."

"So even if we could get in, we would need to get the keys from the guards?" Charlie commented, somewhat at a loss.

"Yes, and doing that alerts them to our presence. We trigger that alarm, and it's over. We would never leave the building alive."

"So getting him from the cell is not an option then," Zoe confirmed. "You mentioned workshops?"

"Yes, the inmates may work for a living. The pay is small. They make fabric items, mostly."

"And you know where these workshops are?"

"No," Sasha admitted, "not yet. And even then, there might be multiple rooms. The one attempt in the mid-nineties had them aiming for the workshop. They got into it, too, but the prisoner had gone to the wrong one. He was in another wing."

Charlie sat back, blowing his cheeks out, letting the information sink in. They'd gone over parts of this before, in the safety of London, around Alex's lounge, wine flowing, games night to come. Then, it had all felt possible. Sitting here, now, in that café, five minutes from the prison in question, and the rose-tinted spectacles had gone. The task seemed too much.

"Do you still think we can do this?" Charlie asked, leaning in close, looking only at Sasha now.

"Charlie, I always knew this would be tough. We are attempting to do something that nobody has done before," he said. "Yet, I'm still here." That seemed to mean something to them both now. Despite him knowing the difficulty, he led the task. "If we get this information, which will not be easy, and we must be careful who we ask, then perhaps we'll see something that others might have missed? Perhaps we'll see a way in?"

Charlie would take *perhaps* given the way he'd been feeling a minute earlier.

"What can I do?" Zoe asked, well aware her lack of Russian stopped her from really helping work through the list Sasha had mentioned.

"We might need a woman," Sasha said, professionally, no hint of mocking in this. He really meant to try every angle with this one, desperate to beat a prison that hadn't lost a prisoner in thirty years. Zoe understood his meaning, accepting it though keeping quiet for the time being. Charlie glanced at her occasionally but she didn't seem to notice.

Lagounov's Hideout, Siberia
Six Months Ago

THE PRESIDENT HADN'T SEEN him since the election, Yuri Lagounov off the radar, very much a wanted man. However, as long as Svetlana Volkov was President, he was safe.

"I have a new idea for a little fun," she said, walking with Yuri, the two of them alone. He'd run the cage fights in the capital at her request, oligarchs gathered to watch the spectacles, producing their own fighters back then, the prize potentially massive.

He looked over to her at that comment. He knew the fun she longed for.

"I have the men for you this time," she said, handing him a list of seven names. Seven men who had defiled her before she had become invincible.

"What do you have in mind?" he asked, aware she always had a plan.

"Use the cat," she said with a grin. That cat was a Siberian tiger, brought in for the last contest, enclosed and lethal. "And we'll play on its turf," she nodded.

"Here?"

"In the east," she confirmed. He considered the prospect.

"You want the animal to hunt them?" he asked.

"Yes," she confirmed. "But one at a time. We'll create six events."

"Six?" he said, glancing at the list. There were seven names.

"One man isn't in Russia. I'm seeing to him another way."

He seemed to accept that. He thought for a moment.

"Outside of a cage, tigers aren't only lethal, they are elusive."

"We will incentivise the animal," she said, then explained what she had in mind. His eyes lit up with the sheer scale of it.

"Brilliant," he said, once she'd finished, though she hadn't said why she was targeting the names on the list.

"These seven? They are a threat to you?" he asked.

She laughed, loudly and with contempt, "Not anymore."

Svetlana walked to the other side of the room, Lagounov calling after her.

"One more thing," he said, Svetlana turning back to him, "I didn't congratulate you officially on winning the election, *cousin*."

21

Sol-Iletsk, Russia
Present Day

Three days later they were no nearer to a solution. Running out of money, short on time too, the longer they hovered around town, the more the risk of capture.

They had a beer and noticed a few guards from the prison standing at the bar. The trio were unknowingly in the same bar in which Anastasia had first met the man who had got her in to see Alex. That man was now dead, Anastasia charged with the murder.

None of them thought she had anything to do with the crime, however. That had been one week ago. They'd been in Russia for seventy-two hours, and nothing looked promising. Everywhere they turned, there were dead ends. Getting information had proved tricky, the town cautious to talk about the notorious institution in their midst. It was soon clear that any stranger asking more than a passing question about the prison would come under instant scrutiny.

The State handled all services at the prison, something not outsourced to private firms as now happened in the UK. The layout and floor plans were under official lockdown, Sasha trying his luck with a lady at the records office, but she'd become defensive when he broached the subject. He now feared this woman might have reported him.

They were getting frantic. Aside from an all out assault––which would take immense firepower, require a large army, and a clear knowledge of the layout of the prison––there seemed no way of getting to Alex. Any such attack might only get them so far. They would still need to escape the country, the biggest manhunt following any escape no doubt underway, all borders watched, every citizen under suspicion. An aggressive escape had never been on the cards. It was stealth or not at all.

And after three days looking at every option, *not at all* was all they had left.

"Get in touch with home again," Sasha said, the three around a table that evening for dinner, possibly their last in Russia, unless they came up with something new.

"And ask what?" Charlie questioned, having been in touch with Anissa most days already.

"See about the SAS."

Charlie shook his head at the idea. "It'll never happen," he said. "She's said Six can't sign off on any action."

"Yet we're still here, aren't we," Sasha pointed out.

"Look, I'll ask," Charlie promised, aware that they were out of options, with time up.

"Do you have enough money for tonight?" Sasha asked, changing the subject now that Charlie had confirmed he would once more approach Anissa, one final attempt to change the odds in their favour.

"If you're settling the bill here, we have enough for the hotel, yes. Breakfast tomorrow we must ignore." They would go to the shop later, get something affordable. Rubles were in short supply, Sasha cautious about having more sent there. He wouldn't use his credit card. That had to be in an emergency only.

"Look, I'm sorry," he said, aware the game was up, the team trailing heavily. No chance of a miracle turnaround now. Those only seemed to happen in sports competitions. "I thought we would find something," he said, knowing being on the ground had been the only way. Charlie knew that too. He'd been the one to buy the tickets.

"I'll let you know what mother says," the Brit informed his Russian colleague. There was little chance the call would alter anything, but it was the only hope to offer the other two right now.

Sasha went to pay the bill, Zoe watching him for a moment.

"It's got to him," she said to Charlie. "I think he believed he could arrange something. Arrive back in London very much the victor."

"Some battles aren't winnable, Zo," Charlie said, the only man she allowed to shorten her name, something she barely noticed he did anymore.

"We all hoped this one was." Leaving Russia, leaving Alex inside the prison felt like the cruelest defeat. To have got that far, only to leave with nothing.

They'd ruled out trying to visit Alex. Whoever went in would only alert the authorities to their presence. Getting another agent taken would rub salt in the wound. Zoe had raised the prospect of getting someone else to make enquiries. They ruled that out too. It would still alert the prison to people sniffing around—whoever they paid to visit the prison would be likely to turn them in if arrested—and that assumed they could find someone willing enough to do it. They might just have run straight to the police and had the trio arrested.

They left the venue in silence, no further words spoken as Sasha went on his way, the other two heading towards their hotel. Another uncomfortable night's sleep awaited Charlie, the floor unforgiving after three nights. He would call Anissa first, catching her probably still at the office, to see what she made of the proposition.

"The SAS?" she exclaimed, half an hour later and not for the first time in their five-minute conversation. "Charlie, you know that's not an option."

"It might be the only chance left," he said, poignantly.

"The DG will never sign off on it."

"Is there anyone who might?" Going around their own Director

General would have them all suspended. That said, the SAS came under the army's supervision, not Military Intelligence.

"Look, I'm not sure," she said. She had connections in the army, she had served overseas before a bullet saw an end to those days. She'd lost touch with most of her commanders since, many retiring or being moved into non-army related desk positions. One served in the House of Lords. She couldn't see how the British could do this. It might be enough to start a full-scale war with Russia, British special forces storming a Russian prison on Russian soil to free a man held there––albeit without trial––but held there because of something he actually did. As much as they all wanted him back, there were only certain lengths to which she knew the UK would go. World War III was not one of them. "Charlie, I'll make some calls, but chances aren't great."

"For Alex's sake," he said, not needing to finish the rest. She got it. She would do her best.

"I'll call you in two hours, is that okay?" She glanced at her watch. It was six in London. "How late will it be there?"

"It'll be fine. Take your time. I'll be awake."

"Stay safe," she ended, knowing their entire operation suddenly rested on her, and she didn't have a clue who to call first.

CHARLIE'S PHONE buzzed gently just after one that night, his mobile lighting up the dark room. Zoe lay sleeping on the bed, tired and having told Charlie she wouldn't last that long. He entered the bathroom, closing the door, before answering the still silently ringing device.

"Not good news," she started, her tone deflated; Charlie hadn't expected any miracles. "It's too dangerous," she added. "I sounded out those I could reach. Bottom-line, they can't send troops into Russia. I'm sorry."

"You tried your best," Charlie said, aware they would have to leave the country the following day, very much the returning team from foreign soil with their tails between their legs after a harrowing defeat.

"This isn't over," Anissa said, realising Anastasia would expect a call, the woman desperate for news and Anissa with nothing good to share. "When you are back, we'll go over everything we know. See if we've missed anything."

"We haven't," Charlie confirmed, knowing their roadblock had nothing to do with a lapse in ability. It was just not possible to break someone out of The Black Dolphin. Not covertly, anyway. With force now ruled out, there was no other way.

"Just bring everybody home, Charlie," Anissa said, her thoughts very much with them at that moment and Alex.

"I will," he promised, catching the time. "Look, it's late," he admitted, not having told her how late it was over there. "We'll call when we're out," he ended. They'd yet to complete their route––they had assumed they would make such a trip with Alex––but Charlie now felt they would stick with what they knew. Anastasia had escaped that way, and it had got them in, too, presumably undetected, since they were still there.

He plugged his phone in, allowing the few hours left that night to top up the battery sufficiently, and he got to the floor, Zoe rolling over in her sleep, the duvet tucked around her. He'd had to make do with blankets, the two agents frantically making the bed again each morning, in case housekeeping came in during breakfast.

After twenty minutes of going over everything in his mind, sleep finally overcame him at last.

He awoke to the sound of the shower, his dazed head seeing the empty bed above him, Charlie rolling back the other way, though none of it was comfortable. He wouldn't miss that about this trip. He checked his phone, no further messages of hope from Anissa waiting for him.

In the bathroom, Zoe hummed to herself, the shower on. Charlie laid his head down, listening to her getting ready. She tiptoed out of the bathroom ten minutes later, hair wet, towel wrapped around her, as she fumbled for something in her bag. Charlie didn't move, his eyes mostly shut, Zoe once glancing his way but satisfied he was still asleep. She knew he'd been up late, the call from Anissa not expected until one. She went back into the bathroom, the steam from the small room misting the mirror. She let the door hang open halfway, her humming kept to herself now, the small mirror on the back of the door able to clear somewhat more quickly than the bigger one in the bathroom.

Charlie could see Zoe's reflection, standing with her back to him, drying her wet hair vigorously. She removed her towel, giving him a complete view of her rear. She had a nice backside. He looked away, leaving her to it, sitting up now on the hard floor, stretching the aches out. It startled her to see him awake, Zoe grabbing the towel like her life depended on it as she walked back out of the bathroom, her hair messy but dry.

"Did I wake you?" she asked, watching him for a moment.

He smiled, thinking about making a witty comment about moonlight or something, but refrained from doing so.

"The light," he said. *That and the bloody floor, too.* She had told him he was being stupid, she didn't mind sharing the bed. He wasn't so certain.

She grabbed some clothes––anything would do, standing there in her towel. Nothing was clean now, the trio travelling light. They had intended to wash everything, though had never got around to it.

"I'll go change in there then," she said, as if making for the bathroom again, to leave Charlie alone. He stood, however, in only his boxer shorts.

"No need," he said, wanting a shower himself. "You take your time," and he grabbed his towel from the back of the chair, hanging it on the door which he pulled only partially closed. She could hear him turn the taps on, Zoe glancing towards the bathroom, the angle not showing her anything, but a familiarity in his confidence with her altogether alluring. She dropped her towel, dressing quickly, but the shower coming on moments later––door still open––told her he wasn't coming out imminently.

Zoe stood at the window looking out when the sound of the water switching off told her Charlie had finished. She caught the reflection in the glass of an arm taking the towel from the back of the door, though she didn't move. She would miss that scenic view from the window, this small town in the middle of nowhere their home for three days. That and the reflection she focused in on every few seconds.

"Have you heard from Sasha?" Charlie asked, coming out of the bathroom barely dry, the towel wrapped around his waist, torso exposed. She turned back to the window before answering, her face somewhat flushed.

"He doesn't rise this early, you know that," she commented. He did. They were due out of the hotel that morning, without taking breakfast, leaving as soon as they dressed. She caught the sight of his reflection in the window, towel off, naked for a moment, before he slipped on his underwear. She watched him closely, not moving as if she didn't know what he was doing, though she'd gone silent. Only when he was dressed did she turn, Charlie not bothered by what she saw or otherwise. He didn't care. That was what seemed to draw him to her all the more. How could he be so carefree about these things?

"You ready?" he asked, Zoe smiling at him, though not moving from the window. A few of her things lay on the table next to the bed.

She hurriedly put them away, Charlie dropping the wet towel on the bathroom floor with Zoe's. He put the blankets he'd used back into the cupboard, throwing his two pillows onto the bed. They picked up their backpacks.

"All done?" he checked a few minutes later, Zoe nodding. She walked to the door and Charlie followed her out. Five minutes later he had settled the bill, and they were outside, wondering where to find at least a coffee.

Various Cities, Russia

It had been a week since the President had instructed Pavel to highlight and then eliminate one-third of the criminal gangs and organisations in Russia.

He'd not yet told her the Spanish operation had failed. He had lost contact with the entire group, the remnants of the Ukrainian-based organisation the first to make it onto Pavel's new list.

He knew all hell would soon break loose.

He had sent the list to Svetlana, via their usual secure route. She would stand to gain the publicity for cutting down on crime. All she was doing was pruning her own garden, making little cutbacks; but knowing the plant would come back stronger, leaner. More streamlined. He didn't begrudge her the limelight. She had all the aces, with the groups desperate for the return of their resources.

Payday would be good that month, for the remaining two-thirds. He would have to pick sides carefully. The more valuable a group, the more there was to gain by their elimination. But they needed the actual numbers on their side too. Needed strength. Needed an assurance of victory before embarking on such a move. There would be a backlash, and it would be vicious, he expected that much. He had to be better prepared, ready to cut them off before they could regroup, before they might band together and make the battle anything longer than a sudden end. He didn't want a war.

The Spaniard, Jose Zabala, was another issue, and not entirely his focus at the moment. Nor was he a target. Zabala, if he had survived, would have his eyes on Volkov. Pavel would get around to warning her at some point. He just needed some good news to share with her first.

Gathering rival organisations together had never been easy. However, Svetlana's call earlier that year had created a blueprint, something Pavel had built upon, appointed by the President in front of them all to act as the go-between. She'd placed her hand of protection on him, making him untouchable.

When the gloves came off, however, and the one-third knew what she had decided for them, he knew her protection would count for very little.

His original plan had been to look for groups that were in competition. In a city where three groups operated, he planned to choose two to work together to eliminate the third. However, most groups existed in their own tight bubbles, and outside the large cities, most had allowed no rival to get any grip in their territory. That made the task harder. They would see the attacks coming before everybody was in place.

War might be all he managed, open gunfights up and down the length and breadth of the country as they looked to take on these criminal groups in their own backyards.

He cursed Volkov, not for the first time that week. It wouldn't be the last, either, he was sure. She'd set him an impossibly complex mission, with an unknown conclusion. Was she also setting him up for his own downfall too? Have them all warring against each other, the military sent in to finish off what remained? He trusted her, somewhat, though the nagging doubts remained.

Timing it all to happen at the same moment was impossible. That had been his first hope. Hit them the same week, give no-one any warning. It couldn't happen.

This was no Hiroshima, the bomb dropped from above, the planes already on their way home when the mushroom cloud rose, victory assured. This was merely the Normandy landings––a strategic push but one the enemy could see coming. One they would fight against when they knew they were the targets. Casualties were likely to be severe on his side as much as on theirs.

Again, the President would come out shining. Even more criminal groups dealt with. Even more political points scored.

Pavel's only option was to think like a general. Gather in the main leaders he would work with, and commission them to complete specific objectives, fighting their own fronts, raising their own forces.

He met with thirty men at the end of that week, ten days since the President had tasked him with this mission, still no clearer on the outcome. Her promise remained. If they completed everything in the next twenty days, the bounty might be all the greater.

The atmosphere around the room transformed as he shared what they needed to do. Some called it a disgrace—they'd all come into line to protect the President—others saw it as an opportunity. They'd wanted a legitimate way of eliminating a competing group. By the end of the day, the thirty had agreed; each man would raise a similar-sized group himself, drawing in the extra groups to oversee the actual attacks in their regions.

It would be a bloodbath, nobody left the meeting with any doubt of that. However, Pavel had assured the thirty he would guarantee their place in the new order. Survive this, and the country was open to them, resources flowing, ground to move in on.

Moscow saw plenty of action the very next day. In three separate incidents, masked men stormed the known premises of three different criminal groups, blasting their way through the building with high-powered yet silenced weapons, before burning each building to the ground, the rising column of smoke and the approach of fire engines the first most normal citizens knew of any situation unfolding.

Other major cities followed in the next few days, the press starting to get wind of the story, known criminal locations now reduced to ashes in what was being called vigilante justice.

Except Svetlana Volkov knew precisely who was behind the attacks.

22

Russia/Kazakhstan Border, Orenburg Region
Present Day

The three agents had hitched a ride in the back of a truck, Sasha telling the driver they were going as far as the village they'd first stayed in overnight four days before. They'd met up shortly after ten, somewhat hungry but at least full of caffeine. Sasha had then purchased a bag of food, enough to see them through the day, he hoped, the remaining cash spread as thinly as he could manage.

Getting off the truck, Sasha thanked the driver who knew the area well, the conversation on the forty-minute journey south open and refreshing. He'd willingly talked about his truck once being used in an attempted prison-break, the ageing vehicle Sasha sat in easily thirty years old. Sasha had dug a little--they were leaving, the driver seemed willing to talk, there was no risk in asking--and the old man seemed to think the same. The unique practices at The Black Dolphin made escape impossible. The prisoners didn't know the building, the guards deliberately keeping it that way. That meant no prisoner could find their way to a safe place from which to escape. He joked over the last few miles that the maniacs deserved to rot inside, elaborating a little about who they had there, though soon it was time to leave.

They would cover the remaining seven kilometres to the border on foot, the roads not leading that way, anyway. They soon got heavily into fields, a long way from the road, away from watching eyes.

"The driver told me they see very few border patrols in the area," Sasha said, he the only one in the cab, the other two balanced on the wooden bench in the rear with their backpacks. "He said the terrain makes it too difficult for people smugglers." They considered that for a moment. It was tough, but not impenetrable.

"You think we shouldn't wait until later?" Charlie asked, second guessing his colleague, but sure it was where he was heading.

"I think making it out is our sole priority now," he confirmed. They could all see the logic in that. "Besides, not having to find our way in absolute darkness might be a lot easier this time. If there is a satellite watching us, staying any longer on the Russian side would not help."

"So it's agreed?" Charlie checked, seeing if they had consensus between the three of them. "We cross as soon as we get into position?" They were aiming for the same bit of river, Zoe having quizzed Sasha about the existence of biting fish, to which he'd apologised, telling her he just wanted to speed her up.

"Okay," Zoe said, not prepared to challenge their logic. She wanted out as much as anyone. The only thing racing through her mind for the final five kilometres was the river crossing. Darkness would not be their blanket this time.

At one o'clock they were standing on the Russian side of the river, in the spot they'd clambered out of the water earlier that week. Russia ended here, just a few more steps of land and then the water would usher them into the beyond.

Zoe was already taking off her shoes, the bag on the ground.

"What's all this?" Charlie called.

"Ladies first, this time," she said. "I'm not being left in Russia on my own." However, she didn't want the men across first and seeing her the last to leave the water. She stripped off, Charlie raising his eyebrows to Sasha who looked his way at the second appearance of her finely toned backside that day, Zoe not wanting to make the same mistake as last time. Naked, she soon lost herself in the water, the bag floating in front, the whole crossing much less daunting in the light of day. It even felt less cold, the sunshine of midday surely not having as much effect on the water temperature as it seemed. They were probably warmer too, having walked nonstop for the last seventy-five minutes.

Zoe heard the two men getting themselves ready—she wouldn't risk sneaking a look, it might cause her to go under. Besides, she would be first out, dressing the quickest she had ever done, drying as best she could. Eyes forward, she pressed for the other side.

Her feet now hitting ground, she finally stood up, pulling the wet bag from the water, though at least the contents were dry. She glanced back at the guys, their eyes forward—they focused on their crossing—but obviously also on her naked form. She stayed low, getting her clothes from her bag, putting her underwear in place while Sasha emerged from the water next, a few metres ahead of Charlie. She couldn't help herself but glance at him as he walked clear of the water.

She felt alive.

Sasha had his boxers on shortly after, Charlie then out of the water, Zoe smiling at him as he unpacked his bag. She went to pull her top on.

"Dry a bit in the sun first," Sasha offered, standing there himself, face turned heavenwards, arms raised as if in worship. She turned to face the sunshine, her hair mostly dry, though the several inches that went below her shoulders had been in the water. Her wet hair clung to her skin for the time being.

Sasha dressed first, Zoe standing there, a freedom she'd never known before, both in escaping Russia, and dressed like that around other men, out of doors. Zoe had seen a different side to Sasha, a man for whom his body seemed not a taboo area like it was in the UK. She cringed at nakedness, her own especially. Yet here stood a man who didn't seem to see it as anything sexual. He'd not flinched when she'd seen him emerge from the river.

Twenty minutes after leaving the water, they were moving from the area, backpacks on, clothing dry. It was not far back to the car they'd left the other day, still perhaps a three kilometre trek.

They booked into the same hotel where they'd visited Anastasia on their arrival and each checked into their own room. Sasha was finally able to put his credit card to good use. Charlie would search for flights home later, he assured them. He would also notify Anissa of their safe escape.

By nine that night, they were each in their rooms, Charlie lying on the bed, exhausted. He would be asleep within minutes, the lack of decent sleep catching up with him now, his mind playing over the sight of Zoe's naked rear the last of his thoughts as he drifted off to sleep.

Various Cities, Russia

As quickly as the story spread around newsrooms, it spread twice as quickly throughout the criminal networks. A purge was underway, and groups not in contact with Pavel now knew they were next.

Three of Pavel's targets in the cities of Kazan, Samara and Nižnij Novgorod banded together, striking out before they could become the next target. Pavel's men who were sent to eradicate them were cornered and butchered before they got the upper hand. The three targeted groups all fled the area, regrouping several hundred kilometres away, trying to work out who was behind it all. When Pavel failed to take their calls they knew it was bad. The order had come from the Kremlin.

"I'll kill him!" the leader of the Kazan group promised, never seeing eye-to-eye with Pavel, a man granted special favour by the new President, a woman he didn't believe in either. "And then that bitch," he added. If they went directly against the President it would cause untold parties to enter the fray; the army, the FSB, even Russia's sharpest shooter, who was now head of security for Volkov herself.

That gave the man who'd survived from Nižnij Novgorod another idea.

"I'll target her team, those around her in the Kremlin."

"I'll take on the sniper," the man from Samara added. He was ex-army himself and aware of the legend, not believing half of it, though Rad himself he would avoid. There were other ways of tearing his life apart without killing him.

Ultimately, Volkov had to see it all coming, unable to stop it, aware she'd caused it to happen. She'd lied to them. They weren't getting their money. They were getting slaughtered, like a bunch of cattle. Expendable in whatever game she felt she was playing.

These three were not the only parties thinking malevolently of the new President. Down in the Mediterranean, another criminal mastermind was doing the same. As the dust had settled on his own battleground, Jose Zabala, security now beefed up, with people watching all the airports for further signs of trouble, was plotting his own response. She'd taken a swipe at him, missing altogether. His father had always drummed into him you never started a fight. He never had. But he sure as hell finished every one.

Forest Dacha, Russia

THE MAN from Samara stood with his men in the forest three hours outside Moscow.

Many months ago, a contact had said to him in passing that the wood yard he worked at had delivered materials to a build happening deep in the forest. The contact recognised Radomir Pajari, former sniper in the Russian army and now head of security for Volkov. He'd not spoken to the man––the contact a mere recruit in the army, serving national service, a nobody to Rad––but the resemblance was uncanny.

Now, standing four kilometres east of Kostya and Olya's dacha, his team of six former army fighters, stood with a map open of the area. The map showed very little detail and none to the east of the dacha. They didn't know if anyone was home, but the word on the street suggested they lived there year round.

The map showed the lake and the river which, given the time of year, might be more like a stream now, the snow long since melted, meaning levels in the lake were a little lower than at other times of the year. The properties did not appear on the map, which wasn't unusual. You didn't live in that part of the forest to appear on general maps.

"One property is here, the other there," the leader stated, jabbing the map with his finger as he spoke, pointing at the two known locations of dwellings in the area. "Our target is this house," he said, jabbing the first again. "We set a course for this zone to the east." The men were going to advance in pairs with one compass between two. "Weapons ready at all times, you know the danger we might be approaching." They did, the legend was renowned. It made the attempt questionable for some, though they saw the value. Any high-value captive such as Rad and they could get a more powerful person to do what they needed. They wanted to send a message to the President. This might be the best way.

"Look out for traps or detection systems," he warned, the traps more likely to be for animals than humans, but either way, it wouldn't be good. Stealth and surprise remained their best chance. Get close enough without them knowing and then they couldn't fail.

"Stay east of the building until we reach this zone," he confirmed, pointing at the rendezvous spot once more for good measure. The main road lay west of the properties, all access points from that side. Apart from the two homes, they knew of no other building that far east, which was why they'd trekked in to that starting point that morning.

"Questions?" he asked, expecting there to be none. It would disappoint him if there had been. They'd fought in Afghanistan and Syria. They could handle a single dacha in the middle of nowhere.

"Good, then lets fan out. One hundred metres apart, three groups, radio silence from here on. We regroup when we are at the perimeter of the target." If gunfire erupted, they would hear, given the proximity to each other, though the tree density meant they couldn't see beyond fifty metres, much less in places. That benefited them. A winter attack and they might get spotted much further away. Not good when there was such a sniper in the area.

They moved into position; the leader remaining central, two men going to the left of his group, the other two going to the right. He checked his watch. One hour should get them into position, from where they would make their strike. They didn't want to have to kill––pressure needed applying, but not blood on their hands this time––although they knew they might not have a choice in this one.

You don't put your hand into a bag of snakes and not expect to get bitten.

Each team had to rely on their compass, the forest an endless copy of itself, boulders passed that they could have sworn they'd already got to––perhaps making them change direction––had it not been the bearing telling them to keep going. They saw no sign of life; no other human life, anyway. Not in the vicinity. There were no paths, no clear tracks, suggesting few people ever came that far in.

The leader's trio was the first to arrive at the perimeter, the other groups were there within two minutes. They could see the wooden structure in the distance, smoke coming out through the chimney, confirming someone was at home.

A woman came out of the door.

"That's the wife," the leader confirmed, his information giving a little detail of who lived where. Crouched in the undergrowth, with many trees in the gap between them and their target, they were all but invisible. They hoped to be in and out within minutes, their exit into the forest as rapid as their emergence from it.

"You two, take the rear. Swing round and cover us from the back. You, watch this spot," the leader said, the game plan forming in his mind, this one of many battlefields he had faced in his time. "The rest of you, we'll take the front door." It was highly likely the door would be unlocked. The wife had now gone back inside, but out there, in the forest, nobody needed to lock their door. Today might have been a good day to start.

"We head for that tree." He pointed at the largest in front of them, at a slight angle, after which was open land, though bringing them in towards the front left corner of the house. The windows on that side might not allow anyone inside to be able to see in their direction. "We keep low, we run fast," he confirmed, something he didn't need to state. They all knew this was the riskiest part. Thirty metres of open ground towards a solid structure of the dacha. If they were spotted and if shooting started, they would have nowhere to hide.

"Make sure you're all in position," he said to the other two groups, who moved off carefully, the leader and his team's life very much in their hands for the time being. "Okay, follow me," he said, once the others had gone. They moved forward slowly, reaching the large tree, a small ditch this side of it allowing them to crouch down, out of sight from anyone looking their way. If the door opened, and the wife walked out again, something they had no control over, then they would be spotted. She would be certain to raise the alarm.

The leader looked to the one man offering them cover––the other two had gone around the rear of the property, out of sight now, but able to help from that position if trouble happened. He nodded to the man, the man nodding back. *I've got you; ready when you are.*

"Okay, on my mark," the man from Samara said. "Go," he hissed seconds later, leading the group as they broke cover for the first time, running at full speed, covering the ground in only a few seconds, getting to the wall of the house where they stayed low, out of sight, lungs heaving for oxygen.

"You get to that window," the leader whispered, pointing at the man in the rear who would offer cover from outside the window once they went inside, the others keeping low, passing underneath a window at the front, which didn't need covering. They would be in the front door which stood next to it, manpower inside better than anyone left standing guard outside. Each man held his weapon ready, the leader reaching up for the handle of the front door. He counted an unvoiced three with nods of his head, stood and then wrenched the door open on three, his men following him.

They covered the lounge quickly, footsteps in the kitchen ahead coming their way, a woman's voice calling out, "Is that you?" He grabbed her.

The leader held a gun to her head, his hand over her mouth. "Where is your husband?" he urged, his mouth to her ear, her eyes wild with fear. A door opening at the back answered that question, two men turning, weapons raised, Kostya staring in disbelief, not quick enough to get to his weapon. The pair were soon on either side of him, a weapon held to his head.

"We're not here to harm you," the Samaran criminal leader said. That seemed rich, each intruder with a gun, three pointed at their heads, entering their home uninvited, in the middle of nowhere.

"Then why are you here!" Kostya demanded, one eye on the weapon at his forehead, the other on the man who'd just spoken to him, who had a gun held to his wife, though he had taken his hand from her mouth.

"We need you to help us send a message," the leader said.

"To whom?" Kostya spat, though the answer seemed more likely the more he took in the situation.

The leader smiled. "That doesn't concern you," he said and, turning to his men, said. "Take them outside."

"Where are you taking us?" Olya demanded, one man with the barrel of his weapon in her back now, urging her towards the door.

"Somewhere safe," the leader smirked.

Any thought of running––not that they had the legs to do so anymore––once outside the door were pushed firmly away as the four men who'd been waiting there now approached, weapons drawn, but aware the capture inside had gone smoothly.

"God, there's more of you," Kostya exclaimed, seven men sent to round up two old folks somewhat an overkill in his book. "You know who we are, don't you," Kostya said, certain now of that fact since seeing them all. The manpower wasn't in case he turned nasty, but in case Rad showed up. You didn't need a squad to collect a lion cub left by itself unless you were worried daddy might come home. However, Rad was not there. He was in Moscow, with the President. Kostya assumed they knew this but wouldn't tell them if they didn't.

"Yes," the leader said; there was no need to say more at that point.

"Then you're a bigger fool than I thought!" Kostya said, as mockingly as he could. Anything to rile them.

The leader put his gun away, but came in close to Kostya at that moment, getting to within an inch of his face.

"Do I need to put a gag on you, *old* man?" he said, his eyes menacing, Kostya shaking his head, message received.

They moved back towards the forest line, returning the way they had come, when the sound of a quad bike came into earshot. It seemed close. They looked towards the track––it could only have been coming from that direction––Olya screaming to Nastya, though given the distance, given the noise of the bike, she wouldn't have been able to hear.

What she saw as she broke cover, however, caused her to hit the brakes hard. A group of men were dragging her uncle and aunt away, Olya struggling, waving her arms in the air, the men looking her way, before setting out towards her. They had guns.

She turned the throttle hard, skidding the bike around fast, sending dirt and dust up into the air as she sped back the way she'd just come. She heard one or two shots fired, ducked as she drove, though she didn't know if the bullets had been close. Her pulse racing, she knew she had to get back to her dacha, had to call Rad.

The leader had ordered his men to shoot the girl, his men giving chase and firing as she made her escape, the diminishing sound of the bike as it raced from there proof enough to the uncle and aunt that their Nastya had got away.

The Samaran leader swore, Kostya gloating at this, though he resisted a cutting remark. He didn't fancy a gag stuffed in his mouth.

"Get them out of here," the leader ordered his men, the group now surrounding the couple again, as they continued their march into the forest. The girl getting away––certain to tell her husband when she got the chance––had changed things. They needed to get far from there, the plan being to hold the couple in a makeshift camp they'd built the night before, four kilometres from the dacha. They had no other vehicles to move them any quicker. The cover of forest would have to do. He hoped he could contact the President before too long, which might be enough to buy them the time they needed. However, he didn't yet know how to contact her. Pavel was no longer an option. He'd tried to kill them that week, on the President's orders, too. This would show them all that they were not men you messed with lightly.

23

Forest Dacha, Russia
Present Day

Nastya sped faster down the track than she had ever gone, the images of her uncle and aunt being dragged away sure to fill her with nightmares for weeks to come. Right now she needed to focus, however. The nearer she got home––only partially fearful that men waited for her there too, though she'd not long come from there, and surely she would have seen them already––the more she worried the two shots she heard hadn't been at her, but had taken the lives of her surrogate parents.

She pulled up at her home, skidding to a halt mere inches from the steps of the front porch, a home Kostya had helped them build, the property now finished, their first child expected in six months. Nastya barely showed any sign that she was pregnant.

She left the bike running, charging up the steps, getting to her phone. Rad answered it after two rings.

"They've got them," she screamed, Nastya explaining through petrified breaths what had happened, what she'd seen, what she'd heard. Rad assured her they would not have killed them. If murder was their goal, they would not have taken them outside as she saw them doing.

"Get your gun, take the bike and get as far away as possible," he ordered. "I'll find you. I'm coming immediately." There was no question about it. Three hours felt like an eternity, however. He grabbed his gun, the call ended, his wife promising to do as he'd suggested. He gave a silent prayer for the life of his unborn child.

"I have to go," Rad said, informing the President what had happened. He wasn't asking for her permission to leave, and she didn't put up a fuss. She knew she couldn't make him stay, and sensed she would hear from the kidnappers before too long, anyway. She wished him success, Rad barely hearing the words as he raced from her office, desperate to get moving, the thought of the Moscow traffic awaiting him something he wouldn't allow to faze him.

As he sat in his third traffic jam less than five kilometres from the Kremlin, he cursed his luck.

London

It took them a proper night's sleep to feel alive enough to face a debrief with Anissa. That would happen that evening at Sasha's, the apartment the perfect base for the four agents to gather outside of the office. Charlie had been desperate for another games' night too; anything to take his mind off things in Russia.

Zoe was the first to arrive this time, Sasha letting her in, Zoe passing him two bottles of wine. They weren't officially on duty, wine not the common refreshment at Vauxhall House, but without question the juice of choice in these contexts.

"Take a seat," he called, taking the wine to the kitchen, the white going into the fridge. "You want a glass now?" he asked.

Zoe had been standing looking at the photos on the wall––all Alex's doing––from when he and Sasha had lived together. Sasha had changed nothing since. It wasn't his to change.

"A glass of red would be great," she said, taking in the photos of Alex, a few at various family weddings, most of him on some rock somewhere, a view of sea or mountains in the distance. Sasha came over and handed her a glass. They toasted.

"To our safe return," he said, not ending that phrase with what ran through his mind that second. *For most of us.*

They stood there taking in the photos for a while, Sasha never having really studied them before, the pair taking occasional sips of wine. A knock on the door finally broke the silence, Sasha swivelling around, placing his glass on the table before going over to let in Anissa, with Charlie not far behind her. She handed him another bottle, Charlie with a bag of snacks, mostly for later.

"You started early," Anissa observed, seeing Zoe with a glass in hand. Anissa eyed Zoe watchfully for a moment. "Shall we get started?" she asked, moving to take a seat on the sofa, Charlie coming out from the kitchen with a half-peeled avocado.

"I was hoping to switch off a little first," Charlie said, his stress level still high, the after-effects of having been back in Russia yet to settle. He opened his laptop after handing Anissa the fruit.

"And what am I supposed to do with this?" she asked him.

"You make a killer guacamole," he said, looking up from his chair. She did, that was true.

"Come on, I'll help you," Zoe said, aware Charlie couldn't wait to play the online game; seeing he needed a mission again, one that they could complete this time. They would soon get onto matters of a more difficult nature.

Anissa didn't seem overly impressed at first, but followed Zoe into the kitchen. Sasha smiled at Charlie as he picked up his controller, switching the television on at the same time.

Zoe watched them both for a few seconds from the kitchen, Anissa washing the remaining fruit and a red pepper. Charlie had purchased all the ingredients. He had laid them out on the side ready for her.

"One game," Anissa called across to them both. She doubted they heard a word, Sasha with his headset on, apparently seeing who else was online, Charlie going over the controls on his laptop.

"Let them play," Zoe said, taking the pepper and starting to chop it up.

"Smaller pieces," Anissa suggested, showing Zoe what she meant.

"WHAT DID YOU SAY?" Charlie exclaimed, the words enough to make the two women look immediately over at him, Charlie only looking at Sasha with a startled look on his face. He wasn't angry––this was something else.

"I said, if we want these guys to let us join them, we must give them something better than they already have," Sasha repeated, something he'd just said as a throwaway line. They were looking to form a larger squad, Charlie's rating as a player too weak for the best teams to take them on. Sasha's avatar was solid––but they came as a pair. Nobody wanted them both. Sasha knew he had an arsenal in his online backpack that he never used.

"You're a bloody genius, Sasha!" Charlie said, springing up from his chair, pacing to the window. "That's it!"

It didn't seem to fit the game, Anissa coming from the kitchen, Zoe following with the dip they'd finished making twenty minutes before, the pair sharing a good conversation over the best part of an entire bottle of wine.

"What do you mean, *that's it*?" she asked.

Sasha looked up, puzzled.

"Alex," Charlie said, the mood changing instantly in the room, Sasha dropping his controller to one side. "It's how we'll get him out." Finally the pieces were slotting into place in his mind. "Volkov has him locked away, and there is no way we can reach him," Charlie said, an assessment they'd not fully shared with Anissa yet––they were there to talk about it all, but had done nothing on that agenda yet. "So we give Volkov something she wants more," Charlie concluded, marvelling that they'd not already thought of it.

Sasha looked blank. The President had everything––arguably she was already the richest person on the planet if the rumours were true, and if she had sole access to a hidden stash of trillions.

"What can we give her?" he asked, aware that, unlike his online avatar, he didn't have a backpack full of President-enticing goodies.

"It's not what, it's who," Charlie beamed, Anissa getting it now.

"Give her Arkady," she said, Zoe's mouth dropping open.

"The whistleblower?" Sasha said, knowing no other Russian by that name.

"Exactly."

"That's bloody brilliant," Anissa said, seeing the play panning out in her mind too. Arkady Petrov had been most vocal against Volkov that last year. He'd given secrets to the West about the goings-on in Russia in a way that had never happened before. She'd rubbished the rumours, but two things were clear once you read between the lines in her many press conferences. One was she saw this whistleblower as a traitor. The other was that she didn't know his identity or location. Adding in the fact she rarely travelled internationally anymore––she knew she wasn't safe––he scared her. She knew his information had hurt her.

And only the four people in that room right now had knowledge of the last known whereabouts of Arkady Petrov. The CIA assumed he was hiding in the USA, possibly in New York. Arkady had used a journalist in that city as a middleman. Jeff McKay was the seasoned reporter Arkady had chosen because of his years of work in the region and had sent on the information to various people. Under Arkady's direction, Jeff had finally been allowed to break the story globally, the crowning achievement to his long career. Despite being harassed by his own government, he'd not given them his source.

That was because he didn't know, not properly. Jeff had suggested to Charlie that Arkady was in Mexico. The MI6 agent had flown there soon after, finally reaching out to the Russian, hearing his story, offering protection. Charlie had learned that Arkady had killed ten of his own men in order to escape from Russia.

Charlie quickly brought them all up to speed on what they knew of Arkady. He'd been the only one of them to meet the man.

"You think she would even accept the trade?" Zoe asked, directing her question to the only Russian in the room.

"Volkov, you mean?" he said, Zoe nodding towards him. "She might," Sasha acknowledged. Arkady made a far more valuable prisoner than Alex. When their crimes were put beside each other, Alex's were nothing compared to what Arkady had admitted doing. It was possible he had more information too, though nothing had been leaked in weeks. Still, the President didn't know that for certain. Getting her hands on him would give her closure.

"And you know where he is exactly?" Zoe said, turning to Charlie now.

"I can find him," he said, aware that Arkady Petrov's capture represented Alex's one final chance of ever getting out of prison. If they lost him, or if the Russians were looking for the traitor and got there before MI6 did, they would lose all bargaining power.

"You need to get there immediately," Anissa said, aware time might be against them. They had a way through now, but didn't know how long that advantage might remain. "You should all go," she said, not wanting to risk just one of them going. "Once you have him, I'll reach out to Volkov."

Anissa had never spoken to Svetlana before, not directly. Now she was the President. Anissa knew Volkov would know all about her, however, no thanks to Filipov.

There was a buzz around the room for the next hour, the wine flowing, the game long forgotten. The men would not play again that evening, the party breaking up by eleven, the food half-finished, the wine gone, and they now had flights to catch. It called for an early night, the three agents due out of London Heathrow a little after nine the following morning.

Forest Dacha, Russia

Nastya ditched the bike after driving for twenty minutes. The tracks would be too easy to follow, and she was far enough from the dacha to get by on foot. She planned to camp out in a spot that gave her a clear line of sight in most directions. She didn't know if they were coming for her as well now.

It would be dark in about four hours. She couldn't tell if Rad would come directly for her or, knowing she was safe, would instead focus on picking up the trail of the others while he still had daylight. She didn't like the thought of him going up against them all on his own. They outnumbered him at least seven-to-one. She wanted to be with him, but she knew she couldn't be. He did what he did, and she needed to let him do that. She might only slow him down, and time wasn't on their side.

She thought of her dear uncle and aunt, the would-be grandparents to her future child. Might her unborn now never meet its *dedushka* and *babushka*?

Nastya walked until her legs started hurting and she needed to rest. Shadows appeared around the place, the sun soon to go down on another day, a terrible day where the troubles that had been out there, had come and invaded their peaceful forest. Come right up to their doorsteps and entered their home. She knew Rad would arrive soon, no doubt terrified himself, though she knew he trained for situations like this one. How many times had he killed? She'd never asked him, but she knew he'd taken human life with that rifle on the battlefield as much as he hunted game in their forest. Was this same forest to become a battlefield now?

24

Mexico City Juarez International airport
Present Day

They had stretched the day with their flight west, local time in the bustling and humid Mexican capital suggesting it was only eight, that same day. Goodness knows what time it really was.

After setting off from London, the trio had checked in at the airport before eight; they had flown to Madrid, making a change there for the direct flight across the ocean.

While Charlie's last known location for Arkady Petrov was in and around Guadalajara––he had advised the Russian to stay put, advice he hoped had been followed but something he doubted the closer they got––it had been connections in the capital that had put Charlie on the right path. He wanted to touch base with these people again. He might need them before the week was out.

The three had travelled on their own passports––Sasha's a British issued one that the government had given him not long after he appeared in London. There was less threat to them all that side of the ocean and south of the border with the US.

Their cover was a holiday. Though much closer to an MI6 remit, this was still not an official mission. Anissa had not even bothered to ask the DG this time. He might have seen the value. He would have wished them luck, regardless. She felt his last words to her covered this operation too. Bring back Arkady and they could deal with any reprimands there might be, though she doubted there would be much.

"I say we keep going for a bit, get some food and sleep it off," Charlie said, his body saying sleep, his mind aware that if he gave in too early, he would be awake at three in the morning wondering why nobody else was up.

"Food sounds good," Sasha said, Zoe nodding eagerly too.

Thankfully, for good food options, they were in the right country.

"Tell me a little more about Arkady," Sasha asked twenty minutes later, a beer each before them, food ordered and expected shortly.

"He's smart," Charlie confirmed. "I'd been watching his house. He doubled back on me, surprised me."

He'd not told them this before.

"He found you?" Zoe asked, not overly impressed with this being shared only now.

"No," Charlie said, aware how it sounded and actually not quite what he meant. Arkady had spotted him watching. "I tracked him down, via a group based here in the capital. That led me to Guadalajara, where I staked out his place." They knew that much, Zoe receiving updates while she stayed in New York, Sasha hearing via Anissa in London. "As you know, I was there to protect him."

As they had discussed on the flight, they were now attempting to do the opposite. Charlie did his best to ignore his sense of betrayal. He'd promised Arkady they were the good guys.

"But he spotted you?"

"As all I could do was watch him, yes, he must have discovered me. He approached me from behind in a group of bushes I was standing in and we talked."

Charlie didn't need to elaborate. They all knew things could have got very messy for Charlie if the Russian had wanted.

"Then what?"

"Then we met up properly. You know that part," he said, having shared it when he arrived back in London.

"And there are no more surprises?"

"That's why we've come here first," Charlie said. That and the flight options. "I want to find out what might have changed since I left."

"Will they know?" Sasha asked, unaware of who Charlie had been speaking to in the city, or whether they had been watching Arkady since.

Charlie didn't answer, the food coming at that moment, the delicious beer not helping on an empty stomach. They ate in silence for the next five minutes, the tastes explosive in their mouths, the experience divine.

Charlie was the first to push his plate away, the remnants that remained just too much to manage, even for him.

"What say we take one final beer, then find a hotel for the night, get some decent sleep, and make this happen tomorrow?"

There was total agreement around the table. Sasha had seen Zoe yawn at least twice, though she'd tried to smother it. His own eyes were heavy.

At ten, they eased into their rooms, one each this time. None of them even bothered with a shower, the air-conditioning on, the bed inviting.

"YOU'RE LOOKING to extract him this time?" the Mexican said, Charlie sitting across from him, Sasha and Zoe either side of their colleague.

"Yes," Charlie confirmed. He'd contacted the man during breakfast at the hotel, the meeting arranged for later that morning.

"Just like that first time we met," the Mexican smiled, his accent strong, his English understandable.

"First time?" Zoe asked, addressing Charlie. He shook his head. As if to say *Not now, Zo.*

"This we can help you with," the Mexican confirmed. "But why the change? Who is he?" He knew as much as Charlie had told him, knew the man was Russian, knew he was the one leaking the information on the President, too.

"That doesn't concern you," Charlie said, knowing that with a man like this one, presenting him with a valuable asset and MI6 risked losing him entirely. The Mexicans would trade him themselves. "He killed his own unit of soldiers," Charlie said, his mind racing with a new thought, based on what he remembered about the Mexican. An old photo from the man's army days hung proudly on the wall just above his head.

"He was in the Russian army?" he asked, his eyes narrowing, his posture tightening.

"Yes. A colonel, with ten men in his unit. He killed them all. Burnt them alive."

"Why?" he asked, horrified.

Charlie paused before answering, wanting to choose his words carefully.

"To escape," he opted eventually, not the impact he had planned, but the look of rage on the Mexican's face confirmed he'd said enough.

"The traitor!" he barked, standing up, pacing a little around his desk. Charlie indicated with eye contact and a shake of the head to Sasha and Zoe––who both seemed alarmed at the sudden dramatic turn––that this was normal behaviour. Charlie seemed perfectly calm. *Relax, he does this all the time.*

"I'm here to see he gets justice," Charlie confirmed, which was true.

"Then you'll get my help," the Mexican said, the change in tone from moments before rather staggering. He took his seat again, picked up his cigar from which he insisted on taking an occasional puff, once again raising a cloud of smoke as he exhaled. Zoe turned her head away momentarily.

"My country thanks you," Charlie offered, the Mexican waving him away.

"We can't have men like this Mr Petrov taking sanctuary in our country when they've done unspeakable things like you've just mentioned," he said, another puff, another turn from Zoe who thought she would break out in a coughing fit any second. Charlie patted her on the thigh––she wasn't sure what that meant; was it okay to cough or would the man react angrily if she did? Had Charlie made that mistake, or was he just being affectionate? In the era of sexual harassment, she doubted Charlie was merely being playful. Not that she would ever take his advances as harassment. *Bring them on.*

"I'll need you to confirm Arkady's still in Guadalajara," Charlie stated, not sure how much interest the Mexican had taken in the Russian since the MI6 agent had left.

"He's not," came the response, only now hinting they had been keeping tabs, just in case. "He's in Acapulco," the man said, with an all-knowing grin.

"You've been watching him?" Charlie asked, a little hesitant to hear the extent of the man's answer.

"No, not really, Mr Boon. But when British Intelligence come looking, it pays to stay ahead of the game, that's all." He pulled a file from his desk drawer and took out a brown envelope, contents unknown. When he placed it on the desk they saw the name on the front was Arkady Petrov. There appeared to be quite a lot of information.

Charlie reached forward as if to pick up the envelope, the man putting his cigar-holding hand firmly on the file before Charlie could take it.

"Let's sort out my reimbursement first, shall we?" he grinned, Zoe unable to hold out any longer, her mini coughing fit seemingly not registering with the Mexican. Sasha stood to get her a glass of water. Charlie and his contact had not taken their eyes off each other. Charlie had come prepared; he'd paid well for information in the past and the Mexican had not failed him yet.

"Naturally," Charlie said, taking his own brown envelope––this one folded in half––and placing it beside the other envelope on the desk. Charlie had drawn twenty-thousand US dollars from his MI6 expense account that morning. The Mexican lifted his hand, collecting the payment, his smile broad and grateful. He put the money in a drawer, no need to look at it, nor count it. Charlie picked up the information, the envelope unsealed, and pulled out the top sheet. It listed an address in the coastal city, a recent photo with a date and several other vital pieces of real-time information.

"You can fly down from here in less than an hour," the Mexican informed them, aware the trio would not need to head to Guadalajara as they might have expected, his information saving them a wasted trip.

Once back outside, which was too hot for them, Sasha agreed to go off in search of tickets for their onward journey south, Zoe heading with Charlie towards a coffee shop in a determined mood.

"What did he mean about extraction?" Zoe hissed, the coffees barely served, the pair tucked into a corner of the busy café.

"Nothing, Zo; he's a little eccentric, that's all," Charlie said, casually brushing the comment away as he sipped his espresso, Zoe having none of it.

"What aren't you telling me?" she demanded, raising her voice, enough for even the always vocal locals to turn an odd head or two their way.

"Okay," Charlie said, his tone placating, not wanting any further outbursts. "I first met him after Zurich," he said, no need to elaborate with Zoe. She'd been there. She'd helped Charlie take out the FSB unit that had killed Anya and left him fighting for life in the hospital.

"You came to Mexico?" she asked, confused. She'd known about further north. "That's why you knew to contact him regarding Arkady, isn't it?" she said, more a realisation than anything. It was obvious why Charlie knew such a man.

"He's the one you turn to if you want answers around here," Charlie said.

"Who is he?"

"That's what you want to talk about, is it?" Charlie asked, mockingly. He knew it wasn't.

"Who did you extract?" she asked. Charlie had brought nobody back to the UK for trial as far as she knew. She had worked with him for several years, predating everything that happened in Zurich and its immediate aftermath.

His eyes were moist. He shook his head. She got it.

"You said you couldn't find them," she stated.

"Well, I did." He couldn't look at her now.

"And MI6 knew?" He nodded. That explained his period in the cold, when she wondered if Charlie Boon would ever come back to MI6, if their working partnership had been merely fleeting.

"But they never reached the UK?" Zoe asked, fearful of the confirmation she felt certain was about to come. His eyes told her the answer before his lips and tongue ever did.

"No."

She swore.

"What were you thinking?"

"Those bastards killed her, Zoe," he said, the emotion building in him now strong, the dam inside barely able to hold it all back.

"You should have told me," she said, more hurt than anything. Hurt that he'd held onto this for so many years. Hurt that they'd worked together closely and yet he'd never deemed her friend enough to handle this.

"I couldn't," Charlie started, a poor use of words.

"Couldn't?" she spat at him in a fury now. "You could screw me in Zurich merely hours after she died, but this... you can't tell me at all?"

He didn't need this; not here, not while they had work to do. His one night with her had happened long before all that. He'd been emotional in Zurich, drunk too. He'd not been thinking. This, however, he'd planned. He'd thought it through. There was no spur-of-the-moment thing about anything he did to the two people who had ordered Anya's murder. MI6 had also sworn him to secrecy, the incident brushed under the carpet by the DG himself. There had been extenuating circumstances to Charlie's actions. The DG had insisted Charlie take counselling before he could come back; the episode put down to a mental breakdown. They ordered Charlie not to mention it to anyone.

"I'm not allowed to say anything," he corrected.

That seemed to ease Zoe a little.

"The Director General said that?" He nodded.

"Part of my terms for coming back." She understood a little more now, though it still felt rough hearing it like that. "You won't mention anything to Sasha?" he asked.

"No, I won't," she said, Charlie taking her hand in his on the table, their gaze locked for a moment.

"I hurt you too, didn't I?" he said.

She couldn't answer. He let her be for a moment, alone with her thoughts, trying to read what was going through her head as he finished his coffee. The humidity of the streets outside right now had nothing on how thick the atmosphere had suddenly got around their little table.

"Look, I'm sorry," Charlie said, aware there needed to be more than that, but the word enough for the moment. She seemed to accept it, looking up at him for the first time now, seeing the sincerity in his eyes. "We didn't get off to the greatest start, perhaps," he smiled. That might have been the understatement of the century.

"We've done okay since," she said, her voice weak.

"Have we?" he posed, confusion on her face now clear. "Us, I mean. You and me, the man/woman thing."

"Oh," she blushed, her thoughts having run through their professional life together since she'd joined MI6. They'd done okay at that for sure. Now her thoughts ran through a whole new list of memories, the most recent glimpses of his naked body perhaps demanding more attention than they warranted.

"You're like a sister to me, Zo," he said, something she hadn't expected or hoped he would have come out with, and nothing he'd ever said to her before. *A sister?* Panic raced through her mind. *Sister? Not a sexy colleague? Not someone to woo?*

"And what if I don't see you as a brother?" she said carefully,

Charlie getting the meaning. He knew her feelings deep down. He knew what she hoped.

"We work well together," he said, off topic.

"And?" she quizzed, not letting him squirm out that easily.

"Sex messes things," he confirmed. Which was true; they both knew that potential.

"It's okay," she said, turning to him, a determination fixed where seconds before there had been hope. "Really, I am."

She glanced at her watch. They should hear from Sasha within half an hour.

Charlie decided not to say anything more. They ordered another coffee, their conversation stilted and somewhat awkward. They would be okay, Charlie convinced himself. It was good they'd chatted like that. Good to get it all out in the open. Good to get some of his past off his chest. He knew he could trust Zoe with what he shared about his past. That connected them in a way now that was special, even if the connection was not all Zoe had hoped it might be.

25

Forest Dacha, Russia
Present Day

Rad took a little under two-and-a-half hours to make the trip, using his army-issued vehicle to break the speed limit; the police were not going to pull him over with those black licence plates.

Even if he had made it in record time, it still gave the others more than a two-and-a-half hour head start, given Nastya had needed to get back home first before calling him. If these men had aerial means, a helicopter waiting in a clearing somewhere, they could be anywhere by now, and he might never find them.

He pulled into the track, ignoring his house, which seemed quiet as he had hoped. Nastya should be miles from there by now. He headed straight to the other dacha, firearm on the passenger seat, his sniper rifle on the backseat, not useful in a gunfight.

He drove right up to the house, waiting for a little while, seeing if his appearance would draw gunfire. Nothing. He suspected they were long gone, which he hoped to be the case. He didn't want an open fight there in the clearing of Kostya and Olya's home. Taking his handgun, he quickly checked the property, which didn't leave many clues, save for a few muddy footprints on the rug in the lounge, a sure sign that unwelcome visitors had come calling.

He soon spotted tracks leading deep into the forest, in the spot Nastya had said she'd first seen the men. The track showed no evidence of vehicles. He wanted them on foot, wanted them hiding deep in the forest. They were playing to his strength.

He assembled his sniper rifle, attaching the scope, and slipped his handgun into his jeans. The tracks showed multiple boots heading east. The expert tracker was on their trail.

As darkness fell, Rad, already using his night-vision equipment for the last half hour, reached the edge of a clearing, though he remained in the shadows. Someone had erected three tents, the trail he'd been following leading directly towards them. He backed away, looking for a better vantage point.

Climbing a tree five hundred metres to the south of the makeshift camp, one large limb about fifteen feet off the ground offered the perfect spot to lie down and scope out the scene. His weapon didn't have thermal imaging, but he had a separate device which offered him that, the screen set up underneath his tripod; the weapon aiming towards the tents. He counted nine separate humans, two of whom would be Kostya and Olya. He didn't want to shoot them by mistake.

Three people occupied each of the tents, some lying down, some sitting, some pacing. He watched them all carefully for a while, seeing if he could tell by movement alone whether it was Nastya's relatives. He figured they would be together, one guard between them. He registered the one tent––two people lying on a bed, one figure standing––as being the makeshift prison cell. He trained his weapon on one of the other two. He had to get the first shot right. Take out one man, and the others would make themselves known, running from the tents, spreading into the forest. He just couldn't afford to kill either Kostya or Olya with that first shot.

He picked the tent on the left, which seemed a little more separate from the other two, though exact proximity from his vantage point was a little difficult to determine. The three figures moving around the tent confirmed they were all young. Rad homed in as best he could with the scope while glancing at the thermal readouts from the device. He took careful aim now, going for the lower risk body shot, enough to kill at that distance, the darkness and unnatural terrain a perfect cover. He was confident he could take out any threats before they discovered his location.

He slowed his breathing, constantly looking between his scope and the device, without which he was shooting blind into a tent. He wanted the first hit to be a success, taking down one-seventh of the threat before they knew he was even there.

His finger caressed the trigger though didn't engage it yet. It had been a while since anyone had forced him to take human life, and this was only the second time on Russian soil. He had no quibble with anything he needed to do to get Kostya and Olya back. These men had it coming.

One final glance and he felt set. His breathing controlled, his mind in gear, he pulled the trigger, the weapon loud, the bullet fast. A body dropped in the tent, chaos ensuing given the movement of the heat images on his device.

Two tents cleared out completely, Rad watching the final tent—a prison for certain, the guard clear. He seemed agitated, walking back and forth around the space, though Rad wouldn't take him out yet.

The five men running around made it impossible to shoot, the time needed to aim and check the thermal device meaning his aim would be wild. None of the men would know where he was, however. Only the flash of a second shot, if they were looking his way, would show where the sniper had hidden himself.

So Rad waited. He wanted them to each find a hiding place, Rad focused on the device only now, tracking the movement of most, trying to be aware of where they would stop. As men snuck behind large trees, the images came and went. If he couldn't see them, they couldn't see him. He would use that, aiming next at a man who had come his way, but was hiding this side of a large tree and looking back towards the camp. Rad couldn't see if the man had night-vision gear on but from his vantage point two hundred metres behind him, he had a clear line of sight. He aimed for the man's head, the shot less risky. It might be the closest kill he'd ever made.

Rad waited. His gun ready, the target barely moving, only the slightest of looks around the tree back towards the camp from which he'd just fled. Rad was waiting for when the other figures vanished, when the other men went behind trees and were therefore less likely to see the flash from his weapon.

Rad fired, taking his chance, the man in front of him poleaxed by the blast. To the right, the shot had caused another to peer around a tree perhaps three hundred metres further along. Rad quickly repositioned the weapon as the gunman crept forward, and he took the shot, barely ten-seconds after the first. Three men down, though now the other three would roughly know his position. The guard in the prison tent had not moved, though the pair on the beds—certain to be Kostya and Olya—were now sitting up. They knew rescue was on its way.

Rad would not move, a scan of his device in all directions showing there were no other people around, besides the ones he'd seen in the camp. Nobody would creep up on him from behind.

The three were moving rapidly, trying to close in on his position, using trees as cover, the only natural wall there was in the forest. Rad focused on the middle of these three men, who might be within a few hundred metres of him now, the other two further away.

The man was running, seemingly aware that Rad had the disadvantage with a moving target in the dark. Rad repositioned quickly, pointed the device in that direction, mirroring the movement with his scope, taking three quick shots, left to right, knowing one of them would cut him down. It did, Rad watching through the scope seconds later as the fourth man fell.

He pushed the device away, reaching for a flare from his bag. With two men left in the open, a little light and the night vision scope of his weapon would be all he needed. He looked up, spotting a gap in the tree canopy above, and fired the flare, the arch of the flame carving a path up through the darkness, before its glow illuminated the scene in front of him.

Rad took two rapid shots, the first to his right, as the man peered around a tree, before swinging the weapon to his left. The other man was lit up in silhouette and the sniper put a bullet clean through his forehead. He scanned the area quickly, deciding to leave his weapon there as he jumped down from the tree. He pulled his handgun out, as he grabbed the thermal device, and started tracking towards the tents, watching all the while for signs of movement from within.

As he got closer, as if sensing his presence, the man pulled up one prisoner––presumably Kostya given the height when he stood––a gun placed to his head.

"I'm warning you," the man called from inside the tent, "I have a gun to his head. You don't want me to kill him!"

Rad stopped ten metres from the edge of the tent, standing still for a moment.

"You shoot, he dies!" the guard said, petrified now, knowing all the others were dead, the silence outside confirmation enough.

Rad slowly pulled his handgun up––the sniper rifle at this range would not have been good––and checking the thermal image, raised his arm. He held the device next to the weapon, at arm's length, dead ahead. His aim had to be spot on.

He took the shot; the guard falling moments later, Rad racing in through the tent, both Kostya and Olya in shock, though stunned to see Rad.

"Were there only seven men?" Rad asked, looking at Kostya, who nodded but couldn't speak. Rad put his weapon away, going over to lead them both from the tent. "Don't look at him," Rad told Olya, who wanted to glance back but stopped at his words.

It would be a long trek and Rad needed to retrieve his weapon first.

"Do they have any vehicles?" he asked, though he knew they couldn't have. He'd followed them on foot the whole way.

"No," Kostya said, looking around at the darkness that had enveloped them. His mind went where Rad's had already gone. They would have to walk out of there.

"Stay here," Rad said, able to fetch his weapon alone.

"Don't leave us!" Olya called, Rad turning.

"I'm not. My gun is in a tree over there," he said, pointing into the pitch black. It might as well have been the other side of the country. "I'll get it and be right back."

"What if there are more of them?" she called.

"There aren't. I got them all," he confirmed. Kostya had counted all seven shots, including the one that had whistled past his head seconds ago, killing the man holding a gun to his head. He took his wife in his arms.

"It'll be okay," Kostya assured her as Rad hurried away from them. He reached the tree again in a few minutes, pulling himself up into the branches and packed the weapon into its bag, though aside from unscrewing the tripod, he kept the weapon in one piece. They might need it on the trek through the forest back to the dacha. These men were not the only predators in their woods.

It was three in the morning before the trio made it into the clearing that formed the start of their land on the edge of the lake. They'd not come across anything to alarm them, Olya weeping as she went in through the door, the emotion now coming out.

"What about Nastya?" she asked, fearful something had happened to her. She knew they'd shot at her.

"She's fine," Rad said, "she's the one who called me." That made sense now. Olya had not thought of that. However, her question reminded him that Nastya was not home. He'd told her to hide, that he would come and find her.

"Why did they do this?" she asked, fully weeping now. Rad had never seen her like this.

"I don't know," he said, which was true. He didn't have a phone on him. Perhaps Svetlana had called, perhaps she had heard from the kidnappers? If she hadn't, he knew she wouldn't hear anything now. Their bodies still lay in the forest, their camp still intact. He would have to do something about that the following day. They couldn't get left there. It would only attract predators. He didn't want the wolves in the area getting a taste for human meat.

Yet Nastya remained his primary focus, she and their unborn child.

"Lock the doors tonight," he said, turning to Kostya now. "You have your rifle here?" Kostya nodded. "Keep it near you. I need to find Nastya. I told her to hide."

They acknowledged this without speaking, wanting him to stay but knowing they wanted Nastya safely home even more. He assured them nobody would come back for them. Not tonight, anyway. He would have to think about how to better protect them all. Someone had known who they were and where to find them.

They locked the door behind him as he returned to the car. He spun around and raced back along the pitch-black track, his body tired, but mind alive. If anything had happened to his wife, to his son… it didn't bear thinking.

26

Mexico
Present Day

The flight to Acapulco had been smooth, the message from Anissa at their confirmation of where Arkady was hiding was far from calm. It worried her to have them travel to one of the most crime-ridden cities on the planet, with the highest murder and homicide rate to boot. Charlie assured her they would be fine. Such gangs coupled with a police force often suspected of being corrupt to the core, despite years of government and military interference to rid it of drug cartel infiltration, might benefit them. A Russian going missing would cause very little alarm.

They had the contact details for a man named Juan––the Mexican they'd met that morning vouching for him. Juan met the trio at the airport, his English limited. He handed Charlie a bag, three weapons inside. Charlie passed two of them to his colleagues in the back seat, Sasha slipping his into his bag, Zoe looking somewhat sceptical before taking the proffered weapon from Charlie and doing the same.

"Es importante," Juan said, the English meaning to his Spanish words understandable. "You need a gun in my city," he added, this time in their own language.

They sat in silence as they moved along constantly changing streets. Some areas seemed a throwback to the 1960s, others now crammed with modern buildings. Rubbish piled high on some corners, gang members hanging out on others.

"You are safe with me," Juan said, seeing them taking in the latest gang as they passed by, this time a few of the gang members looking their way, but there seemed to be no recognition. Perhaps they knew the car already? A burnt out vehicle sat by the side of the road, yet to be towed away.

"Do you know this address?" Charlie asked, showing the driver the sheet of paper with Arkady's details on.

"Not to the hotel?" Juan questioned.

"Can you take us via this address?"

"Other way," the man protested, the instructions he'd been sent that morning being to drive them from the airport to the hotel.

"Please," Charlie asked, aware that having a local drive them, someone who seemed to be on the inside of things with the criminal elements of the city was safer than attempting it later themselves.

The man swung the car around soon after, drawing a few horns from other drivers forced to slow a little, but he ignored them.

"It take ten minute," he confirmed, taking a cigarette from his shirt pocket, popping it into his mouth and lighting it before Zoe could protest, though he lowered the window, his arm resting on the door as he cruised along the coast road with one hand on the wheel.

"It's beautiful," Charlie commented, the man not understanding the words, Charlie smiling, repeating his phrase as he pointed at the beach, the ocean beyond. He seemed to get it now.

"Si," he said.

A few minutes later he slowed, making as if to turn into the address Charlie had mentioned.

"Don't stop, keep moving," Charlie said, pointing with his right hand straight ahead. Juan seemed to respond to the action, his speed reduced, as they passed the building in question, the three agents glancing across. There seemed nothing complicated about the home, which could have had several families living there going by the multiple mail boxes at the front.

"The hotel now?" Juan asked.

"Yes, please," Charlie confirmed, turning to the other two, neither with anything more to add. Sasha checked his watch. He wanted to know how long it would take to drive back from the hotel.

Twenty minutes later they were back up the coast, in the district where all the major hotels stood and the only area where the tourists dared to venture. Foreign tourists no longer came to Acapulco, a haunt for Hollywood stars and millionaires in the mid-20th century but riddled with gang crime in the decades since, meaning only fellow Mexicans now holidayed in the country's largest beach resort.

As they were getting out of the car, Charlie tried asking for the driver's number. They might need him again a few times. He didn't seem to understand, Zoe stepping forward, and in what sounded like near fluent Spanish, she thanked him, asking for his number––which he gave her––and said they would be in touch. Left open mouthed, Charlie followed her and Sasha up towards the hotel.

"You didn't say you spoke Spanish," he said, drawing level with her now.

"You didn't ask," she smiled back. It had been a long time since school, but she'd enjoyed Spanish back in the day.

Sasha opened the door for them both, laughing at the exchange, allowing his British colleagues in first, hearing Charlie tell Zoe it was over to her, Zoe walking up to the counter and checking them all in.

She came back a few minutes later.

"They only have the honeymoon suite available for you and me, *baby*," she winked, Charlie doing a double take. Sasha had noticed the three separate room keys in her hand. Given their conversation that morning, Charlie wouldn't have put anything past her. "Relax," she said after a few seconds of him squirming, "I'm kidding." She handed them both their keys. She could see she would enjoy this.

ARKADY PETROV HAD NOT RESPONDED to any of Charlie's messages, the Brit having written to check up on his safety, promising as always he had the man's back––while in the country to grab him.

Charlie didn't know if someone had tipped the Russian off––he didn't know who might have done that––or, worst still, if others had beaten them to it. That scenario could only have involved Russia, Svetlana's orders.

If that had happened, there would be no hope for Alex.

"You're one hundred percent certain he's here?" Sasha asked, Charlie nodding, knowing the intelligence he'd paid for and the source from whom it came had to be accurate.

"He's here," Charlie said. They'd been watching the building all day, this only their second day in the city. They had opted for a quick extraction rather than a longer, better planned but more complicated one. To delay would risk him running. If he left Mexico, if Arkady did anything stupid, they might lose him for good.

Still, it would be idiotic of them to consider the former army colonel a fool. He'd outsmarted Charlie once; the Brit wouldn't allow him a second shot.

Juan waited close by, the car out of view of the building. Zoe would call him once they went in, the car pulling up, doors open, engine running. They hoped they would have someone with them by that point.

"No shots, remember, not when we're in," Charlie said, the firepower a backup against any local protection the Russian might have purchased, but not to be used on the target. A dead Arkady was no better than a vanished one at getting Alex out of prison. Charlie drew his gun, keeping it low and said, "Call him." Zoe made the call to Juan, the three moving in fast up the main driveway, smashing through the front door without stopping. The inside was communal, a child poking her head out of an open door on the ground floor, Charlie putting a finger to his mouth, as the wide-eyed child watched the three strangers with guns creep past her and climb the stairs.

They stood either side of number three, the address the Mexican had listed as belonging to Arkady. Sasha raised his weapon too, able to tell between a threat and their target if it came to it.

Charlie counted down on his fingers, the signal to charge through the next door and face whatever there was inside. *Three, two, one.*

The weak wooden door offered little resistance, the three moving in rapidly, Charlie covering the hallway, Sasha moving into the room on the left, Zoe right.

The sound of a crashing plate from the kitchen––dead ahead of them and leading off to the left––drew Charlie forward at speed, the other two soon behind him, the rest of the apartment empty. Arkady was halfway across the kitchen worktop, the window open, attempting an escape, despite the height.

"Stop!" Charlie called, rushing over, avoiding the broken china, though some crunched underfoot as he took hold of Arkady's leg. Sasha joined and between the two agents they brought the Russian back to the floor.

Arkady said nothing, just staring Charlie in the face, the presence of the British agent there in his home meaning nothing but danger.

"Is there anyone else here?" Charlie demanded, weapon low, but threat remaining until they knew Arkady was alone.

"Besides you three? Who shouldn't be, I might add," Arkady spat back, shaking his head, Charlie still unflinching. Charlie slipped his gun into his jeans, a car reversing up the driveway outside, the engine straining.

Arkady glanced down. "Is that yours?" he called, frightened.

"I said I had your back," Charlie confirmed. It was better they left the building calmly than needing to drag him out kicking and screaming. "It's not safe here. We have to leave."

Arkady looked Charlie in the face for a moment, took in Zoe who stood by the door, behind Charlie's right shoulder, before turning to Sasha.

"Who are you?" Arkady asked, fear displaying on his face, taking in the dark hair, the Russian complexion. A look Arkady knew well, having been surrounded by it for most of his life.

"He's with me," Charlie said, taking Arkady by the arm, not

prepared to have that conversation yet, if at all. The Russian pulled himself free.

"Who's coming for me? Volkov?" he demanded. If she knew where he was, knew he was alive at all, there was nowhere he could go that was safe.

Charlie took a risk, pulling his weapon––the safety catch on––and placing it square against the man's forehead.

"I swear, if you don't trust me and come now, I'll finish you myself, right here! Blow your worthless brains right over that cactus, so help me god." It worked, Arkady taking a step forward, Zoe turning, leading the way out, Sasha and Charlie bringing up the rear, weapons tucked back into place.

The four calmly walked down the stairs, the same little girl still poking her head out of the same doorway, Arkady even waving goodbye to her as he passed. The girl blew him a little kiss.

"In the boot," Charlie said, the group now outside.

"I'm not getting in there," Arkady protested; another look from Charlie and he raised his hands in defeat. *Whatever you say, okay.*

Charlie shut the boot once Arkady had lain down, glancing around the street, not seeing any overt attention. They got into the car, Charlie once more in the front.

"Let's go!" he called, Juan pulling away at speed, the agreement in place to drive them to a small airstrip forty miles away, where a plane would be waiting for them. It would fly them to the British Virgin Islands, where Charlie had arranged a secure location to hold Arkady Petrov. He would inform Anissa on the flight that they had the Russian, agreements then made to draw the Russians into a deal.

The car pulled up alongside the twelve-seater plane, Charlie opening the boot, Arkady looking around.

"You're flying me out of here?" he asked.

"For your safety," Charlie confirmed, helping him out of the vehicle. The engines of the plane were already warming up. "Come on," he urged, Arkady stepping forward, Sasha grabbing their bags from the back seat and following up behind Zoe, the four of them soon aboard. The co-pilot shut the door, locking it in place.

Strapped into their seats, they lifted off less than ten minutes later, Arkady by himself in the window seat on the back row, Sasha across from him at the other window, Charlie up front two rows ahead of the Russians, Zoe two seats across from him in the aisle. Charlie reached for his phone, typing a message to Anissa to say the package was secure, and instructing her to move on with stage two of the operation.

They landed after dark, a little turbulence on the flight, but nothing they didn't expect. The plane landed on the largest island in the British territory, a car bearing British insignia meeting them on the runway. Arkady felt somewhat relieved to see the obvious presence of an official vehicle. Nothing about his day since hearing his front door smashed in earlier had seemed legitimate.

Arkady sat in the middle this time, no need for the boot. His two minders—Sasha to his left, Zoe on his right—sat either side, Charlie in front next to the driver who was a local man.

They moved through the dark streets in silence, Arkady wondering where he'd gone wrong, how his own government might have found him. Charlie kept looking at his phone. There was no reply from Anissa, the Brit realising the time difference. It was late where he was, meaning she had probably not even seen the message yet. He might have a reply only in the morning.

They pulled through into a gated property not long after, the island not huge, the small airport accessible. No flag poles stood on show, however, hinting that this was no embassy or consulate.

Charlie jumped out first once the car had stopped, opening the door for Zoe, who climbed out. Arkady followed her, Sasha leaving by his door. They ignored the main building altogether, Charlie leading them around the side, Arkady following, sensing he had little choice now.

Charlie stopped by a door, the windows covered by protective grilles on the outside, unlike the main building. The front door opened to another secure door, the room itself one big space: toilet, shower and a small kitchen, next to a metal-framed bed. A television hung on one wall, all three windows, no doubt offering views of the sea in one direction during the day, now only showed the evidence of the security grilles on the outside. The place seemed nothing more than a glorified prison cell.

"You'll be staying here until I hear from London," Charlie said, not stepping far into the room himself, only now pulling what looked like a large watch from his pocket. It turned out it was an ankle bracelet, Charlie crouching down and snapping it in place.

"This will keep you safe," he assured Arkady, the Russian lost for how an electronic tag would be any help if his heart was stopped by a bullet racing through it.

"Am I a prisoner?" he asked. Charlie stood at the door now, securing the inner bars in place.

"You are under our care," was all he replied, closing the outer door, then locking it.

"So far so good," Charlie said. They had the building to themselves, something they had organised in advance. The driver had gone, the gates closing automatically. "You both get some sleep, I'll take first watch," the three of them the ones to protect the building, though they didn't expect trouble.

Checking Charlie was sure, and once they had walked into the main house, Sasha and Zoe went upstairs. Sasha confirmed he would be down in four hours. Charlie sat in the lounge, a clear view across to the other building, monitors relaying the various camera feeds covering the perimeter of the property, one even on the only road to and from the building. That gave them at least five minutes warning should someone head their way.

He switched on the television.

27

Forest Dacha, Russia
Present Day

It had been the following morning when Rad had picked up Nastya's tracks. He found the quad bike, calling her name every couple of minutes as he did his best to follow the trail. She'd done well at hiding.

She came running to him, clothes filthy, face covered in mud, yet she hadn't looked more alluring to him in months. They kissed.

"They're safe," he said, Nastya pulling away from him moments before, Rad reading the question in her eyes before the words could be formed.

"Thank you," she said, letting out a deep breath, "I've been so worried. Who were they?"

"I don't know," he said. "I want to find that out later."

"You caught them?" she asked. He shook his head. She understood.

They embraced for a time, the forest smells alive in her hair, nothing a trekker like him didn't love.

"Let's get home," he said, eventually. She didn't argue, following him back the way he'd come, the path in daylight much easier than in the darkness of the previous night. Reaching the quad bike, she climbed on behind him, their baby tucked safely between the couple, too soon for it to kick, but she knew if it had been big enough, baby would be proud of daddy too.

By nine, they had both showered and changed, eating a little food. They were keen to get to Kostya and Olya soon after breakfast, Rad locking up, setting things in place. Now perhaps it was more crucial than ever to know if anyone might come snooping around. They drove the bike to her relatives, Nastya holding a spare bottle of fuel.

Olya spotted them from the window, coming out of the door before the bike had come to a stop, Nastya embracing her aunt, the two women in tears at the sight of the other. Kostya came out through the door not long afterwards, getting a hug from Nastya as soon as he appeared. Rad followed them in, silently.

"I must clean up the site," Rad said, Olya looking away, though Kostya spoke up next.

"I'll come and help you," he said.

"You need not do that," Rad warned, aware it might not be pretty.

"You can't manage everything on your own," he said. Rad didn't argue, happy for the extra pair of hands.

"Okay. We should leave soon," he said.

"Ready when you are," Kostya confirmed, the couple rising early, sleep difficult that night despite their need for it.

British Virgin Islands

THE VIEWS from the upstairs windows that greeted them that morning were spectacular, clear blue sea, yellow sandy beaches. Everything you could imagine from that part of the world.

The previous night had been uneventful, the reply message from Anissa arriving for Charlie not long before Sasha switched with him,

Charlie pleased to have heard from Anissa at last before he'd taken a few hours sleep. She had promised to get back to him as soon as she heard anything.

"Knock, knock," Zoe called, pushing the door open to Charlie's room, stepping in having apparently showered and dressed already. Charlie lay in bed, but awake.

She looked out of the window. "It's stunning, isn't it," she beamed.

"Then some," Charlie said, sitting up in bed, pulling on a t-shirt after locating where he'd left it the previous night.

"How did you know about this place?"

"Same reason I knew the guy in Mexico," he confirmed.

"I thought this was British?" she said, meaning their current location.

"The car was," he said, Charlie having used that to get them from the airport, no questions asked. The property they were using was something else entirely. "This place, well, it's not," he said, too early to explain. He stood up, Zoe not sure what was about to appear from underneath the duvet but he had boxers on, at least, as he hunted for his jeans. They hadn't packed for the Caribbean.

"Have you heard from Anissa?"

"Yes, last night," he said. "Now we wait."

"We'd better get downstairs," she said. Turning and heading out of the door, Charlie grabbed his phone, glancing briefly through the window.

Forest Dacha, Russia

"WHO WERE THESE MEN?" Kostya asked, him and Rad alone now, the tents finally coming into view. Both knew what they were about to find. The conversation had quickly moved to Rad's attack on the camp.

"I think I'll be able to find that out shortly," Rad said, coming across the first body, no signs that any scavengers had been showing an interest. A bullet through the man's skull, the only wound.

Kostya helped drag it back into the clearing. They would have to burn everything, there was nothing left for it. Nothing would stay buried for long in the forest, not unless they went deep. Given the prominence of clay in the area, neither man warmed to the prospect. They hadn't brought spades, either. Just two axes––for the trees, not the bodies––and enough fuel for their bikes and to use as a fire-starter.

Rad quickly searched the body, nothing of interest found. The man wore army tags, though most men served at some point, the tags often worn years after as proof of their coming of age.

They would throughly search the three tents last, the bodies their main priority.

"How did you manage this?" Kostya asked, recalling the darkness, seeing now that most of the men had been downed by a headshot.

"I have my methods," Rad said, aware Kostya was now observing first hand his capabilities, but it didn't mean they had to talk about that side of his life. Rad liked the fact his home life––family life––had been separate from his other life. How near the two worlds had come the previous night.

He'd yet to hear anything from the President. He'd confirmed to her he was safe, as were his loved ones.

The sound of a telephone ringing caused both men to crouch quickly, Rad reaching for his weapon, the phone continuing to sound. There seemed no sudden movements, however, no-one silencing their ringing mobile. Rad crept forward, warning Kostya to stay low. He got to the body of the man who'd been running straight for him, the fourth kill of the night. The ring tone was still coming from an inside pocket. Rad rolled the body over––the team leader, as he would later discover––the man's face a mess, half blown away. Rad picked up the phone, answering the call.

"God, I thought something had happened to you," the caller declared, Rad looking at the phone's display, which merely said *Kazan* on the readout.

"It depends who exactly you mean by *you*," Rad said, fully alive, the same no longer true for the team sent to grab Kostya and Olya.

There was silence for a moment.

"And this is?" the caller asked, Rad noticing the warning light on the battery confirming power was low. He didn't want it to die. Left on, the phone might tell him all sorts about who these people were.

He hung up. Rad didn't need to give his name, didn't need to say anything stupid like the action heroes did in those American movies. They would know soon enough who he was. They might already have guessed. He dropped the phone into his pocket. If the device died, perhaps the team in Moscow might still mine it for secrets? He loosely searched the body, getting a wallet and map, and the information on himself from the man's inside pockets. Rad had been the ultimate target, the kidnapping intended to force him to pressure the President to back off.

Well, that one had failed.

Kostya came walking over now, hearing Rad's voice answering the call, Rad turning the body over, the dead guy face down, and between them they dragged it back to the tents.

Within half an hour all seven bodies lay side by side on the ground, Kostya setting to work on downing two trees—their proximity meaning they risked catching fire if left where they were. The wood would also help create a fierce fire to burn all the remains. Rad went through the tents quickly, two with little in them, the third with only military style supplies. Rad stacked these boxes next to his bike, slicing through the tents with his blade, the canvas soon piled onto the bodies, the wood of the first tree now holding them in place. He spent the next hour helping Kostya fell and chop up the remaining tree. They piled most of the branches onto the growing mound. They could work on the large sections of trunk, which still needed cutting to size to move, while the fire was taking hold and add the wood in stages, keeping the size of the blaze manageable. The forest wasn't so dry that a widespread fire was much of a risk, but Rad helped Kostya clear a few metres gap in the undergrowth around the area as a final precaution.

Rad doused the wood with the fuel, using half the bottle to soak much of the material, the liquid dripping through to the canvas underneath which covered the bodies. Rad dropped some matches onto the fuel and stepped back, the fire licking into life rapidly after, greedy for the petrol, but soon taking hold in the wood. Kostya went to work cutting the remaining sections of trunk into manageable pieces, Rad pulling his mobile out. He called Pavel, aware that what had happened there––what now lay burning nicely in front of him––had to have been a fallout from the operation Svetlana had put in place.

"Yes," Pavel said, aware of who it was calling him.

"We had visitors last night," Rad confirmed. "Seven men, came to kidnap my wife's uncle and aunt. I presume they would have then got me to speak to the President."

"I take it you intervened?"

"Yes, they're all dead," Rad confirmed. "A call came through from a contact noted as Kazan." Rad mentioned the deceased's name, taken from the man's wallet. "Mean anything to you?"

It did.

"Three groups found out what was happening. The men you killed were from Samara, their leader probably the man whose phone you answered. They teamed with two other groups, one of which is from Kazan."

"Did the President know?" Rad asked, wanting to be clear if she knew of the threat before he did and had said nothing.

"She didn't, no," Pavel confirmed. He'd not told her yet. "She's been in touch since you left, though."

"Okay. Tell me, will they stop?" Rad wanted to know if it was safe to leave his wife alone again.

"I don't know. I take it you haven't heard from the President yet?"

"No, why?"

"The police found three of her staff dead this morning," he said, in what was another focused attack, this one successful.

"Who?" Rad asked instinctively.

"Hell if I know," Pavel said, more pressing things on his mind than the internal workings of the Kremlin.

Rad internally cursed his boss for the first time. She'd brought this on herself, her staff pulled into a mess she didn't need to have started. He also now didn't know what to do. One group had targeted the uncle and aunt. One had successfully targeted the office. What were the third group aiming to do?

"Armour up troops, you have new orders," the Kazan leader shouted, closing his phone, the call to Samara not answered by the man he'd been aiming to reach. That only meant the sniper had stopped them all first.

He'd been most interested in that little mission, the name of Nastya and the uncle and aunt familiar to one of his men. That man had once dated a girl by that name, before she'd fled from Moscow, never heard from again. The leader had promised that man she was his––as long as they took care of Rad first.

Joining them in the back of a second truck, a man sat down, a stranger to most. There was a large cage in the back of the lorry, a sheet covering up the contents. Yuri smiled as his old army comrade from Kazan greeted him––his handshake confirming to the other men that he knew this man. The leader and Yuri Lagounov went back a long way. And Yuri hadn't travelled to this latest hunt empty-handed. He brought with him an animal that hadn't tasted human flesh in quite a while, the man with an understanding over the beast now, though with equally huge respect of its danger. He would conduct his own operation, separate from the others, using the animal to help him hunt.

28

The Kremlin
Present Day

"They failed," Pavel confirmed, updating Svetlana at last on the ongoing efforts, knowing she needed informing of how things had gone so badly wrong in Spain. At least his team had taken out the surviving members of the organisation left in Ukraine, those that hadn't been on the ill-fated mission.

"And you are telling me only now?" she said, somewhat surprised. She'd been talking proudly all week about how criminals were running scared in her country; her stance, in front of the cameras at least, was hardline and determined. She would clean up the country, and they were making great progress. There was nothing more enjoyable than being able to silence the repeated questions that kept cropping up with real-time facts and figures, stats that were impressive. Fewer crimes, fewer murders, much less presence of organised criminal groups right across the country. The questions that arose always linked back to the accusations first leaked by Arkady Petrov, a dissident unknown in the country, but for many an unsung hero.

She never answered their questions directly. She let the stats speak for themselves. Still, she came away from every encounter seething. There she was making the country safer for all, giving them plenty to report on, real progress, real numbers. And yet for some that was not enough. Though the traitor's allegations had never stuck, not properly––she'd won the election by a landslide––she couldn't shake them. They stung, even still. Even after becoming untouchable. Perhaps because of that? She should be beyond reproach by now, safe, secure. Loved. The country should worship her, and while large parts did, that wasn't enough. Instead, they were still going on about a nameless loud-mouth, someone who knew more than she admitted he did.

"I'm telling you as a courtesy," Pavel said.

"You think you are doing me a favour by leaving the fact from me until now that these men failed to kill an old man ten days ago?" So she knew. She must have had someone on the ground, watching.

He didn't know what to say.

"I've focused on your main goal," he said, which was partly true.

"I gave you two objectives; both equally important, both obtainable," she said, which sounded rich coming from her side of the conversation. On the ground, the battle was real. There were no quick solutions to this one.

"The men sent to Spain were nothing to do with me," he pointed out, something that was partially true. He had selected them.

"Do you know what happens to any political leader when someone within their government does something they shouldn't have?" she asked, her tone now as if a professor, he her student.

"No," he said, mostly because he knew she expected that of him.

"It comes back on the leader. Presidents and Ministers the world over have lost their positions because people within their ranks who should have done better somehow failed. The same is true in so many situations."

"You're blaming me for Spain?" he said, the only logical connection.

"I'm not here to point fingers; but these men were under your command, and they failed. I suggest you clean it up, otherwise it will be your head on the line."

"And what about here?" He had enough pressure on his shoulders already with the underground war being fought on Russian soil.

"A good leader learns how to manage situations at home, and abroad," she said, lesson over.

Another thought occurred to her at that moment with the mention of abroad.

"Pavel," she said, checking he was still with her, the man acknowledging he was. "Can I ask one more thing? A personal favour."

It had all been personal as far as he could tell.

"Go on," he said, his tone short, impatient, direct.

"The whistleblower," she stated. "Someone must have helped him cross the border."

"If he needed help," Pavel said.

"Oh, whoever he was, he needed help. My question to you is simple––if he asked for help, someone knows who he is. Someone within Russia. Someone in the criminal world." That was assuming a lot. They might currently be waging war against these very people. The one group, the one person with this knowledge, might already be dead.

"You want me to find them?" Pavel asked, growing angry that another task––probably an impossible one too––was being put on his plate, when he already had more than enough to deal with.

"It shouldn't be too difficult," she said, making it sound like a mere drop in the ocean for him.

"I beg to differ," he said, chancing his luck.

"Fail me again, and begging is all you'll ever do," she snapped, the change causing Pavel to kick himself for speaking out like that. He wouldn't say sorry, however.

He came back to the task in question.

"You want a name?" he said, aware that if someone knew, if someone had helped the whistleblower cross the border, then the person in question––they assumed it to be a man, but they had no proof––was long gone. Tracking anyone beyond the border of Russia was pushing it, even for Pavel.

"His name will be sufficient," she said, well aware she had her own options should she know where to look.

"I'll see what I can do," he said. Offering the name might give one group a reprieve, especially if they were a target. It gave these organisations a get-out––give him the name of the whistleblower and you made it to the safe list. He liked that thought. He would use it.

Svetlana focused her eyes on the desk, a post-it note she'd not seen before coming into view. Written in pen across the middle of the note it said *Anissa from London needs to speak to you* and it listed a private number. The President knew the name of the MI6 agent, the note short on details––naturally. This wasn't a message her office needed to know about.

Forest Dacha, Russia

RAD AND NASTYA sat together with Kostya and Olya in the older couples' home.

"We stick together," Rad confirmed, his own house fitted with an alarm, the track into their properties wired for movement. If anyone came that way, he would know. He'd just told them they would all have to move into the forest.

"We'll take the bikes," Nastya promised, seeing the look on her aunt's face, the prospect of moving through such terrain enough to make her wonder if she could.

"We need to move, though," Rad confirmed. The bikes wouldn't get them the whole way. They didn't have the fuel, either. They could stow them somewhere, ready to use to get home once it was all over. He'd been running through a few rifling tips with Kostya over the last hour. Nastya already knew what she was doing.

They moved out through the front door, a bag packed with food, Olya bringing anything that wouldn't spoil. They loaded the two bikes, Rad driving one, Kostya the other, their wives balanced on the back of each. Olya glanced back at the home longingly. Soon it was out of sight as they went further down the track, away from the main road, the path less likely to show signs they'd driven that way, before veering off the dirt road and venturing through the forest.

At four that afternoon, the first alarms triggered. Rad turned to his phone, the images of one truck and several cars pulling up outside the newly built dacha enough to confirm his worsening fears. At least he knew.

He relayed the information to the other three, Olya putting a hand to her mouth, Nastya close to tears. Kostya instinctively pulled his weapon in towards him. Rad didn't want any of them needing to fight. Given the number of men he'd just seen leaving the vehicles, if it came to a fight, the intruders outnumbered them considerably.

He called Svetlana.

"I need immediate help," he said. She'd just had a worrying call from her cousin, Lagounov. He was near Moscow and said he was going hunting and would be off the grid. She knew what that meant. She didn't yet know where.

"What's happened?" she asked, Rad her primary line of safety. Get through him and she would be next.

"They're here. An unknown number, perhaps a dozen."

She lowered her head. If she deployed special forces and if they caught Yuri, he might lead them back to her. He might admit to everything he knew.

"Look, I'll get everyone there. It'll take time," she warned, Rad looking at his device, men now appearing at Kostya's house too.

"We have little time," Rad confirmed, worry detected in his voice for the first time, Svetlana not used to that in a man who it seemed nothing fazed.

"Look, I believe Yuri Lagounov might be there too," she said.

"How?" He knew all about the legends surrounding Lagounov.

"I have my sources," she said. "He won't be with the others." This was less than a hunch. She knew he always did it his own way. Taking the tiger with him required a unique approach.

"He's alone?"

"Not exactly," she said, Rad picking up the hint she knew much more about the matter than just hearsay. "I believe he's got a tiger with him."

"Tiger?" Rad exclaimed.

"A man-eater," she confirmed, not about to explain how she could possibly know that.

"I don't understand," Rad said, at a loss why they were still targets, why mercenaries, maniacs or tigers even needed to come looking for them.

"I'm not sure I do either," she admitted. "Don't hesitate with Yuri," she said, her lack of a surname immediately informing Rad of a closeness that defied understanding, but he let that thought ride as she finished her sentence. "If you get a shot, take him out. The animal too. I mean it."

"I've no intention of letting anything happen to my family," Rad promised. He would shoot whatever came at them.

"I've issued an all-service alert," she said. That meant all military, FSB and police units in the area would now make a beeline for his location. Given how far away from the nearest city they were, however, he wasn't expecting them to arrive soon. It would also be dark in around four hours. Enough time for them to reach the forest, but that might be about as much as they could manage. Rad knew he would have to hold them off in the meantime. He ended his call with Svetlana, the President wishing him a heartfelt *good luck*. He knew he would need a lot more than luck.

YURI LAGOUNOV STOPPED his truck some way before the entrance to the forest which the others were heading towards. The driver joined the men from Kazan. Yuri was left alone with his cage and the vehicle that would get them off the main road. He checked the wind direction.

The sedative he'd injected into the animal would soon wear off, the tiger already showing signs of life. Getting downwind of their target would be crucial, the animal less of a danger to him once it was released. An electronic tag told Yuri where it was, though he knew it would soon home in on the others. He hoped the men from Kazan didn't get in its way.

He parked the truck two hundred metres back from the lake. Tigers were excellent swimmers, their ability in the water marking them out from nearly all other large––or small––cats. The natural barrier that the lake caused for the men coming in on foot, was nothing for the tiger. Yuri planned to use that to his advantage.

He pulled the sheet from the top of the cage, the tiger now on its feet, taking a swipe at the black material as it lifted, sunlight falling upon the orange fur of the animal.

"Easy, boy," Yuri said, the tiger growling gently, its stance telling him it was hungry. The Russian opened the back of the truck, making sure the path to the lake was clear. He checked the wind direction once again, but the animal had already started sniffing the air. Yuri went back to the cab. He'd raised the animal since it was a cub, but he'd not been around it since it started killing for him. He would open the cage remotely from the safety of the cab, the doors closed, tracking device on.

He opened the cage; the animal took no time to jump down from the truck, landing gently on its front paws, very much the new king in this unusual habitat. It stretched, sniffing the air once more––there could be many food sources available, but the one Yuri had trained it on that last year was human flesh––and it soon darted towards the lake, Yuri confirming it was in the water before he jumped back out of the cab, closing the rear doors of the truck. Taking the tracking device with him, he grabbed a pair of binoculars, a dart gun––which he slipped in his pocket––and a rifle which he hung on his shoulder. He jogged towards the lake, keeping one eye on the screen, confirmation the tiger was moving away from him.

29

Vauxhall House, MI6, London
Present Day

The unknown number displaying for the incoming call on Anissa's private phone could only have been the returned call from Russia. She answered it, pacing quickly back and forth around her office as she spoke.

"Anissa speaking," she confirmed.

"Military Intelligence Six––this is… well, you know who's calling," Svetlana said, her voice instantly recognisable––Anissa had spent countless hours poring over the many press conferences of the last few years. Not to mention Volkov's long and distinguished Hollywood career, before her unexpected move into politics.

The fact she was calling in the first place had taken Anissa by surprise. She hadn't expected her message to have got through, let alone to get a response so quickly.

"I wasn't sure you would call," Anissa admitted, the first time she had ever spoken directly to Svetlana Volkov. By Anissa's reckoning, Volkov was perhaps the single most dangerous person on the planet right then. She had never bought into the President's many press conferences, Volkov always the picture of elegance, of sophistication. The new face of Russian politics, hard on crime, strong on rights and opportunities for women.

"I'm still not sure why I have," Svetlana mused.

"I want to propose a trade," Anissa said, straight to the point. She'd been up all night, unable to sleep since hearing the confirmation from Charlie that they had Arkady. She'd run through this conversation a hundred times. Every time she accused Volkov of something or started by telling the President she knew about Alex; the call always ended abruptly. She had to take a different approach, had to be upfront and open. Svetlana had to hear her out.

"A trade?"

"I have something you desperately want, and you have something we want returned just as much," she said, again her wording picked and ordered such that she drew in the Russian, and got the time to explain what she needed.

An aide had given the President the name of Arkady Petrov only that morning, a soldier thought dead in a terrorist attack which had burned eleven men to death. Yet someone by that same name had skipped the border two days after the attack. Not long after that and the leaks appeared. It had to have been Arkady. He had been senior enough to know everything.

And now the British had beaten her to it.

"You have Petrov?" Svetlana stated, no need to be cautious with the facts here, the call from MI6 highly unusual, the returned call even more so.

"We have Arkady, yes," Anissa confirmed, switching to the first name, proof that she knew exactly who Volkov meant.

"How?" Svetlana asked.

"That doesn't matter," Anissa responded. They could trade spy stories later once they had confirmed the deal. Anissa knew she would never tell Volkov anything.

"May I ask what you want in return?"

"That's easy," Anissa said, keen to drive home her advantage by keeping the information flowing freely. "I want Alex Tolbert released from The Black Dolphin prison, and you get your traitor back." She used the term for Petrov which she'd heard Volkov repeatedly use to refer to the unnamed whistleblower.

"A criminal for a criminal," Svetlana teased.

"Hardly," Anissa pointed out. "Petrov murdered ten of his own men in cold-blood just to escape. That's before we even consider the damage his leaks of confidential information have done to your country, and to you personally."

Volkov laughed, as if the damage was nothing.

"I think your press might have overstated the truth of his words," she said. Overstated or not, both knew the leaks were true, though the Russian didn't yet know to what extent the British understood that.

"They don't yet know about the seven former movie producers who've since gone missing though, do they?" Anissa said, dropping in something fairly new to her. Anastasia's initial tip had helped them piece together the accounts from Moscow, and once they knew the seven names, they'd been able to find the common connection. The men had all worked for the same film studio at the same time. Listed amongst the studio's roster of stars to have come through their doors was a Ms Svetlana Zolnerovic, as she had been then, the studio's own website putting her most commonly known acting name in brackets. Svetlana became Mrs Volkov only a few years after moving on from that studio.

"Terrible business, I hear," Svetlana said, not at all worried by the clear attempt at a threat.

"What did they do to you?" Anissa asked, pressing.

"What makes you say they were anything but decent human beings?" Svetlana stated.

Anissa laughed at this, a genuine one, the sheer nerve of the woman.

"So, this trade," Svetlana added, coming back to the matter in hand.

"Alex doesn't deserve to be there," Anissa said.

"I suppose you believe that; but if the world knew what he had tried to do, I can assure you, many would disagree with you," Svetlana stated.

Anissa shook the thought away. She couldn't allow the Russian to get under her skin.

"Well, the world won't know, just as they won't know anything about this trade."

"They'll know about Petrov, all right," she warned, though she would never admit they'd got him in a trade. "We'll claim we caught him," she confirmed. More good PR for the shining President.

"Will he stand a fair trial?"

"Does it matter?" Svetlana asked, both women aware this man was definitely guilty on all charges.

"One more thing," Anissa added. "When Alex walks, the trumped-up charge against Anastasia Kaminski goes away."

"I see," Svetlana said. "What makes you think she didn't kill the guard?"

"You don't want to go there," Anissa snapped, "not with me!"

"I'll need proof you have Petrov," Svetlana stated.

"We have him. That's all the proof you're getting until we get Alex." She would risk nothing with Volkov. If the Russians got to Petrov themselves before Alex was free, there would be no trade. Charlie, Sasha and Zoe were hardly holding the Russian legally.

"How do I know you won't cheat me?" Svetlana asked.

"Because I'm not the fraud here," Anissa stated.

The President roared with delight, having riled Anissa somewhat. "You think I'm a fraud?" she scoffed.

"I know you are," Anissa said, unable to help herself, not wanting to go this route. Overly goading the President would not serve her purpose of getting Alex traded for Petrov.

"It's just a role I'm playing, sweetheart," Svetlana said, who couldn't have been more than a year or three older than Anissa, though she held her age well. It was possible she was much older.

"A role where people end up dead," Anissa pointed out.

"Everyone dies someday. You, me; we can't live forever," Svetlana pointed out.

A million thoughts raced through Anissa's mind, but this wasn't the time to voice them, even though she knew she might not get another chance.

"So, how will the trade work?" Svetlana asked breaking the silence.

"Alex gets delivered to us somewhere outside of Russia. It doesn't matter where, somewhere in Europe. It can be a bordering country, if you wish. You also arrest the man who killed that guard; announce the news, publicly exonerate Anastasia. Acquit her and you get the location of where Arkady Petrov is being held."

"That's a lot on our side before we get anything."

"I know how this game works; and it's all you get," Anissa said, hoping Volkov's desire for Petrov was greater than her fear of being cheated.

"I had better check if your agent is still alive then," Svetlana sighed, the thought causing more reaction inside Anissa than she thought it would have, though she did well not to vocalise anything; not giving the Russian any reward at the clear attempt to rattle her.

"You'll call me back on this number?" Anissa said, ignoring the previous comment, looking for closure on a deal that seemed all but agreed upon.

"I'll be in touch," Svetlana confirmed, ending the call.

Anissa dropped into her chair, exhausted but utterly exhilarated at the same time. She would call Charlie and update them on the latest news.

Forest Dacha, Russia

SMOKE FILLED THE FOREST, a thick billowing column rising in the distance. Rad knew it had to be an attempt to flush them out, which he kept from the others. Given the rough spot in the forest from which they could see the column coming, the men had most probably burnt Kostya and Olya's home to the ground. He kept that from them too.

"We watch each other's backs the entire time," he said, circling round, addressing Nastya and Kostya, who had the guns, and Olya, who could be an equally good lookout. The news of the tiger caused him more concern than the men.

He pulled Nastya to one side.

"Svetlana confirmed help will come, but it might not be quick enough," he said, his voice low, the other two scouring the surrounding forest for any sign of threat. "She also said they are using animals to hunt us." He would not say what animal, and the hunter in Nastya knew it made sense to use dogs. They had far better smell, able to navigate a path through a wall of forest to their target better than most technology.

"I want you high, off the ground," he said, pointing to a tree close to them. "Can you climb?"

She looked at him, raising her eyebrows as if he'd asked a stupid question.

"Give me a leg up and I'll be fine," she confirmed.

"See if you can reach those higher branches," he said, pointing to a spot several metres up, while supporting her foot with his other hand, as she pulled herself up onto the lowest branch. He passed Nastya her rifle. She made the rest of the climb with relative ease. She had a good view of the forest from there, the lake to the right, the smoke to the left.

"Rad, the fire…" She started, aware now where it was coming from.

"I know," he blurted. "They need not know, not yet; not until this is over." She understood, nodding, a tear for the home that had been her refuge, a building carved by hand by her uncle. She feared what might have become of their new beautiful home too, craning to see further up the lake, though no smoke was visible.

The sound of a helicopter caught the wind, the rhythmic thump of the blades as the aircraft drew closer getting steadily stronger all the time. Gunfire erupted soon after, Rad instantly aware the cavalry had arrived, the helicopter sweeping around, a rope dropping from the open door, men soon descending quickly into the forest below.

"Stay here," Rad called up to Nastya, who hadn't moved, Rad running off in the gunfire's direction, the army now engaging with whoever they had spotted. She wanted to call to him, but he had gone. Her uncle remained crouched behind the same log they'd been watching from, Olya out of sight beside him, the top of her head coming into view occasionally as she circled around, keeping watch in all directions. Increased gunfire started up again, coming from multiple directions.

Rad kept low, the sound of bullets racing through the air nothing new to him, and actually the appearance of the military created the perfect cover. He could creep into position and look to pick them off one by one, their ongoing battle against the recently arrived army personnel blinding them to the danger getting ever closer.

Rad positioned himself in behind his attackers, who had taken cover from their pursuit of him now that elite units had dropped in. A second and perhaps third helicopter sounded their approach in the distance, confirming to Rad the numbers game had dramatically changed in his favour.

Rad took out two men as they loaded their weapons, the shots from behind sure to cause some to turn towards him, but the greater range of his weapon meant their bullets couldn't reach him. He took out three more men. The gang was thrown into sudden confusion, army soldiers cutting them down on one side, an unseen but long feared sniper on the other.

The new helicopters came overhead now, one similar to the first, which unloaded its cargo of elite forces not too far from where the first group had dropped. The second incoming aircraft was a gunship, an attack helicopter that spat rounds into the forest, cutting down more men in its first sweep than the army had managed by themselves that far. It soon circled back, clear that it was preparing for another sweep. Rad fired off another couple of shots, two more men dropping to the dirt.

He surveyed the scene. There appeared to be no sign of Yuri

Lagounov. A scream from behind caused the hair on his neck to stand on end. It had been a woman's scream.

NASTYA HAD SEEN the two latest helicopters sweep in, the second looping over near to where she was, her position covered by the trees. It raced back overhead, opening fire once again.

Then Olya screamed, an ear shattering sound, as she saw the tiger too late, bounding up from the lake, pouncing on her. Nastya turned, startled, almost mesmerised by the flash of orange and black. The animal leapt on her aunt, knocking her to the ground and Kostya twisted, straightening his weapon. A sideways paw from the hungry animal sent him flying, gun dropping the other side of the log.

Nastya pulled her weapon round, the animal barely visible still attacking her aunt. Olya's fate was sealed but Kostya charged forward trying to reach his gun. The tiger clawed at his leg and he too screamed.

She took aim, the scene like nothing she had ever seen before, nor ever wanted to see; her uncle now being dragged by the animal towards the tall grass, his weapon lost, his arms flailing.

His screams as it dragged him along the ground, the razor teeth firmly gripped into the flesh of his lower leg, would live with her forever. He looked up, his face pleading. *Make it quick. Make it stop.*

She took the shot, catching the animal in the leg, sending it running, but not putting it down.

"Stay there!" he shouted, Nastya daring to move––his words stopped her––as she surveyed the scene, no sign of the animal. "It's coming back!" he screamed, this time from another side, Nastya unable to see it now. Kostya's face was fixed in utter terror, a flash of the animal as it jumped on him, his message to Nastya clear. *Kill me. Before it eats me alive, kill me!*

She aimed again, took a shot she never thought she would ever have to take. She hit her uncle clean in the head, the animal once again fleeing at the gunshot––she knew it would be back––the sound in the immediate area returning to silence, the screams of both relatives now no more.

Nastya got low again, pressing herself into the branch, training her weapon in on the grass beyond her now dead uncle. She was certain the animal wasn't far. A flash of orange confirmed her suspicion. She took the final shot, this time taking the animal out; it fell with a blood curdling cry.

Rad came charging onto the scene seconds later, weapon raised, Nastya inconsolable, as he raced over to the log. The tiger was in its final death throes and the fatally mauled body of Olya was on the other side of the log where Rad had stationed her. Following the drag marks on the ground, Rad came to Kostya, the bullet through his forehead telling the sniper all he needed to know. He went over to the fatally wounded tiger, pulling his handgun out, and killed it.

Movement on the far side of the lake caught his attention, Rad instinctively raising his scope. He saw a man standing there looking at a device in his hand then looking up directly at Rad. It was the face of Yuri Lagounov.

Yuri turned, as if to flee, Rad taking in the distance—about a kilometre—automatically adjusting trajectory and catering for wind speed. He took the shot. The seconds between pressing the trigger and impact was always in slow motion for him; the first the target would know, besides the flash of the weapon if they were looking, would be the impact of the bullet. The sound did not reach the other side of the lake until the bullet had met its mark. Yuri Lagounov fell to the ground, dead.

30

Vauxhall House, MI6, London
Present Day

The Russian President's call back to Anissa came a few hours later the same day. Given that the two countries were not in open dialogue--diplomats from both still not allowed in the other capital city--this conversation between Moscow and London was unprecedented.

And nobody would know about it, either.

"We will fly Alex to Turkey. You can plan for his collection in the capital," Svetlana confirmed. "And a press release is being drawn up, clearing Anastasia of all charges." She wouldn't mention not making any other arrest. She had ordered the killing of the guard. She wasn't about to attach her name to any crime.

"When?" Anissa said, scribbling down some notes in her usual fashion, the events now moving rapidly, and far faster than she had expected.

"Tomorrow evening," the President confirmed. "When will you release Petrov to me?"

"Once we have Alex,"--and Anissa knew she would be on that

flight, there to meet him on the ground in Turkey—"I will immediately send you details of Petrov."

"He's secure, I take it?"

"Yes, we have him. Our people will keep hold of him until the agreed time."

"I see," Svetlana agreed, more excited to get her hands on Petrov than she'd been about anything in a long time. He would stand to show her nation how seriously she took traitors. She would use his trial—she knew there would be a trial, public, well broadcast—to give everyone watching a clear message. Step out of line, and this will be you. And with The Black Dolphin about to lose an inmate, there would be space for Arkady. "Then it appears we have agreed on the deal," Svetlana confirmed. "Keep your end of the bargain; and this ends well for everyone."

"Everybody aside from Petrov," Anissa pointed out. If Petrov didn't know that already, he soon would. He would go to jail for the rest of his life in the land he had hoped he would never see again.

"True," Svetlana laughed, the two women getting a moment of common ground, though Anissa didn't allow that feeling to settle. She didn't trust the President. However, Svetlana Volkov had done a much smarter job than most in power at keeping hidden her many flaws. "I guess I'll wish you safe travels then," Svetlana said, well aware Anissa would see this one through and be on that plane to Turkey. Anissa didn't feel in any way threatened by being there, Turkey an ally to the UK as much as it was to Russia. It made the obvious meeting point.

The call ended. She had some planning to do, suddenly aware she was alone. There was nobody in the office to share the news with—her three closest colleagues were all in the Caribbean with Petrov. There was also nobody at home with whom she needed to arrange child care to take a trip at short notice.

She didn't dwell on the thought. She refused to go there. Tomorrow evening, she would see Alex again. That was cause for celebration. She would call Anastasia, the woman desperate to know, Anissa aware she would want to be in Turkey too, and she couldn't really stop her. It would be nice having the company, Anissa the only one to travel from MI6, the scenario far from official.

She went for a walk to the park, pulling out her phone and calling Anastasia not long after entering through the gates. The Belarusian answered after one ring.

Forest Dacha, Russia

HELICOPTERS STILL FLEW OVERHEAD and there was the occasional gunshot, though it seemed as if the threat had been beaten back. Rad sat with Nastya as she wept, the bodies of her uncle and aunt in the distance, that too of their killer. Nastya knew this was only partially true for her uncle. The tiger would have eventually killed him, that much she knew, but she'd beaten the animal to it. Out of empathy; out of compassion certainly. But she'd taken Kostya's life, and there could be no denying that now, her emotions torn to pieces by the desperate situation in which she found herself.

Rad poured the last of the water from the ten-litre plastic container. They had more on the other bike. He passed her some, Nastya drinking, forcing her body to take the fluid, but nothing seemed worthwhile at that moment.

The world had stopped spinning momentarily.

Rad stood and pulled his phone out, allowing Nastya a little time to compose her thoughts, Rad needing to speak to the President. She answered after barely two rings.

"Tell me what happened," she asked at once. A volley of fire from above at that moment told Svetlana the battle hadn't yet finished.

"I killed the tiger," Rad said, the one thing Svetlana had been able to specifically warn him about, though he had yet to understand her reasons. He was going to find out.

"And Yuri?"

"Dead," Rad confirmed, the silence that followed unnatural.

"And?" she said, eventually.

"And?" Rad quizzed, her response not altogether clear given the fact he'd just confirmed he had stopped this monster at last.

"Everything is contained there?" she asked. More bullets, another helicopter flying over, Rad unable to respond until it passed.

"I think so. Look, how did you know Lagounov was coming here?" Silence.

"That doesn't concern you," she said.

"How does it concern you?" he pressed.

"You think he had anything to do with me?" she laughed, though he'd seen her acting skills. She'd been more convincing then.

"I think he told you he was coming. I think he's been in touch with you for a long time," Rad confirmed.

"This is nothing to do with you!" she lashed out.

"I'm your head of security. If the country's most-wanted man is threatening you, it has everything to do with me," he pointed out, Yuri Lagounov far from the most-wanted, but in the top ten for sure.

"Yuri was no threat to me!" she snapped, all too quickly, all too effortlessly. She did know him, he knew it.

She realised what she'd said. There was no comeback to that.

"Who was he to you?" Rad demanded, now wondering if she had even instructed Yuri to set the tiger on them.

"That's enough!" she barked, resolute that she did not have to answer to anyone, especially someone on her payroll. Another helicopter circled back overhead, another thirty-seconds of silence on the phone while the noise died away. "You make sure it's all contained there. Don't leave until it's over," she confirmed, her mind on those still in the forest, dead or alive. They ended the call.

Rad looked over to his wife then up at the sky, the helicopter out of sight but not gone from earshot. He looked at the still visible tail of the tiger near the water's edge, an unnatural sight for sure, an animal with no place being there. The forest was littered with bodies now, even across the lake. Closest of all lay the bodies of the uncle and aunt.

After sitting with his wife in silence for a while––the helicopters eventually fading away completely, the sound of the forest returning, the guns gone--they simply embraced, her tears stopping now. Then, on the horizon came the sound of another aircraft, this a plane and not a helicopter. High above in the sky it appeared, Rad fetching his scope, drawn towards the sound, an impossible sound--given the fact the forest was under no flightpath--but out of place to his combat-trained ears for another reason. Rad knew that sound, knew it from several battle zones. He spotted the plane on a direct course for their part of the forest. His jaw dropped.

The Kremlin

SVETLANA FINISHED the call with Rad, immediately picking up the direct-line on her desk.

"Get me the coordinates of that last call," she said, her team soon to send through the location of Rad's mobile phone, and therefore their location within the forest.

She soon redialled on the desk phone, getting through to the airforce.

"Launch *clean sweep*," she ordered, the confirmation coming back to her that they would be off the ground in five. She said she would have the precise coordinates sent through to them by then.

These came over to her three minutes later, Svetlana forwarding them herself, the airforce acknowledging the target as the high altitude bomber was leaving the tarmac. The three military helicopters were withdrawn as any remaining fighters in the area not already downed were soon to be obliterated with the air blast of the military grade bomb. The detonation above ground level would be enough to cover a significant area, and burn up the bodies in the process. Explaining the dead remains of a tiger that close to Moscow, as well as the fugitive Yuri Lagounov, was not anything the President wanted to do. Now that Rad had guessed she had a connection to Lagounov, he too had outlived his usefulness, much as it pained her to admit it. *Clean sweep* had the sole intention of destroying that entire part of the forest, the explosion enough to destroy the trees without necessarily spreading an uncontrollable wild fire. They would still monitor the situation.

"Aircraft approaching the target," the military commander confirmed, the President on the phone, awaiting the relay. "We have target locked on," the commentary continued. "Five minutes until impact."

Svetlana knew Rad would see it coming. However, given his location was ground zero, he couldn't outrun such a blast. There could be no escape.

"Three minutes to impact."

The President's aide poked her head through the doorway. "Call for you, private line," she confirmed. Svetlana took it.

"Hello?"

"This is the President, I assume," the accented voice of Jose Zabala called, the fact he had that number confirmation he'd pulled several strings. Perhaps he had got it from Roman Ivanov directly?

"Don Zabala, I'm guessing?" she said.

"Alive and very much kicking," he snapped.

Two minutes to impact.

"How did you get this number?" she asked.

"You might like to ask how I am still alive, too. Both answers would be the same. Because you underestimated me," he said.

"I see," she said coolly, aware this had now become a game.

"There are not too many things I detest more than a liar," he said.

One minute to impact. Visuals coming online and the screen in front of the President showed the camera feed from underneath the plane, the edge of the warhead in shot, nothing but forest far below.

The Don continued. "But a liar who gets others to do their dirty work for them would certainly be up there."

"You didn't kill Slava Alkaev?" she confirmed, no reports coming from Germany about the murder of an old Russian.

"No," the Don said. "And you made a grave mistake assuming I would. An even more fatal mistake when you sent men to kill me at my home."

"Are you threatening me?" she demanded.

"Threats? I don't deal in threats," he said, too calmly. "I deal in revenge."

Weapon deployed.

The thought she would send her sniper to take out the Don suddenly occurred to her but the image on the screen reminded her that it was too late for that.

The missile descended ever closer to the ground, the two thoughts joined, panic racing through her mind as she held the phone to her ear, Zabala silent and waiting for a response while she waited for the impact.

"This conversation is over," she said, slamming down the handset as the bomb detonated, the image blanking out before returning to one from the plane.

A vast ball of flame filled the view, a raging fireball bursting out in every direction, hitting the ground. Trees were stripped bare in seconds, a mighty circle of fire engulfing the forest, total obliteration as far as the camera could see.

She sunk her head, still reeling from the conversation she'd just had. Inside the walls of the Kremlin, she was safe. However, with Zabala a known threat, and her ace in the pack now dead, she didn't know how best to deal with a nuisance that could turn into a nightmare.

31

The Kremlin
Present Day

The President stood with Pavel, her chief link with the Russian criminal world. She had agreed to release several million in funding back to his organisation, though it was far from all they had lost. Far from all she'd promised. He'd not completed either task she had set before him, and the name of Petrov––something he had found out––was now worthless. Alex was being removed from prison as they spoke, a plane on standby to fly him to Turkey.

"How is the internal operation progressing?" she asked. Polls suggested her ratings were higher than ever, especially amongst male responders, her ability to produce results on crime seen as the key component. She was getting results.

"Nearly there," he confirmed, what happened in the forest close to Moscow a rare exception. No other group had escaped, no other had formed their own counter-rebellion and threatened violence. Pavel had heard what had happened to the three groups.

"Good. Look, I would like to offer you a role here," she said, something that hadn't been on the cards. "I need a new head of security," though the threat to her, nationally, was at its lowest in decades for any sitting President.

"What happened to the sniper?" Pavel asked, well aware of who Rad was and what he had done for the President.

"He didn't make it," she said.

"I'm sorry to hear that," Pavel said, genuinely. He had met Rad only twice, rather impressed by him, the legend very much fitting the man himself.

"These things happen," she said, showing no signs of sadness, though Pavel suspected, as President, she had to be above such losses. Soldiers died.

"I'm still not sure what I can do for you," he said. Having a gangster like himself, albeit one of the straight-shooting, respectable types, wasn't anything any politician needed.

"Rad wasn't the only one killed from this office," she said. "I need your help, securing things on the outside."

He'd been doing largely that since before the election.

"What did you have in mind?" he asked, sensing a good payday was on offer, and he knew she was good for a lot more money.

"Every castle I ever saw had a moat," she said, initially seeming to go off topic, before drawing it back in quickly. "I need you to be that moat. I need your organisation to be that wall, that watchtower. I'll pay you per month, per year; whatever you need. I'll get someone to replace Rad, but it'll be a token position. They'll be here, my drawbridge. But we both know, when the enemy gets to the drawbridge, the castle's already fallen."

He nodded. "I can do that for you," he said. "How much?"

"How many men do you have for me?"

"How many do you want?"

She smiled. "Zabala's coming," she confirmed, the smile vanishing from her face as quickly as it had appeared.

"Here?"

"I don't know," she said. She knew the visa service would never allow him documents, and the border guard would not give him access to the country. But men like that never bothered with such things. Neither did they often do such things themselves. She couldn't help think in her case he might have made an exception. "I think it'll be when I travel." She had travelled rarely in recent months. However, a President couldn't run the country and never leave, not indefinitely. Deals needed agreeing, invitations accepting. At last, countries were queuing up to welcome a Russian President. Moscow had a part to play on the global stage, and now they were making overtures towards Svetlana to come to their events in person. She couldn't resist them forever.

"Won't the FSB oversee that?" Pavel asked, well aware it was the job of the security service to keep the President safe. Her look to him told him she knew that was a stupid question.

"There are things even they can't do. I want your people on the ground months before I visit. I want you meeting with every criminal in these cities, knowing who they are talking to, knowing before anyone does what threat I'll face. And when Zabala makes his move, it'll be your men who warn me first."

"Or die trying," Pavel stated.

She ignored that comment.

"How much do you need to guarantee my moat?"

"Let's start with two million dollars a month," he said, Svetlana unfazed by that amount.

"Fine," she said, Pavel more shaken by her answer than she was. Perhaps he should have asked for more?

"And if we need any more?" he probed.

"We can talk," she confirmed. "But this stays between us. I don't want you making even the radar of our own FSB, let alone a foreign security service."

He raised his eyebrows at that.

"You'll tell the FSB what we're doing, though?" he asked, her expression telling him to think again. "But they'll see my involvement as a threat!" he exclaimed, Svetlana leaning close to his ear, whispering the final words of this conversation.

"Then don't let them find out."

She straightened, returning to her desk, not looking up from her paperwork, Pavel moving out of the office moments later. With two million of extra funding a month, he could bring his organisation onto a new path. They could make extra money on the side, but mostly he could afford to run everything legitimately now. Why this needed keeping from the FSB he didn't know.

Ground Zero, Forest Area, Edge of Moscow

"Get up!" Rad called, spotting the aircraft closing in.

"What is it?" Nastya asked, immediately aware of the fear in her husband's voice. He never got scared.

"It's a Tupolev," he screamed, scanning the area, nothing but trees on all sides, barring the lake––beyond which were only more trees.

"What's a Tupolev?" she called, Rad reaching for the water container, upending the plastic bottle, allowing the final drops to fall to the floor.

"It's a bomber, Nastya!" he screamed, the plane in perfect line for that part of the forest.

"What's it doing here?" she cried, aware the helicopters had cleared the area already, the fighting deemed over––nothing but sorrow and mourning, after burying their loved ones, to come.

He didn't answer, but his frantic pulling her towards the lake told her it wasn't good. He had no choice but to run past the bodies of both Kostya and Olya, his own head up, straining for the lake, something he'd never attempted to swim across––something there was not time to do now––but a body of water he hoped had depth. Serious depth.

"We need to get under water," he said, floating the bottle out with them, intending to use it to take oxygen down with them, though it wouldn't be easy to drag under the water. It would want to float, to pull them to the surface.

The plane was above them now, the four propellers giving a

constant drone, Nastya glancing up in fear as they reached waist deep in the lake, the sight of the missile deployment nearly taking the strength from her knees.

Rad started swimming, already up to his neck, the lake bottom dropping quickly. He urged Nastya on, pulling the container, the pair going another ten metres as the plane passed over, impact sure to be any second.

"Dive!" he shouted, Nastya down first, Rad upturning the container so that the opening was flat against the surface of the lake, the bottle empty but for the air inside. He dragged it under, a few air bubbles escaping, though as he got under the water, he kept the bottle level, and kicked down hard into the darkness beneath.

Then the sky above them lit up, a huge fireball everywhere. The temperature of the water instantly increased as it absorbed much of the explosion. Even down at fifteen feet, the light flashed, Nastya helping Rad to control the bottle, Rad showing her how to do it, Nastya taking a lungful of air soon after, the bottle filling a little, though with plenty of oxygen remaining.

The surface stayed glowing for a long time, the bottle slowly replacing the oxygen it had trapped with water, as the couple took more and more gulps, losing a little of the life-giving oxygen each time they refilled their lungs. Soon they knew it was time to ascend, the light at surface level returning to normal, though fires raged in the surrounding trees. They kicked upwards, Rad leaving the bottle where it was, the water inside it causing it to hang as if suspended in midair.

They broke through the surface, desperate for another huge gulp of air, the smell confirming that fire burned on the surrounding shore, much of the ground now charred, burnt and ashen in no time, nothing of the shoreline they'd left five minutes before now visible. The explosion had vaporised the bodies of the two relatives and the animal which had killed them, the ground all around only a smouldering mess.

They swam to the edge of the lake as the sound of the bomber faded completely into the distance.

"What about our home?" Nastya asked, visibly traumatised by everything that had happened to her.

Rad glanced in that direction. It was impossible to tell from there. Their dacha was at least six kilometres away, perhaps further. If the bomb had dropped directly above them, it might be safe. That assumed it hadn't been burned down before, as the men had done with her uncle's house.

"It doesn't matter," Rad said, taking his wife in his arms. "We can't go back."

"Can't go back?" she pleaded, tears streaming from her face. She'd lost nearly everything she loved in the last half-hour.

"This was all her doing," he said, looking at the still burning pine trees around, the tops of the trees still sending flames another five metres into the air.

"The President?" Nastya asked, stunned.

"Yes. And she thinks we're dead," he said, the bomb certain to have killed anyone on the ground within a two or three kilometre radius. "Let's keep it that way, for now." His wife was a few months pregnant, not showing yet, but she soon would be. She would need help at some point. She couldn't live in the forest forever. But for now, this would be their home. They would remain off the grid, Rad able to track and hunt, though he could see that his weapon lay burning with everything else. He would find another. Perhaps their home hadn't been destroyed in the bomb? He had firepower locked in the safe. He would double back that way when Nastya was sleeping. She didn't need to see what had become of their beloved home.

"Where will we go?" she asked. "What will you do?"

"I don't know, but we can't stay here. We need to move, we'll go east, delve deeper into the forest." She looked up as he said this, fear in her eyes. "It'll be okay," he promised. He knew it would be.

"What if she tries again?" she asked, the thought of never being safe, a life on the run was not something she had ever contemplated.

"She won't," he said. "I won't let her." He took her by the arm, helping her up past the still burning trees, heading east, deeper into the undergrowth, where the damp of the ground had evidently stopped the spread of the fire beyond the initial detonation. Soon they were walking once more through untouched forest. They would make camp about a kilometre in. He needed to get back to their dacha that night, the trek without torch, weapon or water hard enough as it was, without adding distance. They would be okay, he knew it. They had survived. The thought dawned on him for the first time then too. He was free. He was out. That was something few in his profession ever managed.

32

Etimesgut Air Base, Ankara, Turkey
Present Day

Fifteen kilometres west of the capital, at the military-owned airport, the small unmarked military aircraft taxied to a halt close to one of the main hangars.

Outside, in the dark but warm night, two women waited for the door to the aircraft to open.

Onboard, Alex Tolbert sat quietly in his seat, marshalled on either side by Russian agents of the FSB. They were under strict orders to bring the man to an exchange in Turkey, their task therefore nearly completed. They would then be told where to fly on to next.

Alex had woken that morning in his usual cell none the wiser. The last couple of weeks inside had been tough, though Putin's protection had ultimately saved him from any further trouble. Alex could still not forget the look that the former President had given him as two non-prison operatives––they had to be FSB, working for the Kremlin directly––came and collected him from his cell.

Putin's eyes pleaded *we had a deal to escape from here together,* even while Alex feared they might be taking him to a much worse fate. He thought he was about to die.

Alex had said nothing––there was no time to say anything, nor did he know what to say to Putin––as the two agents escorted him from his cell, standing upright, not handcuffed, heading to whatever future now awaited him.

They'd said little as they drove to the airfield, Alex placed onto the backseat, windows showing him a world he had wondered if he would ever see again. The aircraft was small, powerful and modern, as out of place as anything that had happened to him that day.

It wasn't obviously British, the two pilots in Russian military uniform, causing an element of fear as he took his seat, his minders following him into the plane, though they gave him space. They didn't handcuff him; he apparently wasn't still a prisoner. Then they took off.

Alex dropped off to sleep for a while on the way, waking for what became clear was their descent. He heard Turkey mentioned for the first time, his heart racing now, hope welling up inside. They were freeing him; it had to be that. Outside of Russia, this had to be a release.

Now on the ground, there was only darkness, no sign of any press or waiting dignitaries. He knew his release couldn't be that kind of event.

"Mr Tolbert, you are free to leave," the Russian next to him said, Alex getting to his feet, still in shock, nothing said to him during the flight confirming this outcome until that moment. The door at the front of the plane stood open, Alex spotting stairs rolling into place, the air rushing in. The air of freedom, if not the air of home. That, he knew, could follow.

Alex stood, didn't thank the men––why should he?––and walked towards the opening, stepping out onto the metal landing, a run of about twenty steps taking him to ground level, where two women stood. Alex didn't need to see their faces to know who they were. Anastasia had let out a cry of joy with his appearance at the top of the stairs.

They let him walk down carefully—he'd not used stairs since arriving in the prison, which he'd done with a badly damaged leg. He held the railings carefully, his previously broken leg threatening to give way on one step, and he made it to the bottom.

Both women embraced him, Anastasia not able to let go, the vision of Alex, free and outside of Russia, something she assumed she would never see again.

Down the stairs came another man, one of the two who had collected Alex from the prison. He stopped beside the group, Anissa the first to pull away, leaving the two lovers together.

"You have something for me, I believe?" the Russian asked Anissa. She reached into her pocket, pulling out the details for where they could find Arkady Petrov. They would move him from prison the following morning, a collection time of eleven arranged where Charlie would officially hand Petrov to the Russians. Then the trio would head home. Only Charlie and Zoe would be at the handover, Sasha watching from the outside, there to stand guard, but not showing his face to his countrymen.

"Here," she said, handing over the information. She would call Charlie soon, the trio wanting to send their regards as soon as they had Alex, and she would confirm the Russians were on their way.

"No tricks," he warned.

"He'll be there," Anissa confirmed. She turned to see the end of what had been a long kiss between the British agent and his wealthy Belarusian girlfriend. A romance that should never had been. And yet, there they were. Anissa knew that without Anastasia's help, they might never have confirmed Alex's precise whereabouts.

The Russian FSB agent went back up and into the plane, the Turkish ground crew soon removing the steps, the jet refuelled as the trio moved away from the spot.

"Bloody hell Alex, it's good to see you," Anissa beamed, overcome with emotion herself now, her former colleague thin and hairy, his beard thick, though his eyes spoke a thousand stories. They wept, Anissa embracing him, Alex whispering a silent thanks in her ear,

Anastasia standing to one side, holding his hand, but allowing the two Brits this moment together.

A car pulled up, the driver jumping out, opening the rear doors for them all, two rows of seats facing each other allowing the three to get into the back. Anissa sat facing Alex, Anastasia sliding in next to him.

They pulled away, few words spoken, Anastasia just holding onto her man, a joy upon her like she'd not known in years. A weight had lifted; she knew that much.

Anissa pulled out her phone, pressing the call button, the device put on loud speaker.

"I've got someone here to say hello," Anissa said, holding the phone towards Alex once the call had connected, Alex speaking, an eruption of noise from the other end as three voices shouted at once. Alex recognised the voice of Charlie, and he knew the female voice had to be that of Zoe, his colleague. But it was the accented voice of Sasha that caused a huge smile to spread across his face, Sasha speaking the loudest, the other two giving him time to talk.

"My friend, you do not understand how good it is to hear your voice," Sasha said, somewhat emotional himself, a state the Russian rarely showed to anybody.

"Believe me, Sasha, I'm just as thrilled," Alex said, looking Anissa in the eye as he spoke, his colleague holding his gaze. Raw emotion showed. Alex's release was a small miracle in a process that had slowly ground her down. She too knew a weight had lifted.

"Alex, we'll grab some beers when we get back," Charlie shouted across the miles.

"Absolutely," Alex agreed, nothing to drink but water and an occasional green tea in over three years. "So where are we going?" he asked Anissa.

"The main airport," she confirmed, the call ending soon after that, everyone promising to meet up in London when they were all back, a huge celebration promised.

"I've arranged first-class tickets for each of us," Anastasia confirmed, free now herself to travel, thanks to Anissa's deal. Free to use her vast wealth. Free to be with Alex.

British Virgin Islands

THE HANDOVER the following morning had gone smoothly. By the end of his first week there, Arkady had grown suspicious, given the absence of any British officials, that this had anything to do with his protection, and he feared the worst as each day passed. His transfer that final morning, cuffed and with both agents looking cautious—— Sasha would travel separately——told Arkady all he needed to know.

"You've sold me out, haven't you!" he spat at Charlie, who ignored him. "After all you promised me!"

Zoe looked at Charlie, wanting to assure him this was the right thing to do, Charlie merely looking out of the window, counting down the minutes. Keeping his mind from the feeling of having betrayed the Russian.

They pulled up to a building close to the small airport. Half an hour later, they spotted the Russian jet as it touched down, a car bringing the two FSB agents from the aircraft to the edge of the airport where they were dropped off at the building, Charlie there to meet them.

"You have Petrov?" asked the same guy who'd handed Alex over to Anissa, the night flight allowing a little sleep but his body clock all over the place. They were heading straight back, however.

"He's inside," Charlie confirmed, pointing to the door, the deal being that the British walked away at that point. He handed the FSB agent the keys for the handcuffs. Charlie went over to Zoe, the pair now on the other side of the road. The FSB escorted Arkady Petrov from the building moments later, the man glancing across to Charlie with a look that could kill.

"You've done the right thing," Zoe said, taking Charlie's hand, but he pulled away.

"Have I?" he asked.

"That man killed ten people," she reminded him. "Think of the promises he broke to his unit of soldiers. And he thinks you let him down?" and she scoffed, as they lowered Petrov into the back of the car, both Russian agents getting in beside him, the car pulling away a second later. "His betrayal is colossal, Charlie. Don't you forget that."

They watched the car go, Sasha pulling up a moment later. They had flights out of that same airport two hours from then.

"Did everything go smoothly?" Sasha asked, joining the other two. He'd seen the exchange, nothing about it had bothered him.

Charlie nodded.

"What now?" Zoe asked.

"Now we go home," Charlie confirmed, "after some food." Sasha applauded that idea, the trio going to a small restaurant across the road from the airport, Charlie able to see the Russian aircraft lift off from the runway. He watched it until it went from view, still unsure of how he felt about letting the man down. It would only be the following day late at night when he met Alex again, that those thoughts would finally be laid to rest. Seeing Alex would tell him it was all worth it.

Alicante, Spain

JOSE ZABALA SAT in his favourite restaurant, at his usual table. He ate alone, the wine regularly topped up, the head waiter constantly making sure one of their greatest patrons had everything he needed.

Between the main course and the dessert, one of his men appeared at the door, the Don nodding for him to enter. Jose watched him snake his way through the tables of the venue. He handed his boss a piece of paper.

"Italy?" Jose confirmed. The printout he had handed him listed several dates and locations, the middle one, in Rome in two month's time, with a circle around it.

"She's attending an International Economic Forum there in November," his man confirmed. Svetlana Volkov would not likely be returning to Spain soon. Italy offered them some interesting options.

"Get to work," Don Zabala confirmed, his man leaving as the dessert arrived, and with it a fresh glass of wine, something suited to the dish. He looked down at the information. He might even venture over to Italy himself. He smiled.

Pustosha Village, Forest Area, Russia
Six months later

RAD HAD BROUGHT his wife to the nearest village a week before her due date. As contractions started coming every few minutes, he called upon a *babushka* they'd met a few days before who had been a midwife in Moscow for forty years. She had protested she'd not delivered a baby in nearly fifteen years, Rad insistent they couldn't travel to a hospital.

They'd been living on the edge of the village for months, off the grid, Rad hunting for food, the pair living in makeshift houses.

She had refused to give birth in the forest, refused to put the delivery entirely on her husband.

At three that night, after an eight-hour labour, the cries of a mother in the throes of childbirth were turned into the cries of an infant, announcing its arrival to the world.

"You have a son," the old woman said, handing the baby to Nastya, calling Rad back into the room, having insisted he leave once they got close to delivery. Under her watch, the old woman stated, childbirth was no place for the father.

Rad kissed his wife, the pair looking at that little life, this impossible bundle of legs and arms huddled in the blanket, eyes barely open.

"He's beautiful," Rad exclaimed.

"He has your eyes," the old woman nodded to Rad, Nastya beaming.

"He does, look," she said, Rad unable to see any resemblance.

"He has your skin," Rad confirmed, Nastya's colouring in his tiny complexion, despite being barely minutes old.

After fussing over them a little––the babushka insisting Rad shouldn't get too close––she left them to it, the couple alone at last, with their little boy.

"Do you have a name yet?" he asked her, the pair having assumed the baby would be a girl.

"I want to call him Kostya," she said, tears now streaming down her face, Rad unable to speak, nodding in utter support, the name perfect. They'd talked very little about that day, the day she lost her relatives, the way they had gone. Rad knew she'd taken the shot that killed her uncle.

However, what was clear now, looking at the baby whom they loved even more than they could ever have imagined, was that they couldn't continue to live off-grid. Not now. Working out what to do, and where to go, would require a delicate conversation. That would have to wait, though he knew it couldn't wait for too long. If they had to register the child in the country, that might put them both back onto Svetlana Volkov's radar.

Rad knew he couldn't allow that to happen. They might have to flee. He only knew of one other person who could help. The one person who'd also done that himself a few years before; except getting in touch with Sasha would not be easy.

For the sake of his young family, Rad would try. Getting out of Russia altogether might now be the only way to protect them all.

AUTHOR NOTES AND ACKNOWLEDGMENTS

I'm delighted you have finished this latest book--there is but one more to go in the series now! It all wraps up in *The Lost Tsar,* which comes out before the end of 2020.

Perhaps the biggest unanswered scenario at the end of book six (*The Meltdown*) was what would happen to Alex. I know that was what my wife most wanted to know. It was probably the book most readers wanted to read. If you've read the previous book, you'll understand what I'm about to say. Like a chess player or snooker champion looking three shots ahead, I knew in the instinctive moments of thinking about this book that I needed something more. How do you break someone out of an impenetrable prison?

I didn't want to write that style of a book--this isn't James Bond. A prison is either impenetrable, or it isn't. I knew I wanted to be clever than that. I needed a new character. This is the sole reason that *The Acting President* comes before *The Black Dolphin.* Yes, I wanted a book focused on Svetlana now that she is in the Kremlin, but I also needed to develop the whistleblower, and create a genuine threat that the President would be ultimately willing to trade for. And this is how these two books came to be, in this order. I think they are both stronger for it too.

Now all that awaits is the last book in the series which I've already written, and which, at the time of first publication for this title, is with my editor. Expect it by December.

Can I remind you how helpful reviews on Amazon are and ask you to take a few minutes to please leave your thoughts and a rating?

Now for my thanks––as always, these books are never a solo pursuit, but a magnificent team effort. Thanks especially to Zan-Mari and Fraser Drummond from my ART group for their feedback and corrections. Thanks also to Mike Davis, Wendy Babawi and Netty Mattey from my BETA group for also spotting things that needed changing.

Elizabeth Knight was once again my editor. She particularly liked this book. Thank you for your insight and help.

My wife Rachel also read it later on and, as usual, spotted some important things that needed refinement. It was wonderful to see you reading and hear firsthand your eagerness to see what happens! I'm glad you were not disappointed.

So it's over to my readers now. I don't expect many sales at launch, but I see this series growing in readership down the years and I have this confidence in the quality of each book to know that whenever you read it, you will find a story you love, and an adventure that continues through each chapter of every book right to the very end!

In the last section of this book, at the bottom of the *About the Author* page, there are several ways of getting in touch with me–– please do! If you would like to help me on my author journey, then please look at the Patreon link and discover all the benefits available to you if you support me there.

Now about the Black Dolphin: in case you were wondering, it is a real place! I found lots of useful information online, and thought for those interested, I would share the best links here.

This is the Wikipedia page for the prison: https://en.wikipedia.org/wiki/Black_Dolphin_Prison

Here is an RT report where they were given exclusive access to the prison––it shows you the charge sheets on each prison door, the way prisoners are moved around, the constant watch from above and even the triple doors for each cell: https://youtu.be/OIjFhNYc5Hc

CHARACTER GLOSSARY
WHO'S WHO IN THE HUNT SERIES—AS OF THE START OF THIS BOOK

MI6 Anissa Edison, Sasha Barkov, Charlie Boon, Zoe Elliot, Gordon Peacock (head technician)

Alex Tolbert--former MI6 imprisoned in The Black Dolphin prison in Russia

Svetlana Volkov--President of the Russian Federation and former actress and founder of the Games

Radomir Pajari--elite Russian sniper and head of security for the President

Nastya Pajari--wife of Rad
 - **Kostya & Olya**--Uncle & Aunt of Nastya

Anastasia Kaminski--The Belarusian lover of Alex Tolbert

Arkady Petrov--Russian whistleblower

Roman Ivanov--wealthy oligarch and long-time Host in the Games

Don Jose Zabala--Spanish-based mafia boss whose son was killed recently in Alicante.

MAILING LIST
BECOME A SUPER-FAN!

Loved this book and want to hear when my newest ones are out? Like the idea of getting your hands on free novels of mine when I do a special promotion, or hearing about progress on the books I'm writing in your favourite series? Then become a Super-Fan!

My monthly emails are always fun, full of information and take-aways specifically related to my life as an author, and I only write when I have something to say (or to give-away).

VIP Readers' Group
http://www.timheathbooks.com/books/super-fans

THE NOVELS BY TIM HEATH

Novels:

Cherry Picking

The Last Prophet

The Tablet

The Shadow Man

The Prey (The Hunt #1)

The Pride (The Hunt #2)

The Poison (The Hunt #3)

The Machine (The Hunt #4)

The Menace (The Hunt #5)

The Meltdown (The Hunt #6)

The Song Birds

The Acting President (The Hunt #7)

The Black Dolphin (The Hunt #8)

The Lost Tsar (The Hunt #9)

The 26th Protocol (Due out in 2021)

Short Story Collection:

Those Geese, They Lied; He's Dead

THE BOXSETS—TIM HEATH

The Hunt Series (Books 1-3) - The Prey, The Pride, The Poison

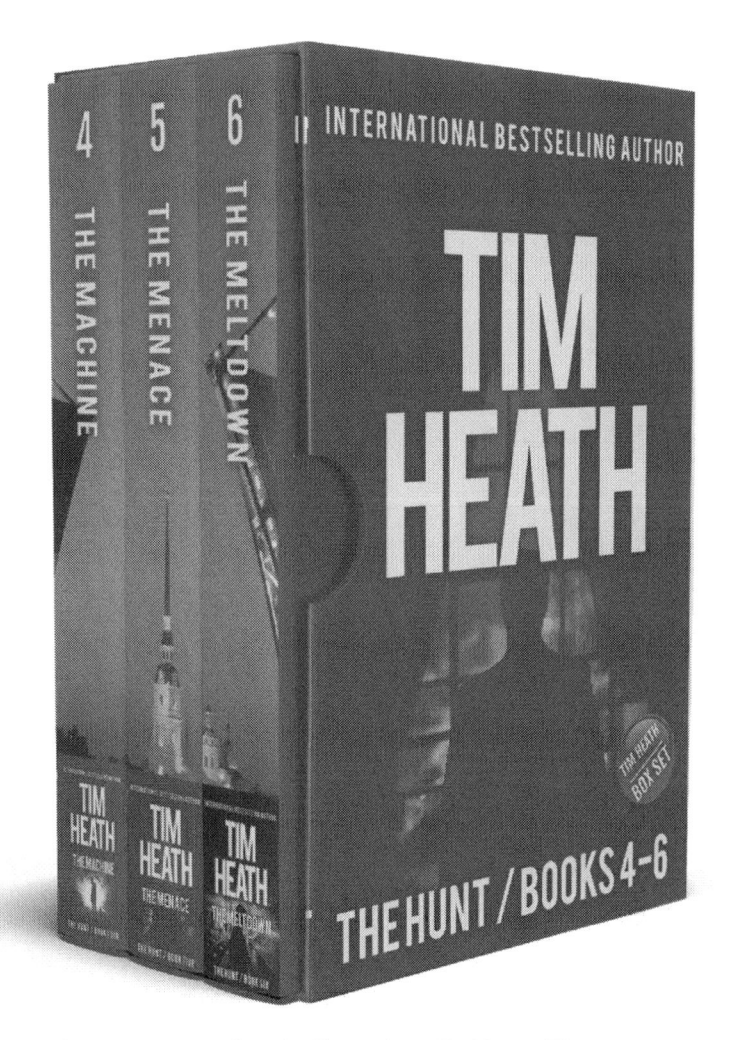

The Hunt Series (Books 4-6) - The Machine, The Menace, The Meltdown

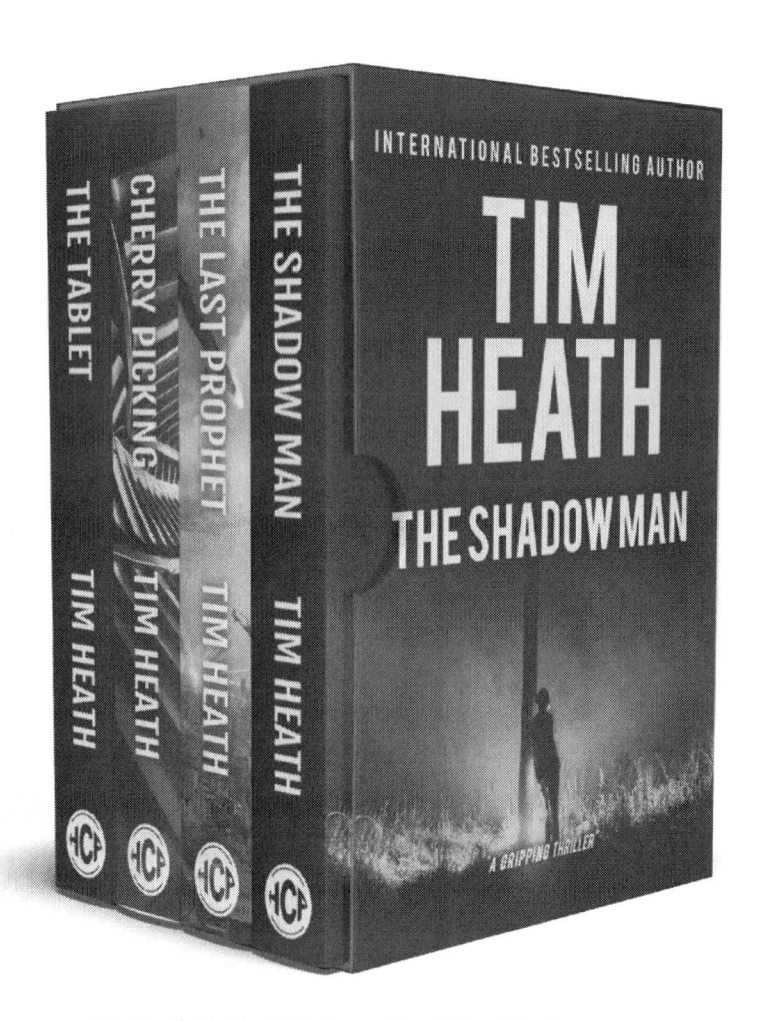

Tim Heath Thriller Collection—4 Stand-Alone Novels - Cherry Picking, The Last Prophet, The Tablet, The Shadow Man

THE BOXSETS—T H PAUL
PEN-NAME SERIES OF TIM HEATH

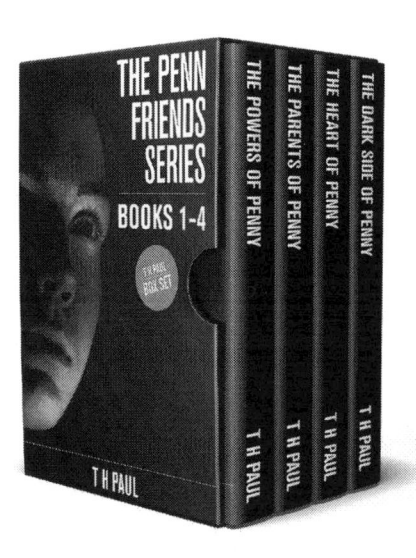

Penn Friends Series (Books 1-4) — Season One Volume One

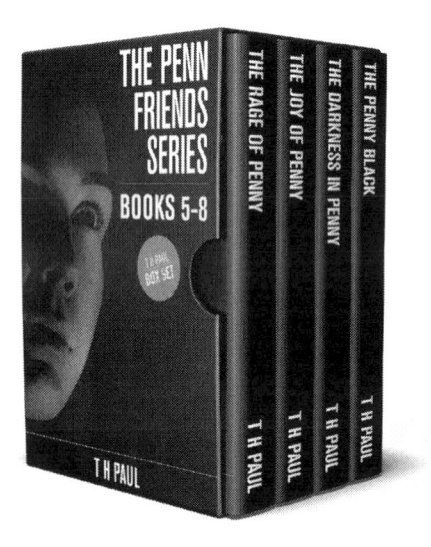

Penn Friends Series (Books 5-8) — Season One Volume Two

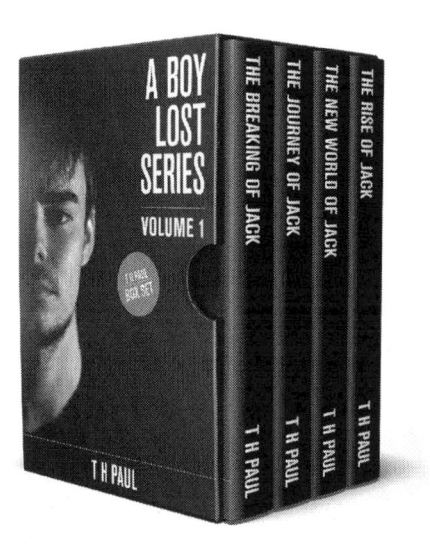

A Boy Lost Series (Books 1-4) — Season Two Volume One

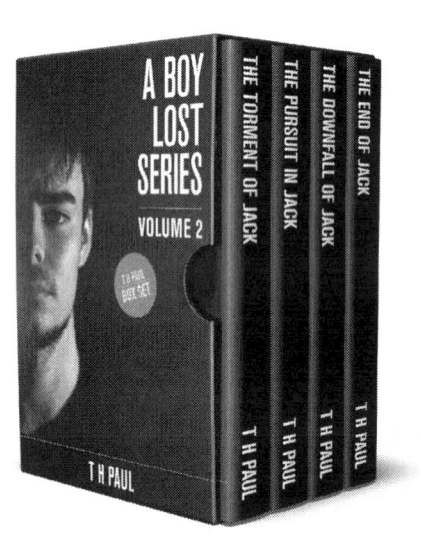

A Boy Lost Series (Books 5-8) — Season Two Volume Two

ABOUT THE AUTHOR

Tim has been married to his wife Rachel since 2001, and they have two daughters. He lives in Tallinn, Estonia, having moved there with his family in 2012 from St Petersburg, Russia, which they moved to in 2008. He is originally from Kent in England and lived for eight years in Cheshire, before moving abroad. As well as writing the novels that are already published (plus the one or two that are always in the process of being finished) Tim enjoys being outdoors, exploring Estonia, cooking and spending time with his family.

For more information:
www.timheathbooks.com
tim@timheathbooks.com

patreon.com/timheath
facebook.com/TimHeathAuthor
instagram.com/timheathauthor
amazon.com/author/timheath
bookbub.com/authors/tim-heath
goodreads.com/TimHeath
youtube.com/TimHeath
linkedin.com/in/tim-heath-83144077
twitter.com/TimHeathBooks